A RELUCTANT BRIDE

At the sound of the rapid knock, Tucker glanced up from the paperwork on his desk. Why did the sight of Sarah always cause his heart to give a small leap? She stood in the doorway, her face red, her body taut. Something was dreadfully wrong.

"Can I come in?" Her voice was polite and brisk.

Tucker jumped up from behind the desk and hurried around to greet her. "What's wrong? You wouldn't have come if there wasn't a problem."

He could see the tension in her body in the way she walked toward him carrying a small tin.

"What's in there?" he asked, afraid of the answer.

"This is what's the matter," she said, laying the tin on the desk and pulling off the lid. Then she reached inside a layer of white tissue paper and pulled out his mother's bridal veil.

Tucker cringed. "I tried to warn you."

Sarah watched him, a frustrated expression on her beautiful face. "I was bluntly honest with her, and she didn't hear me. She had the gall to ask me to wear the thing when I marry you!"

Tucker stared at her, thoughts racing through his mind. How could he honor his plan to help Sarah find another man when his own mother was so determined to see him wed to Sarah? And when all he could think of was the chance to kiss her again. . . .

Dear Romance Reader,

Last year, we launched the Ballad line with four new series, and each month we'll present both new and continuing stories set everywhere from medieval England to the American West—the kind of passionate, romantic stories you love best, written by the most gifted authors. At the back of each book, we'll tell you when you can find subsequent books in the series that have captured your heart.

This month, Martha Schroeder and her passionate *Angels of Mercy* are back! In **True to Her Heart,** a beautiful but penniless young woman finds that her sojourn in the Crimea has discouraged wealthy suitors— and that she wants the one she fears she can never have. Next, the fabulous *Hope Chest* series continues with Paula Gill's **Fire With Fire** as a woman travels back in time only to meet a rugged lawman who sets off an irresistible flame of desire.

In the next entry of the breathlessly romantic *Once Upon a Wedding* series, Kelly McClymer offers **The Unintended Bride.** A shy young woman longs for true love—and when a family friend must offer for her out of obligation, he longs to prove to her that he is the dashing hero of her dreams. Finally, talented Sylvia McDaniel concludes the fresh and funny *Burnett Brides* trilogy with **The Marshal Takes a Wife,** as a female doctor returns to her hometown and discovers that the man she left behind might be the only man to steal her heart.

Kate Duffy
Editorial Director

The Burnett Brides

THE MARSHAL
TAKES A WIFE

Sylvia McDaniel

ZEBRA BOOKS
Kensington Publishing Corp.

http://www.zebrabooks.com

ZEBRA BOOKS are published by

Kensington Publishing Corp.
850 Third Avenue
New York, NY 10022

All Kensington titles, imprints and distributed lines are available at special quantity discounts for bulk purchases for sales promotion, premiums, fund-raising, educational or institutional use.

Special book excerpts or customized printings can also be created to fit specific needs. For details, write or phone the office of the Kensington Special Sales Manager: Kensington Publishing Corp., 850 Third Avenue, New York, NY 10022. Attn. Special Sales Department. Phone: 1-800-221-2647.

Zebra and the Z logo Reg. U.S. Pat. & TM Off.
Ballad is a trademark of Kensington Publishing Corp.

First Printing: July 2001
10 9 8 7 6 5 4 3 2 1

Printed in the United States of America

One

Marshal Tucker Burnett was the last unattached male in a family that had experienced more weddings in the last year than he cared to remember. And he planned on retaining his single status. With a shudder he thought of his two strapping brothers who had succumbed to his mother's matchmaking ways and was more determined than ever to hang on to his freedom.

First it had been Travis, the oldest of the three, and then his long-lost brother Tanner had fallen under the spell of love and settled down.

Tucker shivered, more from the thought of marriage than the cold, as he leaned against the wall of the El Paso Hotel and waited for the stage, his hat pulled down low, shading his eyes, his arms crossed over his chest. He was a wandering man, no ties, no attachments, no ring binding him to forever.

Turning his attention to the present, he cast his gaze to the dusty empty street. His mother had sent him on what he was certain was a fool's errand. For the last month, his mother, Eugenia had made him promise to meet the stage from Abilene, Texas, twice a week, awaiting some mysterious package.

Tucker feared what kind of package his mother was referring to and only hoped it wasn't like the last surprise she had given him, a mail-order bride who had fallen in love with his older brother Tanner. Eugenia's kind of surprises, he didn't need.

After his mother's last attempt at matchmaking, he had warned her to stay out of his business, and he had meant every stinking word. She had promised him that this package was for the much-anticipated newest family member, baby Burnett.

His brother Travis and his wife, Rose, were expecting their first child this spring, and his mother had turned her attention away from finding a mate for her remaining unmarried son, to the arrival of the first grandchild. And thank God she had. Unlike his brothers, he intended on keeping his freedom.

A sharp, cold north wind swirled about the street, picking up dust, stinging exposed skin with a painful reminder that spring was still weeks away. The stage turned the corner of Main Street and came rattling down the road, the horses eager to reach their destination. The wooden contraption pulled to a halt in front of Tucker, the dust settling back to earth. He pushed back his hat and uncrossed his ankles, putting both feet firmly on the ground. God, he hoped whatever his mother had ordered arrived today, so he could quit this silly errand.

Tucker watched as the driver climbed down from the box and dropped to the ground. He placed a small step down in front of the door for the passengers to step on before their feet touched the ground. The driver swung open the door, and a small boy who looked to be around the age of two jumped from the stage to the step, laughing gaily. A feminine hand covered by an emerald glove held the toddler's small fingers securely.

Tucker's gaze went from the child's hand up the arm to the woman who wore the green gloves. His eyes found hers and became lost in those pools of blue sky he had never forgotten. For a moment he thought the ground was going to fall out from beneath him as he stared across what seemed like the thousand miles that had separated them until just this moment.

Dr. Sarah Kincaid had returned home looking more beautiful than when he had left her almost three years ago, and it appeared she hadn't come home alone.

"Well, I'll be damned!" he muttered beneath his breath. He swallowed at the sight of the woman he had chased around the schoolyard as a boy. The doctor who had kept him from dying in Tombstone. The good woman whose bed he had left in the middle of the night.

Dear God, she had returned. After three years would she still be angry?

He let his gaze travel over the blond hair that was carefully coiffed beneath a stylish hat that added a minimal amount of height to her already tall frame. The color matched her green traveling coat which hid the generous curves he knew so well.

Their eyes met and held for what seemed an eternity, and Tucker's mind replayed the memory of Sarah's bare shoulder being kissed by a sliver of moonlight, the sheets tangled about her waist and hips, her breasts peeking from beneath a blond curl.

That one night in her arms had been the biggest threat to his freedom he had ever experienced, and he had left before she tempted him into staying forever. He had left before he knew whether he had ruined a perfectly good friendship by having sex with the lady doctor.

And now here she was proudly standing before him on this cold February morning, shivering, a child gripping her hand.

"Momma," the child said, tugging on her hand, eager to scamper down the step and escape the confines of the carriage.

"Just a moment, son." She stepped down from the coach, her eyes never wavering from Tucker's. She walked toward him, and he met her halfway.

"Tucker Burnett," she acknowledged, her voice stiff and formal as if the night they had made love had never happened.

"Hello, Sarah. How have you been?" He swallowed, his palms suddenly perspiring.

"Just fine," she politely responded, the warm, friendly smile he remembered absent from her full, sweet lips. "I've come to visit my grandfather."

They stared at one another, their conversation stilted and awkward. Tucker resisted the urge to put her back on that stage, shut the door and tell the driver to continue right on out of town. He knew the thought was irrational, yet somehow he didn't care.

That one night with the doctor had made him forget his dreams and act irrationally.

He nodded. "If you'd like, I'd be happy to carry your bags to your grandfather's hotel."

"Oh, that won't be necessary. Lucas and I will manage," she said, her voice polite and cool.

"Lucas?" he questioned.

"My son," she replied, pulling the boy around beside her.

"I didn't know you had married," he said, staring

at the child, who twisted behind his mother, more interested in what was going on down the street.

She was married and had a child; he was safe.

"Mrs. Walter Scott James," she said as she pulled the active boy forward. "Lucas, meet Mr. Burnett."

The boy was dressed in a blue double-breasted overcoat, and Tucker hoped his mother had never dolled him up in such a fashion. The resemblance between Sarah and her son was obvious with the boy's blond curls and fair skin. He couldn't help but wonder about the child's father. Who was he, and when had she met him?

Tucker bent down to Lucas and tipped his hat. "Marshal Tucker Burnett." He gripped the boy's hand and shook it. "Nice to meet you. How old are you?"

The boy glanced up at Tucker, then pulled his hand away and buried his face in his mother's skirts. She patted him on the back reassuringly.

"He's tired and so am I," she said, her voice brusque.

"More reason for me to carry your bags to the hotel." He stood glancing around at the trunks the driver was unloading, wondering which ones were hers.

"Fine," she said, her gloved fingers pushing a strand of blond hair out of her face. He noticed how her gaze kept drifting to the badge pinned to his chest.

"Marshal Burnett? That's a far cry from what you were doing the last time I saw you," she said, a slight edge to her voice.

He saw a flash of anger in her eyes and felt a twinge of anxiety. Dear God, could she still be mad after all these years?

The two good friends had become lovers for just

one long, lonely night, and somehow he was afraid he had damaged their friendship forever.

While she lay sleeping, he had dressed and snuck out the back door, leaving her to wake up alone. Yet he had left dozens of women in the same manner he had left the good doctor. So why should she be any different?

"Not long after you patched me up in Tombstone, I decided it was time for a career change," he told her, the memory of the lonely days he had spent contemplating his life after he left her returning with a poignant pang.

"You're smarter than you look," she said, and turned her attention to the unloading of several bags.

He cringed at her remark, though veiled. He had known when he left that morning nearly three years ago that she would be angry. But a man could hope that time and distance would have cooled her fury. After all, she had managed to hog-tie some poor man into family and commitment.

Once the bags were gathered around her, she glanced back at him. "I'm ready if you'd like to take me to my grandfather. I haven't seen his new hotel."

"Let me check with the driver, and then we'll walk. This is his hotel, but the main entrance is down the street a ways." He stepped over to the driver and asked the young man, "Any packages for Eugenia Burnett?"

"No packages," the driver said.

"Thanks," Tucker murmured. He hoped to God that this wasn't the package his mother had been referring to—that Sarah wasn't the surprise she was waiting for. Maybe she was just pretending to be all wrapped up in this new grandchild. Maybe she was still up to her matchmaking ways.

"Come on." He took Sarah by the arm, and she gently but firmly pulled away. Still, she continued to walk beside him. "Is your grandfather expecting you? I hadn't heard him say anything about you coming home."

"No. He doesn't know. I didn't want to worry him, and I didn't know when exactly I'd be able to get away. I had to find someone to tend to my patients while I was gone."

"What about your husband? He let you come all this way without him?" Tucker asked, his curiosity about the man she had married getting the better of him.

She glanced at him, a sharp, watchful expression on her face. "He didn't care."

Tucker frowned. "How long you been married?"

She turned her lips up, the smile not quite reaching her eyes. "Long enough, Tucker."

He grinned and shrugged. "Never hurts to ask."

He wanted to ask her long enough for what, but he didn't dare. Curiosity about just when and how she had met the man was eating at him; but he knew it was none of his business, and the doctor wouldn't hesitate to tell him so.

She glanced at Tucker, her head tilted at an angle. Lucas was staring at the adults in fascination. "My husband wasn't afraid of settling down. He didn't leave in the middle of the night, without saying good-bye."

"Good for you," he said, picking up her bags.

Tucker smiled and gave her a quick glance. She might not be spitting fire, but she was definitely peeved. From what he remembered of their night together, given even the slightest indication that she was willing, he wouldn't hesitate to charm his way back into her bed for a little frolicking between the sheets. It was a damn shame she was displeased with him and married to boot.

But she had been a threat to his freedom. So in the middle of the night he had run as fast as he could get away.

God had a sense of humor, thought Sarah. After all who would have thought that the first person she would encounter when returning to Fort Worth would have been the last person she ever wanted to see again. But here Tucker Burnett was, walking beside her the short distance to her grandfather's hotel, carrying her bags and chatting as though they were still old friends.

Fear had almost paralyzed her the moment she had stepped off that stage and seen her childhood friend, the man who had broken her heart, the father of her child.

Yet, part of her heart still leaped at the sight of his dark brown eyes and golden brown hair. And that was the part she would love to have surgically removed. They were doing so much now with modern medicine, why couldn't they cut out that piece of the heart that just couldn't get over a man?

Especially when that man was an unemotional, irresponsible, handsome, charming gunslinger—now marshal—who had been the only man to get close emotionally and physically to her in the last five years.

It just proved that tall, ruggedly handsome men, who had high foreheads, twinkling brown eyes and muscles that were shaped to perfection, were not necessarily good for a woman. This man had certainly not been who she thought he was, when he had slunk out like a fugitive in the middle of the night, after spending time in her bed.

"So how's the doctoring business?" he asked. "You still the only doctor in Tombstone? How does your husband like the fact that his wife's the only doctor for miles?"

"My, aren't you the curious one," she replied.

He grinned. "Don't know until you ask, and I've never been afraid to ask."

She shook her head at him. "I just hired a new man to help out," she replied.

She wasn't ready to respond to his question about her husband, because the man didn't care. He was dead. It was none of Tucker Burnett's business, and she would do whatever was necessary to protect her son. She would do whatever was necessary to protect the child she and Tucker had conceived that fateful night almost three years ago.

The son he knew nothing about. Sarah would lie just as long as it was necessary to protect her boy—and herself—for if the marshal knew that Lucas was his child, he would want the right to be with his son. And she couldn't face Tucker every day.

"My practice is going very well. The gunslingers of Tombstone keep me busy, patching up their newest bullet wounds."

He smiled. "You're good at that. I know."

She glanced at his chest, wondering if the wound she had mended for him ever pained him, determined not to ask. Lucas wrapped his fingers in the material of her skirt and gave a sharp tug to get her attention. "Momma, cookie."

She glanced down into eyes that were the spitting image of his father's. The fear that had consumed her the moment she saw Tucker was for the time somewhat subdued, but she knew the anxiety could return at any second.

She smiled at the boy who had changed her life. She hadn't known what to think of motherhood, but having a child had softened her. She was grateful for her son and most of the time managed to block out the memory of his father.

Until today, when she had seen Tucker standing there waiting at the stage depot.

She had never realized just how much Lucas looked like his father. Now it was clearly evident in his gaze and the stubborn set of his chin, and Sarah was amazed that Tucker had not seen the resemblance.

"Just a few more steps and you'll meet your grandpa. Then I'll give you a cookie."

The boy frowned, not quite sure that he liked her response.

"Momma, hungry."

"Lucas, I can't stop and get you a cookie out of the bag. Wait."

"What bag are they in?" Tucker asked.

She sent Tucker her best stay-out-of-this mother's look. "Do you always ignore a mother's wishes?"

"Depends on who the mother is and if I'm trying to charm the child or the mother."

The fear that Sarah had held at bay suddenly returned. Normally, she would have stood her ground, but she was tired, she was scared, and she didn't want Tucker looking too closely at her reactions.

"They're wrapped in a cloth in that gray bag you're carrying."

Tucker smiled that boyish grin he had used to charm his way into her bed, and she almost groaned. She was going to be here for only a month. Just a month of spending time with her grandfather and then she could return to Tombstone, and her life would go back to her practice and her son.

No more Tucker Burnett. She could put up with him for at least a month. Couldn't she?

She watched as he opened the bag and searched for the cookies. He found them and held up a single oatmeal cookie for Lucas. "Is this what you want?"

The boy grinned at him and ran toward his outstretched hand. The sight of Tucker giving his son a cookie touched Sarah so much she had to swallow the lump that arose in her throat and look away.

She should never have risked coming home. If the telegram had not insisted her grandfather was ill, she would not have come back to this city where she took a chance of running into Tucker Burnett, here in this place where they both had lived as children.

But she had come home, and so far Tucker had not tackled her biggest fear. He had believed her regarding her marriage, and she wasn't completely lying. She had been married. But there was no need to tell him she was a widow or that the man she married had died before Lucas was born. There was no need to tell him that she had married Walter Scott James because she had known he was going to die, and she needed his name to give to her son.

Lucas took the cookie from Tucker.

"What do you say, young man?" she said, looking at the boy as he stood between her and Tucker.

"Tank you," he said, grinning from ear to ear.

Sarah's heart leaped within her chest, and she quickly glanced at Tucker to see his reaction.

Sarah watched as he smiled at the boy and ruffled his hair.

"You're welcome." He glanced at Sarah. "Let's get the two of you settled in at your grandfather's place."

What if something gave away the truth that Lucas was his son? What if he counted the months and realized that Tucker had been conceived the night they were together? What if Tucker asked her if Lucas was his son?

She was overreacting. She knew it, but the mother in her worried, while the physician inside her reminded her to remain calm.

Sarah glanced up at the hotel in front of which they now stood. "So this is Grandfather's new hotel. Pretty fancy."

"Wait till you see the inside. Your grandfather went all out on this one."

Tucker opened the door to the El Paso Hotel, and Sarah quickly walked through, her hand wrapped securely around Lucas's smaller one. She felt rattled. She hadn't known that Tucker had come back to Fort Worth, she had never dreamed of finding him waiting for her at the stage depot, and she certainly hadn't expected him to escort her to her grandfather's hotel.

After all, sometime before dawn the night they had made love, he had walked out on her and never glanced back, not caring that his leaving had left her confused and grieving, until she realized she was pregnant. Then she had become angry, before finally she reached an understanding.

Tucker Burnett would miss seeing his son grow into a man, only because he chose not to be with her. And somehow reaching that conclusion had helped her to put his betrayal behind her, until now.

As she stepped into the entrance, her eyes took in the dark wood paneling lining the walls of the lobby, the brass fixtures, and the oak counter. A door led off to the right, and she could see a room filled with people sitting at tables eating.

The door shut behind Tucker, and he called out to the clerk sitting at the counter, "Charlie, this is Mr. Kincaid's granddaughter. I'm taking her to the old man's rooms."

The man jumped up and nodded in greeting. "Welcome, missus. Don't worry about anything; we'll take your bags for you."

"Thank you," she replied.

This was certainly nicer than any hotel her grandfather had previously owned. But then, she had come home to a town that had changed much since she had left. Fort Worth had been merely a spot in the road when she had gone away to college, but now it had grown into a frontier town that leaned just a little on the wild side.

She had seen the brothels, the saloons and the gambling halls as the stage had rolled into town. Fort Worth was no innocent settlement. It was a cowboy's last chance to sow a few wild oats, before he headed up the trail to Dodge City and sold his cattle.

The clerk behind the desk soon had two men carrying their bags to some unknown destination.

Tucker put his hand at the small of her back, and she flinched. No one had touched her there since he had all those years ago. No man had held her—no man had been in her bed—since Tucker.

Not even the man she had married.

She stepped away from his touch, refusing to acknowledge the tingle his caress always seemed to ignite, refusing to pick up where they had left off all those years ago.

Sarah James was a mother, a doctor and a woman who didn't need a man to take care of her. She did just fine on her own. The only reason she would even consider another man would be for her son. But she had yet to find one she deemed suitable, and it wasn't a pressing issue at this time in his life.

"Your grandfather keeps a suite of rooms. Come on, I'll take you to them," Tucker said, leading the way down a hall.

"Thank you," she replied politely.

At the end of the hallway, Tucker stopped before number one twenty-six and rapped on the door.

"Come on in. The door is open," she heard her grandfather say.

Tucker turned the doorknob, and Sarah stepped through the door, her son in tow. The sight that greeted her eyes stunned her. Her grandfather was not sickly looking at all, but rather robust, older, but just fine. He was not near death as she had been led to believe from the telegram she had received from Eugenia Burnett.

Tucker watched as Sarah walked into her grandfather's suite of rooms and couldn't decide if he should stay or back out the door and let them have their reunion alone. But he was reluctant to leave; he wanted to know what had brought Sarah Kincaid home.

The old man looked up from his desk, and for a moment, Tucker was afraid Sarah was going to have to resuscitate her own grandfather. The man's shock was so evident at the sight of his granddaughter and great-grandson standing before him.

"Sarah?" he asked. He stood and slowly came around the desk. "This is quite a surprise."

They met each other halfway across the room and enveloped one another in a hug.

"You don't look sick," Sarah said.

Tucker glanced at Sarah, a frown on his face. What had she just said about her grandfather being sick?

"I'm fine. Who said I was ill? I'm just old," her grandfather said, his arms still wrapped around Sarah. He released her, stepped back and gazed at his granddaughter. "You look wonderful."

"Momma?" Lucas said, tugging on her hand.

George Kincaid leaned down to his great-grandson. "Hey, little man, give your old grandpa a hug."

The little boy reached out and tugged on his mustache and giggled. "Momma?" he questioned.

"It's okay, Lucas. We talked about meeting your grandpa."

"How about instead of a hug, you just shake my hand. We'll hug later," the old man said, trying to relieve the child's fears.

He reached toward the boy and shook his hand. The child laughed as if it were a game.

"I'm glad you're here, but what made you decide to come for a visit?" he asked. "Did you think I was ill?"

"Yes. I was afraid you were dying. I received a telegram from Eugenia Burnett that you were ill."

Surprise almost left Tucker speechless as he turned toward Sarah, shock at her words stunning him. His mother had sent her a telegram?

Tucker scowled, suddenly suspicious that his mother was once again up to her matchmaking shenanigans, trying to get him and Sarah together. But how did she know they had a past. Did his mother know that Sarah was happily married and unavailable to wed her son?

Grandpa nodded and glanced over at Tucker. "Several months ago I was ill, and your mother came to take care of me. But it was only a bad cold."

"Why would she send for Sarah?" Tucker asked.

Grandpa shrugged. "I don't know. Maybe she thought I was sicker than I looked."

"I'm puzzled. If Sarah wasn't married, I would think that she's back to her matchmaking shenanigans, but that's not possible."

Sarah's head jerked toward him. "What are you talking about? Your mother's matchmaking shenanigans?"

Tucker frowned. "My mother has been trying to get all her sons married, and I'm the last holdout. But that's not possible, since you're already married. . . ."

Sarah glanced away from him for just a moment, and then she turned back to Tucker, the light reflecting off her eyes the way the sun glistens on water. "I'm not married, Tucker. I'm a widow."

Two

"Mother!" Tucker called as he strode into the home his family had lived in for over twenty years. The door slammed behind him as he walked down the hall, past the parlor to the bottom of the stairs. He had ridden hell-bent from town after leaving Sarah and her grandfather, determined to put an end once and for all to his mother's interfering ways.

He couldn't believe that once again she had stuck her nose where it didn't belong. Would she never learn to let her children make their own choices and decisions in life?

"Tucker, what are you doing here?" his mother said, as she came down the stairs, surprise on her face.

Eugenia Burnett looked the picture of the sweet little grandmother, but everyone in her family knew that image hid an armor of determination that no knight could have ever penetrated. Tucker pitied any person who stood in her way where her children were concerned. It was understood that Eugenia would do whatever she felt necessary to take care of her family.

"I'm here to discuss your *package*. It came in today from Abilene," he said, his voice gruff with anger.

"Well, where is it?" she asked excitedly.

"I left Sarah Kincaid James with her grandfather," he said angrily.

"That's nice. I haven't seen Sarah since she left to go to that fancy school back east. But what about my package? What does Sarah have to do with my package?"

"Drop the act, Mother. I know about the telegram."

"What telegram, dear?" she asked innocently.

"The one you sent Sarah saying that her grandfather was ill and that she needed to come home," he replied, his voice sharp.

His mother reached the bottom of the stairs and paused, gazing up at him, her brown eyes curious.

"Well, he was ill and he needed her," Eugenia said, turning on her heel and walking past her son into the dining room and on into the kitchen.

Tucker followed her, determined to settle this once and for all. "But his illness wasn't life threatening."

"At the old man's age, who can determine what is life threatening and what is not?" She threw up her hands. "He was very ill."

Tucker reached out and caught his mother by the arm, halting her forward progress. He released her arm and walked around her still form to stand in her direct path, making her face him. "Mother, you lied to Sarah. You made her think that he was about to die. How could you be so cruel?"

"I did no such thing. I told the truth. She chose to interpret that he was dying," Eugenia replied, her hands on her hips.

"What did you say?" Tucker asked, already knowing what was written in the telegram.

"I only told her that her grandfather had been ill, that he was doing poorly and needed nursing care," Eugenia replied.

Tucker stared at her incredulously. "Do you have no conscience? How could you take her away from her patients?" Tucker asked, his temper simmering just below the surface. "What if she had been killed coming here from Tombstone? That's a dangerous trip, Mother."

"I only sent Sarah a telegram saying that her grandfather was ill. Had been ill for quite sometime and was doing poorly. I did not say he was dying, he needed *her* or anything else. The woman made the decision on her own to come, so stop blaming me."

She turned to the stove where a pot of coffee simmered. She reached for a cup sitting on the counter and poured the warm, fragrant liquid.

"Why did you send the telegram at all, Mother? If Mr. Kincaid were seriously ill, don't you think he would have bidden Sarah to come home?" He paused, his eyes narrowing at the way she didn't seem fazed by his accusations. "Or did you think that Sarah would come home and that you could somehow manage to get the two of us together?"

She whirled around to face him. "Now, why would I think there was any possibility of getting a man like you to settle down?"

He glared at her, shaking his head. "Mother—"

"I sent the telegram because if it were me, I'd want my grandchild to come home and take care of me. I also sent it hoping that Sarah would decide to stay in Fort Worth and that she could deliver Travis and Rose's baby. Doc Wilson is getting old, and this town could use a younger doctor. Yes, I hope she stays. As for the two of you getting together, if I were Sarah, I wouldn't have you. You're too damn stubborn to see that you need a wife."

Tucker stared at his mother, speechless. It took a

moment before the words poured forth. "Well, good. I'm glad you see it that way, because I sure as hell didn't want to have to tell you that it wasn't going to happen. I'm not getting married, and you can take that to the bank. You should be happy you got Travis and Tanner married off. But leave me alone."

"Don't worry, son. I wouldn't inflict any woman with your wanderlust ways. . . ."

"Good."

"Or your sour disposition."

The two stood there staring at one another, the room suddenly very quiet. Tucker ran a hand through his hair. His heart was pounding inside his chest.

"I'm serious, Mother. I'm not good marriage material. I know it, and I'm happy living the way I am."

Eugenia smiled and patted him on the arm. "Good. As long as you're happy, I wouldn't dream of imposing on you a good woman who has a fine family, who would make you a good wife and mother for your children. If she's not what you want, I'm sure some other man in town will see her fine qualities and she'll be married soon."

Tucker wanted to roll his eyes, but he resisted. "Did you know that she was married when you sent for her?"

"She's not married. She's a widow."

"So you knew Sarah was available?"

Eugenia sighed. "Sarah is a doctor. Fort Worth needs a new young doctor. I was hoping that she would deliver Travis and Rose's baby. Plus her grandfather was ill, so she would be coming this way already. If by chance you were interested, then I would have killed three birds with one stone. So don't go thinking too badly of me. I was only trying to take care of my family."

"Fine, Mother, but don't try to push Sarah on me. I'm warning you to leave her alone."

"I haven't even seen the girl. She could have become homely for all I know."

"Believe me, she's not homely. But there will be no match between me and Sarah or any other woman. Do you understand, Mother?"

"Yes, I understand. You want to spend the rest of your life alone, free to come and go as you please. You want to die without the benefit of having children and watching them grow up, marry and have children of their own. You don't want a family, Tucker. You want no responsibilities, no ties and certainly no commitments."

Tucker shrugged. "I don't see it that way, but basically you're right. No commitments, no responsibilities."

"I don't approve, but I won't interfere."

She was far too agreeable. It was a terrible thing not to believe your own mother, but somehow Tucker just didn't quite trust her.

"You don't have to approve, Mother. This is *my* life."

Sarah had just gotten Lucas to sleep when she tiptoed back into the living area of her grandfather's suite of rooms, her skirts swishing softly.

She took a seat on the Empire sofa and turned toward her grandfather, who was reading the paper. She sighed, glancing around the very masculine drawing room. Everything was decorated in heavy woods and dark fabrics. There was an air of quiet conservative strength about the room that needed a feminine hand.

"He finally went to sleep," she told the older man, who had raised her since she was ten.

"Good," he murmured behind his paper. "He was certainly a tired little boy." Her grandfather laid down the paper. "Lucas has had quite an adventurous trip."

"Yes, he's not used to being confined, and spending all that time inside a coach was difficult. He probably drove the other passengers crazy, but he was really very good."

Sarah gazed at the man who had become both father and mother to her when her parents were killed.

Her grandfather nodded, his eyes searching hers. "So did you really think that I was dying, Sarah?"

She swallowed, not wanting to admit she had been afraid he would be dead before she arrived. "I wasn't sure. But the telegram said that you had been ill and that you weren't getting better." She flicked at a spot on her skirt. "And because I haven't been home since I left for college almost ten years ago, I decided it was time to pay a visit."

"I'm glad you did."

"You know you could have come to see me and Lucas."

He shrugged. "I intended to visit you and the boy, but the hotel's kept me busy."

"You have people who can run it," she said.

"Just like you found someone to handle your practice, but you didn't want to, did you?"

She smiled, thinking of the turmoil she had been in before she left. "You're right. I hated leaving my patients."

He glanced at her, his eyes filled with sorrow. "I almost came out when Lucas was born. Especially after I found out that your husband had died. But I broke my damn arm and just didn't feel up to the trip."

Sarah looked at her clasped hands and flexed her fingers, willing herself to relax. "Those were trying times."

She sighed and gazed around the room, the memory of her quick wedding to a man who had died before Lucas was born somehow seeming pathetic and hopeless. Everyone in town had thought she was mourning her husband, when in fact she had been pining for the loss of her child's father. She had been afraid of raising a child all alone, right up until the moment the midwife had laid him in her arms. Then she knew that everything was going to be fine.

"Things have been better since Lucas was born."

"Did you love your husband a lot?" he questioned.

She paused for a moment, wanting to tell her grandfather the truth regarding her son, but fear kept her from revealing the tale. For a moment she wrestled with her conscience, then decided to tell him partially the truth. "No. But I love my son more than life."

Her grandfather stared at her, his face full of surprise, studying her. "Then, why did you marry?"

"It seemed the thing to do at the time. He was a kind man, and I live in a dangerous town," she lied.

How could she tell her grandfather that she had married Walter Scott James because she had been pregnant with Tucker's child? That she had wanted her son to have a name without the stigma of being called a bastard.

He stared at her, his expression questioning, but his lips were silent. She felt as if he were attempting to read her mind.

Finally he glanced away. "Lucas seems a wonderful little boy."

"He is," she said wistfully. "And I'm doing my best to be a good mother to him."

"But what about you, Sarah?" Her grandfather paused. "You're still a young woman. You need a man who will take care of you and love you."

She lifted her chin and stared at her grandfather. "I don't need another man, Grandfather. I'm happier now than I've ever been, just taking care of my son and working my practice. Tombstone has settled a bit, and my life is complete."

"But don't you think that Lucas will need the influence of a man in his life? Don't you think that he deserves to have a father? And you deserve a husband."

The image of Tucker Burnett sprang to mind, and her pulse accelerated. Even after all these years, it was obvious he wasn't interested in settling down. "His father is dead. Someday, when he's older, I may consider remarrying just so that he has a man's influence, but until then, I'm not interested in getting remarried."

"Well, at least consider moving back to Fort Worth so that I can spend time with him," her grandfather said.

Could she move back to Fort Worth and live in such close proximity to Tucker and his family? Could she look at him every day and not, somehow, wind up telling him that Lucas was his son?

"I'm happy in Tombstone. I have a good practice, my neighbors watch out for me, my patients care about me, and I don't want to pick up and move back here. I'd have to start over with my practice."

"Just how long will I have the pleasure of you and my great-grandson?"

"My plans are to stay at least a month before we return to Tombstone," Sarah said, wondering for the second time that day if she had been wise to come home to Fort Worth. Wondering if she could avoid Tucker for a month.

"I'm not going to lie to you and say I won't try to convince you to stay while you're here. But I am glad you're here. That will give me some time to spend with my grandson and calculate my battle plan on how to convince you to move home permanently."

"Grandfather, you know you can always come out to Tombstone and be with us," she said, thinking it would be much safer there than here with the presence of Tucker Burnett.

"I know." He gazed at Sarah. "But my life is here in Fort Worth."

"Just like my practice is in Tombstone."

Her grandfather shook his head at her. "Oh, Sarah, you've inherited the stubbornness of your father, I'm afraid."

She laughed. "No. I think I received it from my grandfather. I still remember our lengthy discussions on my attending college. You thought that a woman had no business receiving that kind of education."

"Well, I still think it's unnatural. Most women want to get married, raise a family, and take care of a home. You want it all!"

She smiled. "You're right, I do. But I'm so glad I went to college, Grandfather. Being a doctor has made me happy. It's given a purpose to my life."

"If you're happy, that's all that matters. But I still have hopes that you will find a good man who will be a father to Lucas and a husband to you."

Sarah stared off into the distance. The image of a tall, sandy-haired man with broad shoulders and well-muscled thighs, who wore his guns slung low on his hips, came to mind. There was a man she had once wanted to marry, but he had not wanted to settle down. He hadn't loved her enough to stay.

Tucker let his horse set the pace on his way back to Fort Worth. The ride was nice and slow compared to the frantic pace he had set to reach his mother's place. His horse ambled along, taking its time, while he contemplated the return of Dr. Sarah Kincaid James.

The sun shone brightly, but the breeze that rustled the leaves of the oak trees was brisk enough to have a bite when it grazed his skin. Though the sun's rays were warm, the wind had a winter's chill to it.

For Tucker it had been a hell of a day. First with Sarah returning and then his mad dash to get to the bottom of just what part his mother had played in the arrival of the good doctor.

His mother acted the innocent, but he was no fool. She had hoped that Sarah would come home and that the two of them would somehow fall in love and marry. She knew how Tucker felt about marriage; but to his mother's way of thinking, that was illogical, and she was determined to show him the error of his ways.

Well, it would be a cold day in July before Sarah would take an interest in him again. In fact, the friendship was suffering a severe case of the chills and he guessed he couldn't blame her. After all, the way he had run out on her had pretty much ruined any chance of their being lovers again, let alone companions. He hadn't meant to take advantage of her, but somehow he had gotten in way over his head. When he had awakened in Sarah's bed, he had treated her in the same manner he had all the women before her. He had grabbed his stuff and fled in the middle of the night to avoid any hard feelings or discussions of vows, and rings, and wedding things.

Sarah had the ability to make him forget about his dreams. When he was with her, all he thought about was the way she made him feel, and that had frightened him enough that he had run.

But Sarah apparently had not let his leaving affect her. From the way things appeared, she had barely let the bed sheets cool before she had married someone else. And that man had given her a son.

His Appaloosa gave a snort and shook its head, rattling the halter. Tucker reached down and patted the animal's neck. A wandering man needed a good horse to take him on his travels, but then, he had been in the same place now for over two years, the longest time period he had stayed in any one place since he was a child. Maybe it was time to move on. Maybe it was time he resumed his drifting ways.

But was he feeling this way because Sarah had come home? Surely, after all this time, he could glance at her without remembering the smooth texture of her skin. Surely, he could talk to her without remembering the pleasure of her kiss, the taste of her sweet mouth. The way she made him feel.

He groaned, the sound loud in the gathering dusk. They were friends. She wouldn't be here forever. She would be going home to her practice. She would return to the grave site of the man who had married her and fathered her child.

Just who was this man she had married?

Tucker couldn't help but be curious about the man who had made the trip down the aisle with Sarah, shortly after he himself, had left. Hadn't she missed Tucker at all after he had gone? Or had she been so angry that she had resolved never to get involved with a rambling man again, and had run straight into the arms of some do-good, sweet-talking cowboy who would have promised her the moon just to get in her bed?

His horse snorted in the early evening air, sending up white clouds of vapor into the cold. He shivered, remembering the month he had spent in Tombstone with Sarah. Even though he had been hurt, the memory of being ministered to by the good doctor, of getting to know her better and the laughter they had shared together, was a special one. They had always been friends. Even when they were kids living and attending school in Fort Worth, he had enjoyed being with Sarah.

Only today, when she had stepped off that stage, had there ever been any friction between them. The tension had reminded him of waking up beside a woman, the morning-after awkwardness he tried to avoid, but this time that morning had occurred three years ago. Yet somehow it felt as if it had been just yesterday.

But sometime after he had left Tombstone, while he was out searching for trouble in the name of fun, she had found someone new, and this time, she had promised this man forever. While he had been sampling the West and all the decadence it offered, she had been taking care of her own chance at happiness. And though her marriage had not lasted long, she had a son. Sarah Kincaid James was now a mother.

He couldn't help but wonder if she would ever remarry. After all, she had a child—a boy who was going to need a father figure, someone to teach him the things that a man needed to know in order to survive. He was a cute kid, who looked a lot like his mother, though what must be traces of the father could be detected in his features.

Dr. Sarah Kincaid James was still beautiful, still very much someone Tucker would like to spend time with. But she wanted forever, and Tucker was not a man who could give that to any woman. He couldn't even promise he would be here tomorrow.

That night they had shared so long ago was still a pleasant memory. And before that night they had been friends for many years. She was a beautiful woman, he was a man, and they had made a mistake that one night in Tombstone. Maybe, just maybe, he could salvage the friendship.

Maybe she would show him the door and tell him to get lost, but whatever happened, he had to talk to her, had to attempt to salvage the friendship he had lost.

Three

Several days later, Tucker sat eating lunch with his two brothers and their wives, wondering what had happened to the men he had grown up with. His strong, manly brothers had become lovesick fools since they married.

Tucker watched as Travis leaned toward his very expectant wife. "Would you like some dessert, Rose? I'll order it if you want some."

At this late stage of her pregnancy, Rose was being treated by her husband as though she were a fine piece of china, fragile and delicate.

She smiled up at Travis and patted him on the arm. "Thanks, but the way this baby is kicking me right now, I don't think that's a good idea."

"So when is the baby due, Rose?" Tucker asked, thinking the woman couldn't get much bigger.

"In about three to four weeks according to Doc Wilson."

Tanner whispered something to Beth, and she smiled up at him and said, "I thought you were going to wait."

"I can't." He grinned sheepishly at everyone around the table. "Beth and I weren't going to tell you just yet; but Mother's not here, so I'll let you in on a little family secret." He paused. "Beth and I are expecting a baby in November."

"Wonderful!" Rose cried. "I'm so happy for the two of you, and the two babies will be close in age. They'll be able to play with one another. This is so exciting."

Beth laughed. "It is wonderful, isn't it?"

"Congratulations," Travis said, grinning at his younger brother. "And you haven't told Mother yet?"

"No. We're waiting until after your baby is born, so she can't drive us crazy for nearly as long," Tanner replied, then turned to Rose. "You and Travis have amazing stamina where Mother is concerned."

"She's not bad," Rose replied. "You just have to understand that you boys come first in her life."

Beth glanced at Travis. "Was Eugenia always so focused on the three of you when your father was alive?"

She didn't ask Tanner, since he had been missing from his family for well over ten years and had not been here when their father passed away. He really couldn't answer many of his very soft spoken, level-headed wife's questions.

Tucker glanced around the table at the women his brothers had married. Rose was a vivacious woman who had drawn out his brother Travis and made him a more approachable man. While Beth, Tanner's wife, was quiet and determined, more reserved. But he knew from past experience that she had a will of iron that had helped his middle brother put his past behind him.

Both men had married strong women who would be good partners through life.

Travis frowned, deep in thought, reflecting on Beth's question. "You know Mother's always been involved in our lives, but now that I think on it, she wasn't quite as caught up in our business before Father's death. I think Father probably buffered us from her interfering and most likely told her when to leave well enough alone."

Rose glanced at Beth, a startled expression on her face. "Beth, dear, I think you've just found the solution to our dilemma. Eugenia needs a man in her life. Someone to focus on besides her children."

There was a chorus of groans from the men.

"Please, don't you think it would appear a little hypocritical to do to our mother exactly what we complained she's done to all of us?" Travis asked.

"She hasn't matched up Tucker!" Beth pointed out.

Tucker frowned. "You know very well she's tried, not once, but twice."

Travis laughed. "Beth, you weren't there the other day when Tucker came in with a burr up his backside. Seems Mother sent a telegram to a certain young friend of his in an effort to get her to come home."

"We're friends, nothing more," Tucker informed the group.

Though if the truth were known, he would like to be more with Sarah, just nothing that said forever. But she wasn't the kind of woman who could dally without the promise of "I do," and he was definitely the kind of man who didn't believe in forever. That one night had been a mistake.

Tanner frowned. "Anyone we know, Tucker?"

"You knew her as Sarah Kincaid. Since she left Fort Worth, she's married and had a little boy. Her name is Dr. James now."

"She's a doctor?" Beth asked.

"Yes," Tucker said, feeling very uncomfortable as

he could see this information had become very intriguing to his sisters-in-law.

"She came home after your mother sent her a telegram?" Rose asked.

"She's here," Tucker said, not wanting to reveal too much to his brothers and sisters-in-law. He didn't need them all joining forces with his mother. "Her grandfather is George Kincaid, owner of the El Paso Hotel."

Rose looked at him curiously. "So what was in this telegram to bring her home?"

Tucker shifted uneasily in the chair. "Mother told Sarah her grandfather was sick and she needed to come home. She thought he was dying."

"Oh, no, look out, Tucker. Momma is on a mission to end your bachelor days," Tanner said, laughing.

"You're not telling me anything I haven't considered. Though Mother denies that's the real reason she sent for Sarah."

"It would be nice to have a woman doctor in town. Doc Wilson is good, but he's just so old," Beth said, not paying any attention to the men.

"She's not staying," Tucker quickly informed his sister-in-law.

"That's a shame," Travis said, his eyes twinkling with merriment. "You better keep a close eye on Mother, because you'll be saying 'I do' if you're not careful."

"I'll tell you just like I told Mother: I have no intention of settling down," Tucker said to his brother.

Rose leaned toward Tucker. "Then, you better help us figure out just who would be a good husband for Momma Burnett. Or else she won't rest until you're married."

Tucker groaned. "I'm so afraid you're right, Rose."

* * *

After Tucker returned to the jail, he couldn't help but reflect on his brothers. Funny how in the last six months life had suddenly changed for all of them. Eugenia was going to be absolutely thrilled when she found out about Beth and Tanner expecting. Now there would be two babies in the house, and Tucker could only hope that her interest would turn away from interfering with his life.

The life he had chosen wasn't meant to be shared with a wife and family. A roaming man had no room for permanent ties. Sarah's image came to mind, and he quickly pushed it aside. Not even blond doctors, whose looks were tempting enough to cast his future to the wind, could change his course.

He turned his attention to the paperwork that lay strewn across his desk. This was the part of the job he detested. Being marshal was often exciting, but filling out paperwork was tedious and boring. Tucker liked action. He liked the thrill of the chase, finding the criminal and making the arrest.

A knock at the door had him glancing up from the forms he was working on. Federal Marshal McCoy, the man who had worked with Tanner to bring in the Bass gang, stood in the doorway.

Tucker jumped up and came around the desk. "Hello, McCoy, good to see you. Come on in." He reached out and shook the older man's hand. "What brings you back to Fort Worth?"

"I'm here on an errand and thought I'd drop by to give your brother his pardon. How are Tanner and his wife?"

"They're doing fine. Tanner's busy building them their own place down the road a ways from the main house, and I just found out today they're expecting a baby."

"Sounds like Tanner really has settled into married life," McCoy replied.

"Yes, I think he and Beth are very happy."

"I wanted to stop by and see how things were going with you."

"Things have been almost too quiet. Not nearly like when I first took on this job. I was hoping Tanner would want to come work with me here as a deputy, but he's been helping Travis around the ranch."

"I guess he got his fill of law enforcement when he was running from the law. I'm going to be in town for several days. Why don't we get together and have a beer? I may be needing a new man. One of my men is considering getting married and settling down."

Tucker nodded.

"This isn't the kind of job a family man needs," McCoy said. "You're never at home."

"Besides being dangerous," Tucker replied.

"Do you like being the marshal here, Tucker?"

Tucker was taken aback by the question. "Yes, I enjoy being in law enforcement."

The marshal twirled his hat in his hands. "I could use a good man like you, Tucker."

Tucker sat up, suddenly feeling a spark of interest. "Tell me more about the job."

"Most of the time I'm off on special assignment, following some particular criminal. The way I was assigned to your brother. I never stay in one place long, so this is not a job for a man who has commitments or family, unless you like being gone from them."

Tucker shrugged. "I'm not tied to anyone or anyplace.

I like being able to pick up and go at a moment's notice."

The marshal nodded. "I understand. Like I said, the man may be getting married."

"Keep me in mind," Tucker said. "I'd like a different opportunity."

"I will."

A deputy suddenly burst into Tucker's office, interrupting their conversation. "Marshal, come quick, there's been an accident."

Tucker stood and grabbed his hat. "What kind of accident?"

"It's the doctor!"

His heart skipped a beat as the image of Sarah splayed on the ground and bleeding came to mind. A shudder passed through him, and his legs felt leaden.

"What happened?" he asked, moving toward the door.

"Some rowdy cowboy shot off his pistol, and the doctor's horse got spooked. Dragged the poor doctor for over a block before the man's boot came off and released him from the stirrup. He's hurt bad."

"Doc Wilson?"

"Who else?" the deputy asked.

Tucker ignored the man's question. Relief that Sarah was unharmed went through him, and just as quickly he wanted to kick himself for jumping to the conclusion that she had been hurt.

"Excuse me, Marshal McCoy, while I take care of business."

The marshal stood and nodded. "I've got to go anyway. We'll get together for that beer before I leave town."

"Good to see you," Tucker said, and hurried out the door to his office, walking briskly. He stopped outside the door of the jail and gave directions to his deputy. "Run down to the El Paso Hotel and tell Dr. Sarah James that I need her. Ask her to bring her medical bag."

"Sure thing, Marshal. The accident is one block over on Main Street in front of the Red Slipper Saloon. When I left, a crowd was gathering, and Charlie stayed with him."

Tucker sprinted the short distance to where the accident had occurred. When he arrived, Tucker knew the doctor was hurt badly as he lay unconscious, his leg twisted at an odd angle. Suddenly he was afraid for the man. What if he didn't live?

The town needed a doctor, and Doc Wilson was the only one they had. Who was going to deliver Rose's baby if Doc Wilson died?

Tucker pushed the thought out of his mind while he began clearing the people from around the older man. "Everyone step back and give the man some breathing room. We've got a doctor on the way."

"Who?" a man yelled from the crowd. "We don't have another doc in town."

"Just step back," Tucker said firmly.

He glanced down the street and saw his deputy hurrying alongside Sarah, her black bag in hand. She was brisk and businesslike as she walked quickly down the street. She didn't look like a doctor, but more like a refined lady, her blond hair swept off her neck with tendrils softly curling around her face.

Tucker made room for her to come through the growing crowd, and she rushed past him to the prostrate doctor. She knelt beside the man, her full skirt flowing around her. She picked up his wrist and checked for a pulse.

Softly she called, "Doc, can you hear me?"

Receiving no response, she opened her bag, reached in and pulled out a vial of smelling salts. Quickly she passed the ammonia beneath the doc's nose.

He coughed and sputtered, but his eyes opened. "What in the hell? Where am I?"

She laid her hand on his shoulder and warned him, "Lie back, Doctor. Don't try to move. You've been hurt."

With a groan he laid his head back in the dusty street.

"Can you tell me where it hurts?" she asked.

"My head is splitting," he said, shutting his eyes against the bright afternoon sun.

Quickly she checked for broken bones, frowning when she came to his leg.

"You've taken a nasty fall. I know your leg is broken, probably several ribs, and I'm worried you may have internal injuries."

She stood and walked over to Tucker. "I need a stretcher to carry him back to his office." She looked back at the doctor. "Your office is where you still keep your hospitalized patients?"

He nodded slowly.

"Okay, I'm going to need a wagon to take him to the hospital."

The doctor moaned, then turned and retched in the street, losing the contents of his stomach.

Sarah hurried back to her patient and tried to make him more comfortable. She glanced up at Tucker. "Now. Get moving. We need to move him inside and get him as comfortable as possible."

Tucker, who until that moment had been staring at Sarah, amazed as she went about taking care of the doctor, turned and yelled orders to his deputy. "Run down to the doc's and get that stretcher I know he uses. Charlie, can we borrow your wagon?"

"Sure!"

In a matter of minutes, the wagon was in place, and the deputy arrived with the stretcher. With care they lifted the doctor and placed him on the litter, then loaded the injured doctor into the wagon, while Sarah climbed up beside the man.

"Is he going to make it, Sarah?" Tucker asked quietly, so his friend couldn't hear his question.

"I don't know yet. He's got a concussion, a broken leg and possibly some internal injuries. Not to mention the scrapes and bruises. We'll know more in the next twenty-four hours. Do me a favor and tell my grandfather I'm at Doc Wilson's if he needs me."

"What about Lucas? Who's watching him?" Tucker asked.

She turned and gazed at him, her blue eyes luminous in the bright sunshine. She swallowed. "Grandfather is with him. I left them playing on the floor."

"Okay. I'll check on you later."

"Fine." She glanced up at Charlie, who was sitting in the driver's seat. "Let's go."

Tucker stood back from the wagon and watched as it rolled down the street. Now that their only resident doctor was hurt, what would the town do if Doc Wilson died? What would they do if Sarah left?

Thank God she was here. His mother had tricked Sarah into coming home; now if only they could somehow convince her to stay. But would she, considering their past?

Two days later Tucker walked into the doctor's infirmary, his hat in his hand, and found Sarah sitting at the desk.

"Hello," she said, as she glanced up from the notes she was making.

"Good morning," he said, noticing the way the blue dress she wore heightened the color of her eyes, reminding him of the lavender growing in his mother's garden. Sarah's eyes were not only beautiful in color, but they were warm, expressive and, most of the time, friendly. "How are you?"

"Fine. Other than using outdated equipment, the doctor has a nice practice here." She laid the ink quill down and looked up at him. "If you want to see the doctor, he's resting. I've set his leg and it should heal, but I'm still concerned about him. He's still dizzy, and he broke two ribs, so I had to put a binding around his chest. He's pretty banged up."

"How soon before he can see patients again?" Tucker asked.

"As his physician I don't want him working for six to eight weeks, longer if there are internal injuries."

Tucker walked around the room, glancing at all the cabinets, the examining table and the different tools lying out. "He's the only doctor we have in town."

"That's what he told me." She pushed back away from the desk and watched him as he strolled around the room. The feel of her eyes on him was pleasant.

"You know, he was thinking of retiring and now this happens." Tucker held his hat in his hands and twirled it around. "It just doesn't seem fair for him to be so hurt."

"Life isn't always fair," Sarah replied calmly.

The words he had to say wanted to come tumbling out, but he knew he had to move slowly or Sarah was likely to bolt, and he needed her to stay in Fort Worth.

"We need a doctor in this town, Sarah. You're the only one we've got right now, and you're just visiting."

Her eyes grew large, and her face tensed. "Don't ask me to stay, Tucker. You know I have my own patients back in Tombstone. The man sitting in for me is new to the town."

Tucker walked to where she sat, forcing her to look up at him. "What about the people you love? The friends you grew up with? What about my sister-in-law? Her baby is due in the next few weeks."

"Your sister-in-law can get a midwife. I'm concerned, but I can't stay."

"Why not, Sarah?" he asked. "Your husband is dead. Your grandfather is older. He could need medical attention."

Tucker felt like a hypocrite; hadn't he yelled at his mother for using this same tactic? Yet he wanted Sarah to stay. Needed her to remain in Fort Worth for the town, not himself.

"Your son is not old enough to care whether you're here or in Tombstone. Why can't you help us? At least until we find another doctor."

"I . . . I just can't."

Her facial expression was blank as if there were no emotion, and he knew something was wrong. He walked across the room and placed an arm against the window frame, leaning to gaze out into the street, not really seeing the people pass by.

She was going to leave because of him. Something was eating at her and though he wasn't sure what, he had a pretty good idea. He turned and stared at her.

"Is it because of that night we shared together?" He paused. "You won't stay in Fort Worth because of me."

"What night are you referring to?" she asked, as though she didn't know what he was alluding to.

"I never meant to hurt you that night," he said, twirling his hat nervously in his hands. "It just happened."

She shrugged and tried to pretend indifference. "I don't regret that night."

How could she ever regret that night? That was the night her son had been conceived, and she loved Lucas more than she thought possible. Yet because Tucker had walked away without saying good-bye that night, she'd come to the conclusion that he had never cared for her.

He stared, disbelief all over his face. "You aren't mad?"

"No. That happened almost three years ago. It's in the past. I got over you, Tucker."

Inside she cringed. She had gotten over him, and if she repeated the phrase enough, maybe she would believe it. But for her son, she could do just about anything.

He gazed at her. "You did, huh?"

"Yes," she said, unable to meet his gaze. The memory of his big, strong hands caressing her breasts had her jumping up out of her chair. She wandered around the room, picking up objects and setting them down again.

"Is that why you married your husband so quick?"

She frowned. She didn't need him checking dates and figures. If he started counting days and months, he could possibly realize that Lucas was his son. And that was her biggest fear of staying in Fort Worth.

Her fear of Tucker finding out that Lucas was his son made her want to pack her bags and catch the next stage out of town. The fear of someone recognizing Lucas as Tucker's son, the fear that her son would somehow be hurt if this knowledge ever came out, woke her in the middle of the night and left her sleepless.

Tucker wouldn't take the news kindly regarding the fact that he had a son, and she didn't need his family interfering in Lucas's life in the next few weeks while she visited.

No, Doc Wilson's patients were easy enough to handle, but her own concerns of being near Tucker and the secret of Lucas's birth made her nervous.

She certainly didn't need Tucker worrying about dates or why she had married so hurriedly.

"Yes, I met and married my husband quick, but what concern is that of yours?" She stood. "Frankly, it's none of your business what I do. I moved on with my life and put thoughts of you behind me."

He was quiet as he stared at her from the window. Tucker was so devilishly handsome that just looking at him filled her with wanting. When he had left her in Tombstone, it had nearly devastated her. Now here they were three years later in almost the same situation. But instead of him being hurt, Doc Wilson needed medical care, and this time Tucker needed her for the town they had both grown up in.

"Then, why won't you stay?" he asked, his voice earnest, almost pleading.

"I wanted to visit my grandfather, spend time with him and my son, not work," she said, looking into eyes the color of an oak leaf in fall. It wasn't a complete lie.

"Look, why don't you help until we find someone else? I'll get started right now putting ads in other cities' newspapers that we need a medical doctor. It shouldn't take but a couple of weeks; then you could spend the rest of your time here visiting your grandfather," he said, his words rushing out.

"At least be realistic. It's going to take more than a few weeks. It will probably take at least two months, if not longer."

"But the doctor could be healed by then," he pointed out.

Oh, God, she wanted to stay, the magnetic pull of being with Tucker almost irresistible. She didn't want to stay, the memory of Tucker's desertion still a painful wound. But most of all she wanted to protect Lucas.

She worried her bottom lip. Yet how could she leave family and friends without a medical doctor? Did she really have any choice?

But who was going to protect her heart?

"Okay. I'll stay for two months. By that time either Doc Wilson will be healed enough he can take over or you better have found another doctor for the community."

Tucker smiled, took two steps and pulled her to him. He lifted her off the floor and spun her around, holding her in his arms. Shocked, Sarah smiled, her face tight as an uncomfortable feeling filled her at his touch. She had steeled herself not to let him past her guard, but when he touched her, it was difficult at best.

Unexpectedly, he reached up and pressed his lips to her cheek.

"Thanks, Sarah!"

"Two months, that's all."

He set her back on the floor, and for a moment her knees felt as if they had turned to gel. She glanced up at him, and for a moment her heart stopped as she stared into the welcoming warmth of his brown eyes. Eyes that reminded her so much of Lucas.

She stepped out of his arms, needing to put distance between the two of them, the imprint of his hands on her body like sunlight on skin, warm and invigorating. She had just agreed to stay here two months, and she couldn't let herself get involved with Tucker again. There could never be anything between the two of them. Never!

Four

Tucker rode back to the jail, suddenly fearful of what he had just done. Having Sarah here in town for more than just a visit was going to complicate things between the two of them. Not to mention he had just given his mother all the ammunition she needed to make his life miserable.

She was going to believe that he had asked Sarah to stay because secretly, deep down, he wanted to marry her, and Eugenia would spend the next two months doing everything in her power to unite them in wedded bliss.

Was he crazy to give his mother this opportunity?

But what choice did he have? Without a doctor in Fort Worth, there would be no one to supply medical attention if anyone became hurt. And what about his sisters-in-law? Didn't his new niece or nephew deserve a doctor to take care of its arrival in the world?

The town needed a doctor. Sarah was a beautiful doctor, who he considered to be a great friend. And it felt good to have her back home where she belonged. But friends were all they could ever be.

If he were inclined to settle down, Sarah wouldn't be a bad choice, but he had no intentions on tying the knot with any woman. He was a rootless man, and from what he remembered, Sarah was a forever-after kind of woman. The kind who wanted commitment, wedding rings, babies and roots. And the last time he checked, he wasn't a damn tree.

But how was he going to convince his mother he hadn't asked Sarah to stay because he was in love with her? Words never seemed to have much effect on Eugenia. In fact, she gave new meaning to the expression falling on deaf ears.

He rode his Appaloosa up to the hitching post and saw Travis sitting there on his horse, waiting patiently for him.

"What brings you to town?" Tucker asked. "Everything okay at home?"

"Everyone is fine. No baby yet. Had to make a trip over to the mercantile for Rose and the ranch," he said, stretching in the stirrups. "Rose doesn't feel much like getting out right now. Got time to get a beer?"

"You bet. Hell, I could drink the entire keg right now."

"Troubles?"

"Just with women," Tucker replied.

They turned their horses and headed down the street to the Cowboy Saloon. A cold northerly wind whistled down Main Street sending a chill down Tucker's spine.

"Damn, but it's been cold this year," Tucker said, shivering in his coat. "I'm ready for spring to get here."

"You and me both. This baby needs to get here. Rose is miserable, and I ache with sympathy every time I look at her," Travis replied.

"Well, when your stomach starts protruding, then I'll get concerned," he told his brother.

Tucker sighed. He had done the right thing in encouraging Sarah to remain in Forth Worth. Rose and Beth needed her, but what a price to pay for his sisters-in-law and the townspeople. Putting up with his mother's matchmaking just to keep a doctor in town didn't seem quite fair. That was the reason he had asked her to stay, the only reason.

They arrived at the saloon, tied their horses outside and walked into the establishment. Tucker glanced around at the patrons as they took a seat at the bar. The usual crowd of ranchers and cowboys filled the saloon. Upstairs, one of the finest brothels in town operated. Most of the time he left them alone; but occasionally the mayor and the city council would get their dander up, and he would be required to shut them down and run the girls into the city jail.

"I heard about Doc Wilson. How's he doing?" Travis asked, while they waited for the bartender to bring their beers.

"Not so good. He broke two ribs, a leg and has a concussion. Sarah says he'll be unable to work for at least two months."

"Hey, I've got a baby coming in the next month. Who's going to deliver him?" Travis asked.

"Calm down. I thought of that. And I've talked Sarah into taking on the doctor's responsibilities for the next two months." He paused, lifted his hat and ran his hand through his hair. "My biggest concern is that Doc Wilson won't be back to work, that he'll go straight into retirement. Or even worse, Sarah says he's still not out of the woods."

"That bad, huh?"

Tucker gazed at his brother, his hat pushed back

on his head. "Yep. So I coerced Sarah into staying for two months, and then either the doctor will be back or I'm supposed to have someone else lined up to take her place."

"You scared me for a moment. I know we could get a midwife, but I want a doctor to deliver my son."

"You're awfully damn certain this is a boy."

"Of course."

"What are you going to do if it's a girl?"

"We're having a boy."

"You're pathetic," Tucker said, shaking his head.

"So could this woman trouble have anything to do with the doctor?" Travis asked, as the bartender set their beers in front of them.

"Our matchmaking mother."

"What's she done now?" Travis asked, sipping from his beer.

Tucker glanced at his brother, resisting the urge to accuse him of being stupid. Couldn't he see the problem that Sarah's staying in town presented?

"Mother is going to see Sarah's extended visit as her golden opportunity. That fate has given her a chance to bring us together."

Travis started laughing.

Tucker glared at his older brother. He wasn't trying to be a comedian. He needed his brother to defend him. Hell, he needed all the help he could get to win this battle with their mother.

"I'm sorry for laughing. But you are so right. She's going to jump on this like a bass on a june bug," he finally said.

"It's not funny. The city needs a doctor. Hell, your own wife needs a doctor, but I'm scared to death that mother is going to run Sarah off with her antics.

I'm telling you this woman won't put up with our mother's interfering."

"Then, there's nothing to worry about."

"That's easy for you to say. You're not the one she's trying to saddle with a wife. She's already gotten you leg-shackled."

"You know I didn't think anyone besides myself could be so stubborn when it came to settling down. But you're more bullheaded than a bull at branding time." Travis shook his head, a silly smile on his face. "The more you resist, the more Mother is going to hone in on your fears. You better throw her off track somehow or you're looking square in the face at a speeding locomotive, and you're tied to the railroad track."

"Thanks! But if I act interested in another woman, then she'd just turn her attention to that lady. Then I'll still have the same troubles, except it won't be with the good doctor."

"What about Sarah?"

"What do you mean?"

"Well, what if Sarah had someone else she was interested in?" Travis asked.

Tucker stopped for a moment, taken aback by the question. Someone started to play the piano in the background, and he blocked the tune from his mind.

Maybe someone else for Sarah was the solution. Maybe it would at least derail Eugenia's train for a little while.

Sarah with another man . . . It didn't have to be anyone that would be permanent. Just long enough to keep Eugenia from trying to throw them together.

"You know, Travis, you might be on to something here." He sipped from his beer. "What if I introduced Sarah to someone else. They could have dinner, and maybe she would fall for him, and the mystery man might even convince her to marry him and stay here."

"Now you're carrying this a little far. Isn't Sarah the woman that you kept reminiscing about? Isn't she the one you told me about?" Travis asked.

"Yes, but we're just good friends. She knows I'm not interested in forever. I need her attached to someone. . . ."

"Why can't you promise her forever?" Travis asked, eyes questioning.

"Because I don't want to be tied down to anyone. Not Sarah or any other female I know," Tucker said, with as much determination as he felt.

"Tucker, I'm here to tell you that settling down with Rose has been the best thing that ever happened to me."

"Well, I don't want to get married. I want to see the rest of the world, find out what's over the next ridge of mountains, and see how other people live. I've only been home since Father died. It's time I left again."

Travis nodded. "You're right, you don't need to settle down if that's the way you feel. It's just a shame though, since I think in your case Mother just might be right. But it's your life, and I'm not about to interfere."

"Thank you! Sarah is not the only female in town, and when I need companionship, I know where to find it."

Though Tucker would never admit it to his brother, there had never been a woman he enjoyed being with quite like the good doctor. Their one night together had frightened him so badly, he had run as soon as Sarah fell asleep. But he reminded himself again that they could never be.

Travis shook his head. "It's not the same and you know it."

"Maybe not, but it offers relief without all the promises and commitments for tomorrow."

"So what are you going to do about Mother?" Travis asked, sighing.

"I'm going to warn Sarah about Mother. Then I'm going to explain to her how it would be beneficial for her to meet an eligible suitor while she's visiting," he said, thinking what an awkward meeting this could be.

Oh, by the way, would you like to be courted by some men I know? If the good doctor didn't throw him out on his ear, he would be lucky.

"Do you think she'll be very receptive to the idea?"

"I don't know. Our friendship has been strained since she came back into town. It's just not the same as it was when we were in Tombstone."

Travis glanced at his brother, his forehead furrowed in a frown. "Why do you think that is?"

Tucker sighed and looked away from his brother. His fingers did a tap dance on his beer mug. "Friendship is a strange thing. Sometimes the least little thing can change it forever."

Travis sighed, and held up his hand. "Don't tell me. There are some things that are better left unknown."

Sarah chased Lucas around her grandfather's suite, his excited giggles making her feel warm and fuzzy. No matter how busy her schedule became, she always made sure she spent time with her son every day and attempted to tuck him into bed each night.

A knock sounded on the door, and she wondered who would be calling this early in the morning. "Who is it?"

"It's Tucker," he replied.

She reached up and checked her hair, pinched her cheeks and smoothed her skirt. When she realized what she was doing, she frowned. Why was she primping for this man? He couldn't care less how she looked. And no, it didn't bother her.

Crossing the room, she opened the door and gazed at the man she had tried to forget all these years. He stood with his arm braced against the door frame, the tin star twinkling on his chest. His golden brown eyes met and held her gaze, until Lucas ran to the open portal.

"Hi."

He greeted his father, a big smile on his baby sweet face. His eyes, so much like his father's, twinkled at Tucker.

Sarah felt her heart swell, and she wondered how long she had before someone realized the truth. How long before someone recognized the likeness of father and son. Or was she the only one who could see the resemblance?

"Well, hello there, young man," Tucker said, then raised his eyes back to Sarah.

His gaze was warm as he took in the sight of her morning gown. "I thought that you would be at the doc's this morning, but you weren't there."

"I haven't left yet. I was playing with Lucas while Grandfather took care of some business. Later he's going to take Lucas for a ride in the buggy, and then I'll go down," she said, her voice deliberately restrained. She could not afford to let herself get too closely involved with Tucker for any reason.

"That's nice. I guess your grandfather is enjoying spending some time with the boy," he said.

"Yes," Sarah replied. "So why are you looking for me?"

"Can I come in?"

"Of course."

Tucker stepped into the room from the hallway, his hat held loosely in his hand. He strolled across the hardwood floor, his gaze nervously scanning his surroundings.

"Have a seat," she invited.

"Thanks, I think I will," he said, sitting down on the sofa.

"So what's wrong?" she asked, noting how nervous he appeared.

He cleared his throat and twirled his hat in his hands. "Uh, we need to talk."

Sarah sat down across from Tucker. "Okay."

"Remember how I kept complaining about my mother and her matchmaking shenanigans the other day?"

"Yes."

"Well, I wanted to warn you, I think she's trying to put us together." He took a deep breath and slowly released it. "One of the reasons my mother sent you that telegram was to bring you home to marry me."

Sarah's heart skipped a beat, and then she laughed, the sound strained. It was a wonder Tucker was still in Fort Worth. It was a wonder he hadn't bolted for his horse the moment he realized what his mother was up to.

"She doesn't know you very well, does she?" Sarah said. "Even I know better."

"I've told her over and over that we're just friends, but she refuses to listen." His hat was becoming misshapen in his nervous grasp. "We've been friends since we were kids. Nothing's changed that. But we both know we could never marry."

Did he really believe their friendship hadn't changed? Did he think he could just crawl into her bed, dizzy her with his incredible lovemaking, leave in the middle of the night, and still be good friends the next time they saw each other? God, he was a stubborn, foolish man.

That one night had changed her life forever, and if he would let himself, he would know how much it meant. But he refused to acknowledge to anyone the importance of that night.

"Of course we're just friends," she said, feeling like a liar. How could they ever be just friends when they had a child together? A child he knew nothing about, a child he didn't recognize.

She shook her head, trying to rid herself of the unjustified anger that always seemed to be present when she thought of Tucker. She was being illogical, but she couldn't help it. She saw Tucker everywhere in Lucas, and that frightened her. From the color of his eyes to the sound of his laughter and even his persistent nature, he reminded her of his father.

Lucas giggled and handed Tucker his favorite toy, a wooden soldier. He took the toy from Lucas and, much to the child's delight, acted as though he was playing with it.

The child grabbed the toy back and ran across the room giggling.

Tucker watched him and smiled. "I've been thinking about you staying in town and how my mother is going to react to this news."

Sarah almost laughed, but refrained. He had left her grandfather's hotel room so upset the other day over the telegram his mother had sent her. He had repeated over and over that she was up to her matchmaking shenanigans once again. Now Sarah understood.

"With you remaining in Fort Worth, she's going to do everything in her power to find someway to arrange for us to be together," he said anxiously.

"Why?" Sarah asked.

"Because she's desperate to get me married."

"That can only happen if we let it. And we both know it's not going to happen." Sarah couldn't help but wince inside. The thought of her and Tucker married, together with Lucas, was heart wrenching. But there was no second chance, and she could not give her heart to Tucker a second time.

"My mother is determined, Sarah."

"I'm not afraid of your mother, Tucker."

"I know. But she's a strong-minded woman who has succeeded with my other two brothers." He paused. "Actually, I have an idea that might just throw her plans awry."

"What's that?" Sarah asked.

She watched as he sighed and glanced down before lifting his eyes back to hers. "I thought that maybe you might consider seeing someone while you were here. You know, maybe do some courting, and consider staying permanently. I could help you."

"What?" she asked, stunned at the sudden turn in the conversation. Was he offering to help her find a husband?

"Are you suggesting that I court other men just to keep your mother from pestering you?"

"Well, it would solve the problem, but . . ."

"Are you suggesting that I let you help me find a husband?"

Tucker grimaced and shrugged his shoulders. "Kind of."

He was offering to help her find a husband when for so long he had been the man she dreamed of. She almost burst out laughing at the absurdness of his suggestion.

Only she felt like hitting him even more.

She watched as he shifted uncomfortably on the sofa. "I know it seems kind of forward of me, but you might find someone from here that you'd be interested in marrying."

"No," she said emphatically, suddenly almost angry that he was so blind. "I'm not interested in courting. I'm not interested in staying in Fort Worth. I have my son; I don't need a man."

Tucker nodded. "I know. I just thought that maybe you'd want the boy to have a father."

Lucas had a father. He had a father who was an idiot . . . a total and complete ass to think of suggesting that he help her find a husband.

"Absolutely not."

"Well, I just thought that maybe if there was someone else you were interested in, Mother would leave us both alone."

"I'm not going to rearrange my life just because your mother doesn't know the meaning of the word 'no.' I'll deal with her directly."

"You're sure?" he questioned.

"No doubt."

"All right, I just wanted to warn you. If you change your mind . . ."

"I won't!"

He sat on the couch, watching Lucas play with the toy soldier. Finally he looked up and gazed at her. "So how's the doctor been doing?"

"He's about the same. At least yesterday he seemed to improve a little. I really need to get over there," she said, suddenly anxious for Tucker to leave.

Tucker stood. "Okay, I'll be going then, but if you need me, you know where I'm at."

"Yes. I know."

Tucker went to the door, and as he stood there, Sarah couldn't help but remember images from their night together: the feel of his muscles beneath her hands, the way his skin glowed, the strength of his embrace and the power of his kiss. She stared at his lips, remembering the way they had felt covering her own, making their way to her breasts. . . .

She closed her eyes for just a brief moment.

"I don't know how to tell you to be prepared, but I know Mother is going to try something."

"I'll handle it," she said quickly. All she knew was that he had left her in the middle of the night. Even knowing that he probably left every woman that way, so as not to face her in the morning, it still hurt. Somehow she had imagined that what they had shared was different.

"We wouldn't even be having this conversation if it weren't for my mother. I don't plan on ever marrying, but if I was going to marry anyone, you'd be my first choice."

She glanced up at him, and for a moment, she felt the urge to put her lips on his—kiss him once again, find out if her memories were really as good as she envisioned—then permanently shut the door on her memories and forget her experience with Tucker.

"Don't flatter yourself. You're not a marrying kind of man, and I'm not getting involved with anyone like you ever again," she said. "Are we clear on this subject now?"

He grinned. "That's one of the things I've always admired about you, Sarah. You know your own mind, and you're not afraid to speak it."

The smile she had summoned felt as if it would crack from the strain. "Get out of here," she said playfully, though she meant every word. "You're a man full of false promises, and I don't want to hear them."

"No, I never make promises, Sarah." He tipped his hat and walked out the door. "Especially ones I can't deliver on."

Sarah closed the portal and leaned against the wood. Yes, he was right; he had never made her any promises. God, how could she spend two months in the same town with this man without letting her feelings slip through? And his mother. She surely didn't need Eugenia nosing around and finding out the truth.

She laughed. He had asked her to see other men! What a homecoming!

Sarah heard the knocking on the doctor's office door, but was checking her patient's wounds. She hurried through the hallway connecting the house and the office and heard the voice she had been dreading.

"Yoo-hoo, is anyone here?" Eugenia called.

"Hello, Mrs. Burnett, how are you?" Sarah asked, as she strolled into the office area. "I'm sorry I didn't get to the door, but I was changing the doctor's bandages."

"I'm fine, dear. I must say you are looking lovely. I haven't seen you since you left for that fancy college you insisted on attending back east."

"That was a long time ago."

"Yes, it was, but I'm so happy that you're here and that you're replacing Doc Wilson." Eugenia took a breath and paused. "I'm really worried about him. How is he?"

"He's seems to be improving a little bit each day. It's just going to take time." Sarah smiled at the older woman's ploy. "But I'm not replacing him. I'm just filling in until he's strong enough to resume his duties or the town finds someone else."

Eugenia shook her head. "Whatever you say, dear. Tucker told me that the two of you have been getting reacquainted. I'm so glad to hear that. Since you've been back in Fort Worth, I've noticed some nice changes in him, and I'm hoping that's because of you."

"Don't give me credit for any changes in Tucker. We really haven't been getting along all that well since I've returned."

"Well, he's like his father. Stubborn as they come," the older woman said. "You know, it's been ages since you've been out to the house. Why don't you bring your son and come for a visit."

Sarah decided it was time for some frank discussion with Tucker's mother regarding her matchmaking and the telegram that had brought Sarah home. "Eugenia, Tucker came by and warned me about your intentions regarding the two of us. I also assume that's the reason you sent me that telegram about my grandfather. You know, I really did not appreciate being scared into coming home."

"What, dear? I didn't mean to scare you, but your grandfather was ill. I took care of him, so I would know. As for Tucker, he's so confused about what he wants and needs right now. I hope that you can help him."

"Tucker does not want to marry, and I'm not about to get involved with your son again." As soon as the words were out of Sarah's mouth, she wanted to retract them.

"Again?" Shock rippled across Eugenia's face—followed by a smile.

Sarah wanted to kick herself. Why had she let the word "again" slip when she knew Eugenia would jump on it? She could almost see the thoughts scampering across the woman's brain like a stampeding herd.

"What do you mean 'again'? When were the two of you involved?" Eugenia asked.

"I meant a man like Tucker."

"Oh." She stared at Sarah. "I bet it was in Tombstone."

"Eugenia, Tucker and I will never be married. Please don't try and push us together."

The woman completely ignored her.

"Like I was saying, why don't you bring your son, Lucas, out to visit with us? Tucker could teach him how to ride a pony, and you could meet my daughters-in-law, Rose and Beth."

"We're really very busy," Sarah said, trying to politely refuse the woman.

"I insist. Rose's baby is due in four to six weeks, and you're going to be her doctor. So when you come out to see Rose, bring Lucas and we'll make a day of it."

"If I do as you request, you have to understand that there will be nothing between Tucker and me."

"Oh, right, dear. That's between the two of you. Whatever you say."

"I mean it, Eugenia. You sent me the telegram to get me home. Granted, I should have come long before now. But I'm here, and nothing is going to happen between Tucker and me."

"Well, I understand how you feel." Eugenia held her reticule in her hands.

"Would you like to see the doctor now, Mrs. Burnett? I'm sure he's up to having visitors," Sarah said, feeling the need to rid herself of this woman as quickly as possible, before she made some other remark.

"No, dear, I just wanted to come by and tell you welcome back and how delighted I am that you're going to be our new doctor. Tucker and I both are happy to see you."

"Thank you, but it's only temporary."

"Well, I will be going, but I do expect you to come out soon to see Rose and be sure to bring your son."

"We'll see," Sarah said, refusing to commit herself to Eugenia's invitation.

Eugenia walked back to the door. "Tell Doc I said hello."

"I will."

She was half out of the door when she stopped and turned back to Sarah. "I know you don't believe me, but you and Tucker are meant to be together. Toodoloo, dear."

Sarah watched as she stepped out of the door and closed it firmly, effectively cutting off any reply that Sarah might have given. This woman was stubborn enough to make Tucker look like an amateur.

For two days Sarah kept replaying Eugenia's visit over and over in her mind. God, if the woman knew that Lucas was Tucker's son, she would probably have them both kidnapped and taken to the justice of the peace. Anything to get them joined as man and wife, whether they wanted to be together or not.

Funny, Sarah had never thought of herself being with any man but Tucker. Even before Tombstone he had been the friend to whom she had confided all her hopes and dreams, the man on whom she had practiced her first coquetry, and the one she had missed when she left town to go to medical school.

Now his mother was on a mission to get them together permanently, and Sarah saw only heartache looming in the future. Eugenia's meddling seemed to push Tucker further away, but the woman was too determined to see that her interfering did more harm than good.

A man like Tucker only ran faster the more dogged someone nipped at his heels, and right now he was poised for the race of his life. And Sarah couldn't help but think that maybe she should be the one to run. Maybe she should pack up and take Lucas home, right now.

Life was full of choices, and she was not a woman who let convention stand in her way. She could leave right now and return to Tombstone without helping the people of Fort Worth. Or she could try once again to reach Eugenia and make the woman understand that she and Tucker would never be married. Or she could reconsider Tucker's proposal of finding someone to court her while she was here.

She tossed the ideas around in her head for several moments, thinking about each of them, searching every possible angle, tossing out the impossible ones.

She couldn't leave Fort Worth and the people she cared about without medical help. No matter what happened, she was a healer, and she took her profession seriously. She could not leave until either the doctor was well or someone else took her place.

Yet trying to make Eugenia understand the futility of a relationship between her and Tucker seemed impossible. The woman was a cyclone blowing in and out of people's lives, leaving behind damage and destruction, never intending to hurt, never intending to do harm. The woman just plain refused to listen.

Then there was the possibility of Tucker finding her someone he thought she could marry. But she didn't want to marry. Though the thought of two months of Eugenia pushing her and Tucker together, while his mother only drove them further apart, was not exactly appealing either.

And though Sarah was loath to admit it, she didn't know what she wanted with Tucker, but she certainly didn't want the chance of them being together totally destroyed. Yet Eugenia was on a course that was destined to make Tucker run as far from Sarah as his long legs would take him.

A knock on the hotel door interrupted her thoughts. She stood and went to the door, turning the lock slowly before she opened the portal.

One of the hotel messengers stood before her, a package in his hand with a hand-delivered note.

She signed for the package and shut the door. There was no name on the outside of the parcel except her own. Curious, she ripped open the tissue paper and tossed the lid aside. She reached inside the tissue-lined tin box and pulled out a white wedding veil with lace and pearls trimming the headband. Immediately she knew whom the package was from.

She tore into the envelope, fury making her fingers tremble.

Dear Sarah,

I've always dreamed of one of my daughters-in-law wearing my wedding veil when she weds my son. I'm sending you this veil so that you will know the faith of my belief that you and Tucker are meant to be together. Though I don't expect the wedding to be held tomorrow, I do think eventually you will marry my son. Please do me the honor of wearing this veil when that day comes.

Sincerely,
Eugenia

Stunned, she stared at the white veil that had been lovingly wrapped in tissue and preserved. Oh! Sarah crumpled the note in her fist. The woman had nerve. To send her wedding veil to an almost stranger with a note regarding her son? How could she be so bold?

Well, Sarah could be just as stubborn. She would return the veil at once to Tucker and tell him to tell his mother in no uncertain terms that there would never be a match between the two of them.

Eugenia had set her sights on her goal, and she was determined she would succeed, but Sarah was suddenly just as determined to put an end to her matchmaking ways. Sure, at one time she had wanted Tucker. But she wanted him to love her, not make a vow because his mother imposed upon him enough that he finally catapulted into marriage.

Maybe Tucker was right. She should meet the men he was willing to introduce her to, not to marry them, just to keep Eugenia off balance. With her involved with other men, she hoped Eugenia would give up on Tucker and Sarah being together.

Or maybe Tucker would consider that he could lose

her to another man or maybe this would keep mother and son from driving Sarah crazy while she was here.

Whatever happened, it appeared that the next two months were going to be interesting, and Sarah was going to have a full social calendar for the first time in years.

Five

At the sound of the rapid knock, Tucker glanced up from the paperwork on his desk. Why did the sight of Sarah always cause his heart to give a small leap? She stood in the doorway, her face red, her body taut. Something was dreadfully wrong.

"Can I come in," she asked, her voice polite and brisk.

He jumped up from behind his desk and hurried around to greet her. "What's wrong? You wouldn't have come here if there wasn't a problem."

He could see the tension in her body in the way she walked toward him carrying a small tin.

"What's in the tin?" he asked, fearing her answer.

"This is what's the matter," she said, laying the tin down on his desk and pulling off the lid.

She reached inside the white tissue paper and pulled out a wedding veil.

Tucker stood to the side of his desk, shock paralyzing him as he stared in horror at the white piece of material. Suddenly he remembered where he had seen this lacy material. He recognized the garment from a tintype of his parents' wedding day. It was his mother's bridal veil.

He shook his head. This was beyond what even he had expected from his mother. Just how far was she willing to go to see him wed?

He ran his hand through his hair. Oh, God, was he in trouble. He glanced at Sarah and noticed the tautness around her mouth, the grim determination in her features. What could he say to her?

"I don't know what to say," he mumbled, taken aback.

"She came by the clinic the other day, and I thought I had made it abundantly clear to Eugenia that you and I would never marry. She sent this veil to me to show her faith in just how much she believed we belong together."

Tucker cringed and shook his head in disbelief. "I tried to warn you."

Sarah watched him, a frustrated expression on her beautiful face. "I was bluntly honest with her, and she didn't hear me."

"Did she send a note with the veil?"

"Yes. She had the gall to ask me to wear the thing when I married you."

Tucker burst out laughing. "Well, she's going to be waiting a long time."

"I'm glad you find this amusing. I've been rather annoyed."

"I'm sorry. Even I never thought she would go this far," he said, wondering if anything he said to his mother would do any good.

Sarah sighed. "I attempted to talk to her, let her know that we would never be a couple, but she obviously chose to ignore me."

He cringed. Sarah's words sounded so final, yet that was what he wanted.

"I'll talk to her again, and tell her to leave you alone."

"What makes you think she's going to listen to you?" Sarah sighed. "I hate to admit this, but I think you're right about your mother."

She stared at him, the blue of her eyes reminding him of a clear bright sky, where he wanted to lose himself.

"I've been reconsidering your suggestion."

"Oh?" Tucker said, suddenly uneasy. Maybe the idea of her courting other men wasn't such a good idea after all.

"Maybe it would be good for me to be seen with other men. Maybe then she would understand that there will be nothing between the two of us and leave us both alone."

"That's what I was thinking," he said, but somehow the scheme just didn't seem quite as agreeable as before.

The thought of her being with one of his friends made him wince. How could he look at the two of them together without remembering how it felt to be in Sarah's arms? How could he look at Sarah without thinking even the slightest nod in his direction would have him back in her bed, as long as there were no commitments, no promises.

She looked damn good standing here, her blue eyes sparking with indignation, her blond hair pulled up off her delicate neck. He wouldn't hesitate at an opportunity to kiss her succulent lips. Hell, he wouldn't hesitate at an opportunity to share her bed again.

"Okay, I'm willing to try this idea of yours just so she will leave me alone. You line up the men, and I'll agree to have dinner with them, be seen with them," Sarah said. "I'm willing to try this at least once."

Tucker stared at her a moment, thoughts racing through his mind. How could he back out of this plan? How could he admit to her that he didn't want to see her with other men? He couldn't.

"I've already got the first one in mind. I'll contact him and see if he's interested," Tucker agreed, ignoring the apprehension he felt at her seeing other men. This was what he wanted. Right? He couldn't back out now.

"All right. In the meantime, what do you want me to do with the veil?" she asked.

"Keep it."

"The veil is your mother's. I'll return it to her when I go to see Rose. That way I can tell her to her face just how her plan isn't going to work."

Tucker picked it up and looked at the pearl headdress. "I'm surprised she didn't send you the entire dress."

"Maybe we were never the same size," Sarah acknowledged.

Tucker couldn't help but glance over Sarah's body. No, he doubted very seriously if his short, plump mother had ever had as many curves as Sarah, or was ever built to make a man dream about running his hands over her generous breasts and small waist.

The urge to wrap her in his arms and let his fingers glide across her velvety skin engulfed him. He wanted to feel her naked flesh beneath his fingertips, caress her satin skin and explore her body just like he had done before.

He took a deep breath and tried to bring his mind back to the present. Back from the memory of Sarah to the realization he was going to give her to another man. "You're probably right."

"Well, I'm on my way to the clinic and just wanted to show you the latest matchmaking shenanigan your mother has pulled and tell you I had changed my mind."

He put the veil back into the tin box and replaced the lid on the container and handed it back to Sarah. "I never thought she'd go this far."

Sarah sighed. "I wouldn't be a bit surprised if she tries something else."

"Oh, no. This is her last matchmaking shenanigan."

She started walking toward the door, and the urge to stop her and take her in his arms and kiss her full red lips almost overcame him. But instead he walked alongside her to the open portal.

At the door he stood there and gazed down into her eyes, which reminded him of a warm spring sky. Unable to resist touching her, he reached out and laid his hand on her arm, his fingertips tingling.

Sarah stopped and gazed up at him expectantly, eyes warm and questioning, and he wanted to lose himself in her gaze.

"I . . . I'm sorry that this has interfered with your homecoming," he said, watching as her tongue nervously flicked across her bottom lip. Not really caring what he said as long as she stayed for just a moment longer.

She shrugged. "It's not your fault. Well, I guess I better get down to Doc Wilson's and see what's going on there."

"I'll come by later and let you know if the man I have in mind is willing."

Tucker had to go through with this plan; he had

no choice now. He was the one who had suggested this damn scheme, and now he would be forced to endure it. But it was the right thing to do, he kept telling himself. His mother would leave them both alone, and maybe, just maybe, Sarah would find a man who would keep her in Fort Worth. He needed her to stay, for the town's sake, but did he really want her to find another man?

"That's fine." She stepped out of his office and walked across the hall and out the front door.

Tucker watched her go, his mind full of images of how her skin had glowed in the moonlight, the thrust of her naked breasts and the taste of her lips.

Was he crazy to hand her over to another man? Or just crazy for torturing himself with the memory of the feel of her in his arms?

Sarah walked into the clinic and saw a young red-haired woman standing at the door.

"Yes, can I help you?" she asked.

"Mrs. James, I heard you were sitting in for Doc Wilson . . . and I . . . I thought that maybe you being a woman doctor, that you could help me."

She glanced at the woman, who was so nervously standing at the doorway. She tried to put her at ease. "Come in, Mrs . . . ?"

"It don't matter what my name is. I just wanted to see if you could help me."

Sarah tried to reassure the pretty young woman whose green eyes barely meet her own. "There's no one else here but me and you. Come on in and we can talk about whatever is bothering you."

"I work down at the Silver Slipper. I'm . . . I'm a calico queen, Dr. James," she informed Sarah.

"You're also a woman who needs a doctor. I'm a physician," Sarah said slowly. "Now, how can I help you?"

The woman sighed and stepped into the office, shutting the door behind her. "You don't mind me coming to see you?"

"Not at all," Sarah said warmly.

"Well . . . I keep having this problem."

For the next several minutes Sarah listened to the woman describe her symptoms, knowing immediately that what she was describing sounded like a fungus.

"What is it, Doc?"

"I don't think it's serious, but I would like to take a look at it. Why don't you go into that curtained-off area, remove your pantaloons, wrap a sheet around you, and then I'll come in and take a look at it."

"Okay," she said nervously.

Sarah gave the woman a few moments before she went in to see her new patient. She walked in and tried to be quick about looking at the woman's legs and groin area.

"You have a fungus that is transmitted sexually," Sarah told the woman. "I'll give you a jar of cream, and you will need to apply it twice a day until the rash disappears."

The woman breathed a heavy sigh of relief. "I was so afraid. I feared I'd gotten the clap."

"You know, in your occupation, you run a very high risk of catching a disease," Sarah said, trying not to sound judgmental.

"Yes, but a girl's gotta earn a living, and I don't know any other way."

Sarah nodded in understanding, not wanting to alienate the woman. "I understand. Why don't you get dressed and then we can talk some more."

She left the woman to dress and found the cream

in the doctor's drug cabinet. She also opened her own medical bag and reached inside for a condom.

When the woman came out, Sarah handed her the cream and then showed her the sheepskin. "This is a condom. You put it over a man's erect penis and it protects you and him from catching a disease. It also will help keep you from getting pregnant, though it's not foolproof."

"What is it?" the woman asked.

"It's the dried gut of a sheep, and you can reuse it."

"Oh! But will my customers agree to use it?" she questioned.

"If you're honest and tell them that it protects them from catching a disease from you, why wouldn't they?"

"I don't think they want to hear me talking about the clap when they're paying me for sex," she said.

"Then, just slip it on them before they enter you," Sarah suggested. "Make it fun and in the end they'll thank you for it."

The woman reached out and took the condom from her. She let her fingers run over the soft skin. "This will keep me from catching a kid?"

"It will help," Sarah said. "Rinse it with soap and water after every use. And when you need another one, come see me. I'll be here for two months."

The woman glanced up from the skin she held in her hand. "Thank you."

Sarah smiled. "You're welcome. Now, come back and see me if the cream doesn't clear up the red patches."

"You know, most people don't want to have anything to do with women like me. Even Doc Wilson wouldn't help us, 'less he just had to."

"I'm a healer. If this condom helps keep you from

getting sick, then I've done my job. You tell the other women, I'm here for the next two months, and I'll be happy to help anyone."

The woman nodded. "By the way, I'm called Buckskin Sue."

"Nice to meet you, Sue."

She took the cream and put it in her reticule, then took out a few coins and handed them to Sarah.

"Is this enough?"

"That will do. Come back to see me before I leave, Sue."

"Thanks, Doc, I will." The woman stepped out the door.

Sarah watched her from the window walking down the street until she noticed a small figure in pants, with a straw hat, standing at the edge of the house. She walked outside to where she could get a better look at the boy and see what he needed.

He backed into the shadow of a tall cedar bush and slinked around the corner of the house. Sarah followed, suddenly curious about what the lad was doing.

She slowly moved around the corner of the house to a small shed where he huddled in the darkness, hiding.

"Please don't be afraid," she called. "Come out and talk to me."

The small figure came into the light, but all Sarah could see was the top of the hat and the white shirt and pants. When the boy raised his head, she stared into the battered and bruised face of a young Chinese girl.

She almost gasped at the sight of the poor girl's bruised and swollen face, but managed to restrain her outcry.

"Hello," she said, trying to recover from the surprise that it was a girl and she was so badly beaten. "Can I help you?"

The girl just stared at her.

"Do you need medical attention? I'd be happy to take a look and make sure you're all right," she offered, trying to let the girl make the first move.

The woman-child opened her injured mouth and tried to say something. A tear rolled down her cheek. "Hur . . . t. Don't let . . . hurt me."

Sarah wanted to take her in her arms and comfort her, but was afraid any sudden movements and the girl would bolt. And she could see only the young woman's face. What did the rest of her body look like?

She laid her hand on the girl's arm and touched her gently. "Come inside with me and let me help you. I won't let anyone hurt you, I promise."

"Wo Chan, he will find me. He will hurt me," she said, her words halting and mumbled through swollen lips.

Sarah shook her head. "Come in. We'll go through the back door. No one will know. I'll keep you safe. You have my word."

The girl stared at Sarah, and the lady doctor saw the pain and bewilderment in her dark eyes. Slowly the girl nodded in agreement, and Sarah hustled her as fast as she could through the back door of the doctor's house.

Tucker knocked on the door of Doc Wilson's office, astonished it was locked. He glanced up in surprise as Sarah peeked through the window at him. He heard the lock turn and watched as she opened the door for him.

He glanced at her, puzzled. "Are you so afraid of my mother now that you lock the doors?"

"No." She motioned for him to come in the door and then quickly shut the open portal behind him, turning the key in the lock. "I'm so glad you came by. There's something I need to talk to you about."

He smiled, noticing for the first time she appeared tense. "Well good, because I needed to tell you about your first date."

He cringed inwardly at the thought.

She shook her head, her blond curls swaying. "Later. First I have to tell you about Kira."

"Who?" he questioned, gazing into the blue softness in her eyes. God, why did he always feel the urge to take her in his arms when he saw Sarah?

"This afternoon after one of my patients left, I noticed this young boy standing outside by the back of the house in the bushes. Only it wasn't a boy; it was Kira." She paced back and forth across the small office, her skirts swishing with a quick rhythm.

"Who is this Kira person?"

She raised her hands excitedly. "She's a young Chinese girl. Tucker, you've got to do something. She works for Wo Chan, and he beat her badly."

Tucker swore and felt the hair rise on the back of his neck at the name of Wo Chan.

Sarah pleaded with him. "She can't go back there. I had to put stitches in the cut above her eye, and I think he broke her nose. She's frightened, and I told her she could stay here as long as she liked."

He tensed as fear suddenly lodged in his throat. Wo Chan ran an opium parlor on the west side of town. Several times Tucker had tried to close down the opium den, but had been told by the members of the city council that as long as the man paid his fines and his taxes, to leave him be. Though Tucker disagreed, one of the reasons he got along with the council was because he listened to their suggestions.

And now Sarah wanted to risk her life by keeping one of Wo Chan's girls with her. He shuddered to think of what the man would do if he found out. Somehow he had to convince Sarah that this was one do-good project she should leave alone.

"You can't keep her here."

"Why not?"

"Because he'll find out, and then he'll want her back. She's one of his girls, and he's not going to let her go."

"He beat her until she could hardly stand. It's a wonder he didn't kill her, and you want me to send her back? She's sixteen years old!"

God, this was all he needed. Sarah had always had a bleeding heart; it was one of the reasons she had become a doctor. And now she was turning her attention to a young girl who was working for a man who would do anything to get back what he thought belonged to him. Unfortunately this man was known for beating his girls into submission, and there wasn't much Tucker could do to stop him.

"Look, it's a damn shame, but unless she decides to get away from him, there's not much I can do. He's not going to let her go," Tucker said bluntly.

Sarah grabbed his hand. "I'll pay him for her; then she can be Lucas's nanny. I've been considering hiring one for months and just haven't done it. She can watch over him."

"Sarah, listen to me. He's going to be insulted that you interfered. He's going to want her back. He won't take your money, but he will hurt you."

Somehow he had to talk her out of helping the

girl. Somehow he had to keep Sarah from getting involved with someone like Wo Chan. Somehow he had to protect Sarah at all cost.

"Well, he's not getting her back. And if you don't want to help me, then fine." She released his hand. "Now excuse me."

Damn! He didn't like Wo Chan hurting the girl, but his concern was for Sarah.

"Wait! I didn't say I wouldn't help you. Let me see the girl."

Sarah led him through the office area down a short hall to the clinic beds. When they stepped into the room, he gasped at the sight of the young girl's face. Her eyes were red and puffy with rings of black and purple surrounding them. Her lip was cut and swollen, and she had a bandage across her left brow.

Tucker clenched his fists, the urge to leave and find the person who did this to her almost overwhelming.

"Kira, I'd like you to meet my friend, Tucker Burnett. He's the marshal."

The girl's eyes grew large with panic, and she glanced at Sarah as if she had betrayed her.

"It's okay," Sarah assured. "He's a friend of mine. He won't hurt you."

Kira watched him, her eyes wary, never letting him out of her sight. Tucker nodded to the girl. Someone had hurt her badly, and the sight of her blackened face left him furious.

He took Sarah by the elbow and guided her out into the hallway. "Okay, I understand why you want to help her. Hell, I want to help her, but I'm telling you, Wo Chan is going to try to get her back."

"Well, he can't have her."

"Are you willing to endanger yourself, your

grandfather and your son? Are you willing to risk their lives for hers?"

Sarah frowned. He could see her thinking rapidly and watched as her blue eyes reflected her worry. He didn't like the thought of Sarah being in danger. He didn't like Sarah taking chances. But what could he do?

She stood before him, her blond hair pulled up off her neck exposing her slender throat, her blue eyes gazing up at him with resignation.

"I don't have any choice. I can't let another human being go back to a situation like that. He'll eventually kill her. I'll keep her safe until I leave. When I return to Tombstone, she can go with me."

Tucker groaned. He knew she was right and even thought her decision a fair evaluation, but that didn't mean he had to like it any.

"Okay. But you've got to be careful. Maybe he won't find out who has her until then, but I doubt it. For now, keep her indoors and don't let anyone else know that you are protecting her."

"All right. I'll start being extremely cautious."

He stared at her, his hand reaching out involuntarily and brushing back a loose curl. He took a deep breath and released it slowly at the feel of the silken tendril beneath his fingers.

Why was he feeling so much anxiety about the dinner he had arranged for Sarah? This was what he wanted? He had suggested this stupid idea.

"The reason I came by was to tell you about your first courting."

"Oh? Who is it?"

"Neville Smith, the schoolteacher."

* * *

Sarah James stood in the doorway of the restaurant and glanced around the room. What was she doing here? The temptation to turn around and go home was intense as she gazed about the crowded dining room. If Tucker could set her up with another man, then she was going to at least meet him, just to show Tucker she could play his game and beat him at it.

Though she wished to God it wasn't so, there was still this attraction between them. She could feel it, and she knew he did, too. And while she didn't like his mother's tactics, Eugenia wasn't the main reason Sarah had agreed to see other men.

She glanced around one more time and almost groaned as she saw a man heading toward her. He wasn't bad looking; he was about average, though short and thin with a hairline that receded into next week and spectacles that covered his dark beady eyes.

"Mrs. James?" he asked.

"Yes," she replied, reminding herself that looks weren't everything.

"I'm Neville Smith. Tucker said you would have dinner with me tonight." He pushed his spectacles back up his nose.

"Yes," she said, swallowing, a fixed smile frozen on her face. She resisted the urge to run the opposite direction as fast as her legs would carry her.

"I went ahead and took the liberty of getting us a table. You don't mind, do you?"

"Oh, no," she replied, thankful at least that maybe this dinner would be swift and she could escape back to the hotel.

He took her arm and led her to their table where he pulled out a chair for her. The dining room was filled with people, and hopefully someone in this room would take the news back to Eugenia. That was the reason she was doing this, right?

"I'm so pleased to make your acquaintance, though I must admit you're not at all what I was expecting," he said, gazing at her with an almost shocked expression. "You're much better."

What had he been anticipating?

"Thank you. I'm going to take that as a compliment."

"Please do," he said. "I hear you're filling in for Doc Wilson. I've never heard of a woman physician before."

Sarah felt her nerve endings rise to attention. "Yes, I'm filling in for the doctor. But back in Tombstone I have my own practice."

"How is the doctor?" he asked, ignoring her response about her own practice.

"He's doing better."

"Good, then he should be back to work soon." He picked up the menu. "Let's order. The pot roast is very good and so is the meatloaf. I'm getting the meatloaf and would recommend that you do the same."

She glanced at the little man sitting across the table from her. He would recommend that she do the same? "I was considering the pot roast."

"Too greasy," he informed her.

She frowned at him, just as the waitress walked up.

"We'd like two meatloafs," he replied, ordering for her.

They had known each other less than five minutes and already she was annoyed. "Excuse me, I don't want meatloaf. Make mine the pot roast."

He frowned, clearly irritated. "If you insist."

After the waitress walked away, she glanced at him. "I detest meatloaf."

"Well, for the price difference, you were better off with the meatloaf."

She was astounded by the man's actions and couldn't help but wonder if this was the reason he had yet to find a companion.

"I'll pay for my own if it's a problem," she said, growing more and more certain that this dinner was a huge mistake.

"No. I just try to be thrifty with my money. A teacher's salary is small."

She nodded, grateful for the opening to change the subject, determined to find something positive to talk about. "Tucker told me you teach school. That must be a rewarding experience."

He shook his head. "Teaching these children is like trying to whip dogs into shape. Their parents obviously have not disciplined them. They send them to school and expect me to try to make something out of them."

He took out a handkerchief, held it to his nose and blew noisily. "Spare the rod and spoil the child, I always say."

"Children have such active minds; I would think they would be extremely enjoyable to teach," she said, refusing to think that teaching could be such drudgery.

"Mrs. James, it's obvious you know very little about children. They are rude little buggers who get into things, run screaming and yelling, and engage in the biggest tiffs with one another. They have no manners."

Sarah sat there a moment feeling rather stunned at the audacity of the man. "You're absolutely correct, Mr. Smith. I know nothing about children. But my two-year-old son teaches me new things every day, and even a bad day is more wonderful than the last."

He sat back, disapproval in his beady eyes. "You have a son?"

"Yes, didn't Tucker tell you?"

"No."

Just then the waiter brought their food and placed their plates in front of them.

"Does it make a difference that I had a child with my husband?" she asked. "Since you teach school, I wouldn't have thought it mattered."

She took a bite of her pot roast and felt her stomach recoil.

"Well, I only have a two-bedroom house, and my mother takes up one room, so it would be difficult."

Sarah shuddered. They had just met.

"I see. Well, since we've just met, it's not something that we need to worry about at this point," she said, knowing beyond a shadow of a doubt that this would be their only meeting.

She picked at her dinner, pushing around the entrée on her plate. Why had she agreed to do this? Wasn't it bad enough that she had decided to stay in town an extra month? But now she was playing some kind of game with Tucker to outsmart his mother, and she was the one suffering.

"The meatloaf is excellent!" he said. "It's the most economically priced item on the menu, and you get the most for your money."

"How nice. Are you always this frugal, Mr. Smith?" she asked, thinking this was just more insight into his character and not liking what she saw. It was certainly one thing to be economical, but this man was downright cheap.

"A wise man knows where every cent goes," he said. "So eat up, you've got plenty left there on your plate. You need to clean your plate and not waste all that food."

She was going to kill Tucker Burnett. String him up and strip pieces of hide off of his muscular body while she slowly replayed this evening's event for him.

If Mr. Smith was an example of the men Tucker was going to find for her while she was here, she would just deal with Eugenia directly. She didn't need the aggravation or the headaches someone like Mr. Smith had provided for her this evening.

Finally she pushed back her chair and laid down her napkin. "That's all I can eat."

"You didn't clean your plate, so no dessert for you," he said accusingly.

"Don't worry, I hadn't planned on asking for any," she said, clearly annoyed.

How could she politely tell Mr. Smith to take whatever food was left and stuff it into any orifice that he chose?

"You know, I'm rather tired, and I think it would be a good idea if we cut this night short," she said, her smile frozen in place.

"That's fine." He picked up the check and started adding and subtracting the dollar figure that the waitress had written on the bill.

"Is there anything wrong?"

"No. You spent over a dollar for your meal. Mine, which was the special, was only seventy-five cents," he said, with a smile.

"I insist on paying for my own," Sarah said. The image of Tucker hanging suspended from a doorway, while she took perverse delight in torturing him, came to mind. He was going to pay dearly for introducing her to this man.

"Oh, no. I'll pay it."

They rose and walked to the door. Sarah was just

about to start the somewhat short stroll back to her grandfather's hotel when he spoke up.

"It's not safe for you to walk the streets of Fort Worth at night. I'll take you back in my buggy."

"Thank you, that would be nice."

He helped her into his phaeton buggy and then stepped in and took the reins. "I saved a long time to buy this rig. And it cost a lot of money."

She smiled in the semidarkness. "I'm sure it did; it's very nice."

Within a matter of moments they pulled up to the side of the hotel, and at first Sarah thought he meant to let her out here. She watched as he set the brake and then turned toward her.

"I had a really enjoyable time tonight. I hope you did, too," he said.

"It's been interesting," she replied, thinking torture would still be too nice for Tucker.

Before Sarah had time to prevent the little man, he had pulled her into his embrace and had planted his mouth on hers. Sarah was revolted as she opened her mouth to protest and he slid his tongue between her lips.

She brought her arms up between them and pushed with all her strength, sending him sprawling back. Quickly, before he could object, she jumped from the rig and called, "You're a rude man, Mr. Smith. Don't call on me again!"

As she walked up the wooden sidewalk, she shuddered with revulsion. Yes, slow, painful torture was exactly what Tucker needed, and she had just the right equipment to make it agonizing.

Six

Tucker showed up at Doc Wilson's the next morning, curious as to how the meeting between the school-teacher and the doctor went. If their get-together was successful, then he would have solved his problem with his mother, but somehow that didn't excite him. And he was thrown off by the fact that he felt irritated and confused. He didn't know if he liked Sarah seeing other men he knew or not. He had been unable to sleep last night, wondering about the two of them.

All he really knew about the schoolteacher was the fact he was looking for a wife. And Tucker wanted Sarah to stay in Fort Worth. So why wouldn't he want them to marry?

Because the schoolteacher wasn't good enough for Sarah.

After several rapid knocks, she opened the door of the doctor's clinic. When she saw it was him, she frowned.

"Good morning," he said, watching her expression.

She stood in the door staring at him as though she wanted to shut the portal on him.

"You know, I thought about you a lot last night. I

kept having dreams of just how I'd like to use several of the tools in my amputation kit on you," she said, a smile on her beautiful face that didn't quite reach her eyes. "It's a good thing that I'm a rational, sane woman or you'd be missing something vital this morning."

He smiled. "Was it that bad?"

"Worse." She stepped aside for him to enter the clinic. "Now I remember why I'd decided never to marry again, never to become involved with men anymore."

"You're not quitting, are you?" he asked, anxious that she was giving up.

"No, but have you ever considered introducing your mother to Mr. Smith? They would get along fabulously."

"He's a little young for her, but I'll keep him in mind," he said, recalling the conversation with his brothers and their wives about finding someone for his mother.

"So I guess he's not a man you'd like to see a second time?" he asked, watching the way her skirts swung to the sway of her hips as she moved across the room to the desk.

"Absolutely not, unless I can take along one of my saws to chop off his wayward hands," she said matter-of-factly.

Tucker felt the skin along the back of his neck tighten. "What are you saying? He'll answer to me if he got out of line."

Sarah turned and gazed at him, a smirk on her face, shaking her head as if she couldn't believe he was serious. "Your concern is duly noted. But I'm quite capable of taking care of myself. I handled the situation, and I will not be seeing that gentleman again, regardless of your mother."

He felt a sense of relief that disturbed him.

"Well, I'll start working on candidate number two, then," he said reluctantly.

Sarah nodded and then turned back toward her desk. "And who would that be?"

"Don't know yet. I've got someone in mind, but I have to talk to him."

She glanced at him, her expression serious. "Just make sure that he understands that I'm a doctor and I will be carrying my surgical instruments with me this time."

Tucker laughed as he glanced around the room. He wasn't ready to go. He wanted to stay and be with Sarah. "Where's Lucas?"

She looked up from the desk and stared at Tucker. "He's with Kira. Why?"

"I haven't seen him since that day over at the hotel, and I was wondering where he was. I kind of like the little guy," he said, twirling his hat in his hands.

He watched as she stared at him, a guarded expression on her face. "Kira has been watching him. The two of them get along great."

"That's good. I've been asking around town, and so far all I've heard is that Wo Chan is looking for her. He hasn't realized yet where she is."

Sarah sighed. "Good. Let's hope it stays that way for a while."

Tucker knew that his business with Sarah was finished, but somehow he wasn't in the mood to leave. He wanted to spend time with her; he didn't want to go back to his office and read reports. He didn't want to leave her here vulnerable, alone. But he knew she had work to do and he was disturbing her.

On impulse he suddenly said, "I need to ride out to the ranch this afternoon. I was wondering if you'd like to go along. You could check on Rose and take back my mother's veil."

Sarah glanced up at him. The soft pink dress she wore made the blue of her eyes shine brighter, and he thought he could become lost in her gaze as she stared at him.

She was a danger to his wanderlust, yet he kept putting himself in the position of being with her.

"We could take Lucas and Kira if you'd like," he said, knowing that he was offering to take them, but somehow wishing they could be alone.

He scolded himself for having that thought. He didn't have any business being alone with Sarah. Already his thoughts spent way too much time thinking about the lovely young doctor and just how much he had enjoyed their night together.

"That would be nice. I could meet with Rose and try to squelch your mother's enthusiasm for the two of us. I need to do some things around here. What time did you want to leave?" she asked. "I don't think we'll take Kira and Lucas. I don't want Kira out where anyone can see her, and Lucas can stay with her."

"How about you meet me at the jail around one o'clock," he said, suddenly excited at the idea of spending time alone with Sarah.

"That's fine. I'll see you this afternoon."

"Don't forget to lock up after I leave," he warned as he walked out the door.

"I won't," she said, once again returning to her paperwork.

Sarah sat finishing her notes on the patients she had seen this morning, anticipating the afternoon with Tucker. She was nervous about leaving Lucas, but her grandfather was there in the hotel and would watch over the girl and the young boy. Sarah hated not being close enough that someone could find her if she was needed, but she should go out and check on Rose to make sure the woman's pregnancy was progressing well.

Plus she had this irrational fear that Eugenia would realize that Lucas was Tucker's son. But how? She kept telling herself that her fears were not logical. How could the woman recognize her grandson if she had never seen him before? If she didn't even know he existed? But Sarah wanted to postpone their meeting as long as possible.

If Eugenia even suspected that Lucas was Tucker's son, then Sarah might as well pack up and leave town now, for she would never have any peace if Eugenia found out the truth.

Yet Tucker had seen Lucas, and he didn't realize the boy was his son, though she had had a brief moment of panic this morning when he had asked about the child. She had been surprised at the question, and her heart had almost stopped beating when Tucker admitted to liking him.

She didn't need him paying attention to her son. She was frightened of him finding out the truth. But she was the only one who knew who Lucas's father was.

The door opened suddenly, and she glanced up as a Chinese man strolled through the portal without knocking. She had forgotten to lock the door.

"Good morning, Doctor."

"How can I help you?" she politely asked, refusing to show fear, anxious that she knew who the man was and the reason he was here.

"I'm looking for a young girl that was seen close to your office several days ago. A young Chinese girl with dark hair and eyes, about sixteen years of age."

Sarah stared at the beady-eyed man and considered his question. She felt no guilt at lying to him about Kira. He had mistreated her and would do so again. "I don't recall seeing a young girl fitting that description around here."

"I'm offering a reward for her return," he said, staring at Sarah as if he could read her mind. "If you should know of her whereabouts, I would like to find her."

Sarah shrugged and leaned back in her chair. "I'm sorry, I can't help you."

He smiled, his eyes cold and impersonal. "I will be most unhappy with anyone who tries to keep me from her."

She took a deep breath to steady her nerves and nodded at the man. "I understand, Mr. . . ."

"Wo Chan," he acknowledged, bowing toward her.

"I'll let you know if I see her," she said.

"Thank you." He headed out the door. "Good day."

"Good day," she called.

As soon as the door closed, she stood, crossed the room and bolted the door. With a reward being offered, it wouldn't be long before the man found out where Kira was hiding.

Her hands began to shake suddenly when she realized her son was in danger. The man ran an opium den, he had beaten a young girl and he wanted her back. This man was dangerous, and Sarah was now truly frightened by the seriousness of her situation.

* * *

Tucker looked up as Sarah came rushing into his office, her face ashen.

"You were right," she said, breathless from running.

"Twice in the same week, that's got to be a record." He grinned.

She glared at him. Something was seriously wrong for her to completely lose her sense of humor.

"What's wrong?"

"Wo Chan came to see me this morning. He's looking for Kira, and he wants her back."

Instantly Tucker grew serious. "He didn't hurt you, did he?"

"No. I lied to him and told him I hadn't seen the girl. He's offering a reward. He will find out about her."

"What do you want to do?" Tucker asked. "Do you want to return her to him?"

"I can't," Sarah said. "I gave her my word I would help her."

"We've got to get her out of your grandfather's rooms. We've got to hide her."

She nodded slowly. "You're right. Someone will turn her in just for the reward that's being offered."

"We'll move her to the ranch," Tucker replied, knowing the buggy ride he had wanted alone with Sarah was not going to occur this afternoon. "I'll bring the wagon over to the back of the hotel. We can hide Kira in the back of the wagon and then slip out of town."

"Thanks, Tucker. I knew you would know what to do, and I didn't want to leave town without Lucas."

"Let's get going."

They hurried out of the jail to the waiting wagon and drove around to the back of the El Paso Hotel.

While Tucker stayed with the vehicle, Sarah went upstairs and brought down Kira and Lucas.

"Momma. Go bye-bye?" Lucas asked, as she carried him to the waiting wagon.

"Yes, son, we're going to see a ranch, see the cows and horses," Sarah told Lucas as she sat the boy in the middle of the empty seat. Tucker helped her up into the conveyance, his hand on her arm to steady her.

Kira lay down in the back of the wagon, and Tucker covered her with a blanket.

"Stay hidden until we reach the ranch," he told the girl.

She nodded. As he looked into her big, dark eyes that had green and black marks around them from where she had been hit, Tucker shuddered to think what the girl must have gone through. He admired Sarah for the strength of her actions, but he worried for her safety. Wo Chan would not take the disappearance of one of his whores lightly.

Tucker stepped up into the wagon and unwrapped the reins from the brake handle.

"Giddy up!" he called to the team of horses, and they pulled away from the hotel.

He glanced over at Sarah and enjoyed the way the wind teased wisps of hair away from her face. She had her arm about her son and a smile on her face as they headed out of town.

The memory of her head thrown back in passion, her blue eyes dilated and glassy as she called out his name, returned, slamming him with a sense of longing he didn't think he could deny. He swallowed and watched her as she buttoned Lucas's jacket to keep the chill out and wished that he could feel the cold air instead of this inner heat that raged within him.

God, if he could experience being in her arms just once more, just lie holding her one more night and feel the passion they had known, surely then he would have gotten his fill and could leave these memories behind once and for all.

Tucker swallowed and glanced over at the woman he had known all these years. "What does your grandfather think about you staying in town and filling in for Doc Wilson?"

"He wishes I would move back. He keeps telling me that Lucas needs a male figure in his life, and since it doesn't look like I'm ever going to remarry, then it has to be him," she said, shaking her head.

"You don't agree?" Tucker asked.

"Lucas is a toddler. A father figure is nice to have, but right now I'm the most important person in his life. Eventually he will need a man, but not now."

Tucker flicked the reins, urging the horses to go faster as they pulled away from town. "See, I'm telling you, if you married one of these men I'm introducing you to, then you'd have a father for Lucas, you could stay here in Fort Worth and you'd have a man in your life again."

"What makes you think I need a man in my life?" she asked.

"Well, it certainly couldn't hurt. You're beautiful; you're young. Don't you want more children?"

"Sure I'd like more children, but not at the expense of my freedom," she said. "Why do I need a man? I have control of my life, I have my son and I have my practice. What more do I need?"

"Most women want love, a little romance."

She nodded. "Most women. But I'm not like most

women, and if I require those things, I could have
them without marriage."

"Oh," he said, stunned. So she didn't want to marry
for love? He was confused. Didn't all women want to
marry, settle down and have children? Wasn't that exactly what he was running from?

If passion was all she wanted, then maybe she
would agree to share his bed one more time. Maybe
they could experience the delight he remembered so
vividly between them once again.

The countryside passed by for several miles without either one of them saying anything. Kira lay in
the back with the blanket covering her face, while
Lucas laid his head in his mother's lap and slept the
time away.

"You know, Sarah, you're a unique woman."

She glanced at him. "I guess I am different."

"Most women would have joined forces with my
mother to get me to the altar, but not you. So why
aren't you helping my mother?"

She stared at him. "Tucker, at one time in our life,
I wanted to marry you. But you didn't want to get
married then, and you obviously still don't want to
marry. So why in the world would I want to force
myself on someone who doesn't want me? What kind
of life would that be?"

"You wanted to marry me?" he asked, surprised.

"Once. But now, now you don't strike me as the
marrying kind. You've got that wandering bug, and
I've got a son I have to think of. We're friends, nothing more."

He glanced at her to see if she was telling him
the truth or just speaking words that he wanted to
hear. She gazed back at him, her blue eyes never
wavering from his face.

"Damn, Sarah, you almost sound cold," he said, confused by her obvious disregard of their relationship.

Her words left him stunned. She had wanted to marry him? But he wasn't the marrying kind. She knew that. And what could he offer the doctor?

"You know you don't know what you want." She raised her brows. "Now you're upset that I'm not joining with your mother to force you into marriage. Would you rather I lie and tell you that I want you desperately. I can't live without you?"

"No, but what about that time in Tombstone?"

She glanced at him, looking as if she wished she could pick something up and throw it at him.

"Tombstone was special. But you left without saying good-bye, without so much as a 'so long'. I woke up to an empty bed and a night filled with memories. It meant very little to you if you could walk away so easily."

He stared at her, stunned that she had expected more from him that night. He had only left in the middle of the night to avoid the awkwardness of having to face her in the morning.

"I couldn't stay."

Sarah was unique. She wasn't like the other women he had known. She was his friend, someone he had known for years, and they had crossed a line they never should have gone over.

The two-story white ranch house where Tucker had spent his entire life came into view.

"I think it's for the best if we drop this subject for now. I don't think that either one of us wants to give your mother any more ammunition than she already has to try to bring us together," she said, her voice very polite.

He glanced over at her and nodded. "You're right, but we're not through discussing this."

"Maybe so," Sarah said, as the wagon pulled to a halt. "But that was three years ago, and this is today."

Sarah couldn't believe the conversation that she had had with Tucker on the way out to the ranch. Part of her had wanted to laugh, and part of her had wanted to rail at him. Was he so blind that he couldn't see that she still cared for him? Was he so afraid of commitment that he couldn't acknowledge the attraction they both were feeling? And he was feeling the magnetism, because she saw it in his eyes, in the way he watched her. She had felt it in his touch.

Tucker came around to the side of the wagon and put his hands on Sarah's waist and lifted her to the ground. He reached up for a sleepy Lucas and handed the boy to Sarah.

"What a nice surprise," Eugenia called from the porch that ran along the front of the house. Sarah could see the woman's mind filling with all kinds of thoughts regarding her and Tucker.

"Tucker was coming out today, and I rode along to check on Rose," Sarah said, climbing the porch beside Tucker, Kira following along behind.

Sarah turned and introduced the girl. "This is Kira. I'll let Tucker explain the situation to you."

Eugenia raised her brow and then smiled at Kira. "Welcome to the Bar None."

The young girl tried to smile, though her face was swollen.

"And this must be Lucas," Eugenia said, reaching out and touching the child Sarah held in her arms.

The fear that Eugenia would recognize Lucas as

her grandson seized Sarah as the older woman stroked Lucas's face. It was all she could do to keep from yanking the boy away from Eugenia. Would Tucker's mother recognize her son in Lucas's features? Would she know he was her grandson?

"You look so much like your mother," Eugenia said, as she patted him on the arm. "Come in out of this cold air. I bet Cook has some cookies hidden somewhere."

Sarah almost sighed with relief.

"Cookie!" the child demanded.

"Yes. I'm so glad you all are here," Eugenia cried excitely. "Rose is upstairs lying down. She's been so tired lately that she usually naps in the afternoon."

"That's good," Sarah said.

"Come into the house and let me fix everyone something warm to drink to take the chill away," Eugenia said, heading toward the door of the house.

Tucker touched Sarah's elbow and guided her through the front door and into the parlor. The feel of his fingers lightly pressing against her skin left her warm and tingly. He seemed to want to touch her whenever he was close, and the feel of his skin against hers always reminded her of the way his naked flesh had felt against her own. It was a sensation that had lingered in her memory, like a warm bath on a chilly evening.

God, she didn't need these thoughts now, not even when she was alone. He obviously was drawn to her, but didn't want her on a permanent basis. Just another quick tumble, another baby and then he would be on his way.

"Would you care for coffee or hot tea?" Eugenia asked, bringing Sarah back to the present.

"Thank you, I think a cup of hot tea," she replied,

watching as Tucker nervously paced the parlor while Lucas explored his new surroundings.

"I'll be back," Eugenia said, and Kira followed her into the kitchen.

Tucker glanced at Sarah and leaned against the wall, a smile on his face. "Should I tell her we're engaged, just to stir things up?"

"You do and I promise you'll be limping back to town," Sarah threatened.

He laughed, the sound of his voice settling over her nerves like a warm balm.

"We're trying to help her realize that we're never going to marry, not give her more reasons to think there's a chance. Please, Tucker, behave."

He shrugged. "I was only teasing."

Travis came in the front door, shivering, and walked into the parlor where they were all gathered. "Hey, Tucker, I thought that was you."

He glanced over at Sarah and Lucas. "Hello, Sarah, it's good to see you. Nice-looking boy."

"Thank you. He's pretty special. I hear you and Rose have a baby on the way," she said.

"We're very excited, but I'll be glad when it's all over with," Travis acknowledged. "I guess you came out to see Rose."

"Yes, I wanted to check on her and make sure everything's going okay. I didn't want to wait until you needed me," Sarah said.

"Rose is resting right now," Travis said. "But after Tucker and I run out to the barn, maybe she'll be up. I want to show Tucker the new foal born two days ago."

Tucker glanced at Sarah. "Is it okay if I leave you alone with Mother?"

She smiled. "Go ahead. Actually, that would be

good. I'll talk to her, and then I can go up and see Rose. Take your time."

"Are you sure?" Tucker asked.

"Positive. Now go."

Tucker followed his older brother out the door, leaving Sarah alone waiting for Eugenia to return. It wasn't long before their hostess hurried back into the parlor, her arms laden with a tray that held a teapot and several cups.

She set the tray down on a table and then turned her attention to the child.

"Lucas?" she called. "I brought you an oatmeal cookie. Does he like oatmeal?" she asked. "They're Tucker's favorite, so I try to have some baked when I know he's coming."

"Lucas likes them well enough," Sarah replied hesitantly, knowing it was her son's favorite cookie, but not about to share that information with his grandmother.

The boy saw the cookie in Eugenia's hand and danced excitedly. "Cookie, Momma, cookie."

"Yes, son, you may have the cookie."

The child took the sweet from Eugenia and smiled at the older woman.

"He's so adorable. He reminds me of when my sons were small. Toddlers are so cute at this age."

Sarah felt her heart race with panic. Surely the woman couldn't tell anything just by looking at Lucas. The urge to pick up the child and run was strong within her, but she took a deep breath and tried to relax. What could the woman do?

Sarah cleared her throat, anxious to change the subject. She picked up the tin box and handed it to Tucker's mother. "Eugenia, I am returning your package to you. I cannot accept your gift."

"Why ever not?" the woman asked, as she poured the tea into the cups.

"Because I have no intention of marrying your son. And if there was even the slightest possibility of us ever getting together, you are pushing him away by your constant interfering."

"But that's why I'm contacting you, dear, not Tucker. I think he's always had a crush on you, though he knew you wanted to go away to that fancy school, so he let you go. But now you're back, you're a doctor, you have a son, and I'm sure you must want to settle down."

Sarah couldn't believe this woman. "Eugenia, I'm going to ask you to quit trying to force us together. He's a man who wants to travel. He doesn't want to settle down and have a family. I have Lucas, and I must look out for his best interests."

"Oh, pooh, dear. You and I both know that Tucker is no more a traveling man than either one of his brothers. He's just being stubborn, and he thinks roaming the countryside is what he wants to do. It's up to you to show him that's not what he really wants or needs."

"Me?" Sarah asked, surprised.

"You're the only one who can, dear. Haven't you been listening? Tucker has had a crush on you for years. I've watched the way his eyes change and glow at the mention of your name. Today, the first thing I noticed was how different he is when he's around you. He's happier, more settled. And, Lord, when he looks at you, I blush to think of my son's thoughts."

Sarah sat stunned at her words. Was it that obvious? Seldom in Sarah's life had she been speechless, but for just a moment she was.

"Mothers know these kinds of things, dear, just

like you'll know who Lucas is attracted to long before he does and even longer before he tells you."

Sarah considered her words. "If it's true about Tucker not really being a man who likes to roam, then he will have to discover that on his own. I can't help him make that realization."

Eugenia thought for a moment, her head tilted to the side. "That's a very astute observation. I think that's true. But you, dear, are the catalyst to set him in motion. I would wager that even now his thoughts are centered on you. He isn't ready to declare himself or set the wheels of matrimony in motion just yet. He's fighting his attraction to you with all the strength the Burnett boys are known for."

"Oh, please, Eugenia. Why am I listening to you? Tucker doesn't want to be with me; he proved that years ago." Sarah stood and began to pace around the parlor. "If what you're saying is true, then why in the world would he be introducing me to other men while I'm here? Why wouldn't he be pursuing me himself?"

"Like I said, dear, just part of the Burnett boys' resistance to getting entangled. Why do you think I've resorted to matchmaking? If I'd waited for any of my sons to succumb to marriage, they would still be single, and I'd be no closer to becoming a grandmother."

"What if I'm not interested in him? Have you considered that I might not want to marry your son?"

"Yes, I considered it. But our meeting the other day convinced me that you are very interested in my son. So much, in fact, that I sent you my veil."

"I'm not going to marry Tucker, Eugenia. I've returned your veil, and when I leave town, I want you to remember we had this conversation. Plus, I plan on taking advantage of Tucker's idea of seeing other men while I'm here."

Eugenia only smiled and sipped her tea. "Go right ahead, dear. I think it would be good for Tucker to see you with other men. I think it's a great plan to push him closer to proposing."

Sarah stared in awe at the woman. She had never felt so frustrated in all her life. Tucker's mother just refused to see reason. She refused to even consider that Tucker and Sarah would never be together.

"I think I hear Rose moving about upstairs, if you'd like to go up and see her," Eugenia volunteered. "I'll watch Lucas if you want to leave him here with me."

Sarah swallowed and glanced around the room for Kira. She had gone to the kitchen with Eugenia and never returned, leaving Lucas alone with Eugenia and Sarah. How could Sarah refuse Tucker's mother? Yet she was nervous with Lucas and Eugenia in the same room. God, she didn't need her to find out about her grandson, or she would never give Sarah a moment of peace.

"Okay. I'll be back down shortly," Sarah replied, walking out of the room, determined to return as quickly as possible.

Sarah hurried up the stairs, anxious to see her patient, not wanting Eugenia to have too much time alone with Lucas.

Tucker came in from the barn and noticed his mother watching Lucas in the parlor.

"Hello, son," she said. "I'm so glad you brought Sarah and Lucas out."

"Where's Sarah?" Tucker asked.

"She's upstairs with Rose, and I'm playing with Lucas."

His mother was down on the floor with the boy, and they were playing with some blocks that Tucker remembered he had played with as a child.

"Mother, why did you send Sarah that wedding veil? Wasn't it bad enough you scared her into coming home by sending her that telegram?"

"She told you about the veil?" Eugenia asked, placing a block on top of the tower that Lucas was building.

"Of course. I'm not going to marry Sarah or any other woman, so I wish you'd just leave us alone. Fort Worth needs a doctor, and you're going to keep bothering Sarah until she leaves and goes home. Then who is going to deliver Rose's baby?"

"You're exaggerating, son. Sarah is going to be with us for quite a while. I promise you this: I won't interfere anymore as long as you bid on her basket at the church auction."

"Why do I have to bid on her basket?"

His mother smiled at him. "Because the church needs the money, and if you up the bid, it makes Sarah feel welcome. And you need for your loving mother to quit interfering."

Tucker groaned, wondering how it could be so easy. He had already planned on bidding for Sarah's basket, but if this was what it would take to make his mother quit her interfering, then he could easily play her game.

"Okay, I'll bid on her basket, but don't expect me to buy it. And you've got to promise me that you won't interfere anymore."

"I won't as long as you don't tell her why you're bidding on her basket." His mother gazed up at him, her eyes sparkling with merriment. "You know, Tucker, in case you haven't noticed, Sarah is not a young girl anymore. She's turned into a beautiful woman."

Lucas knocked the blocks down, clapping his hands in delight at the destruction. "Momma?"

"She'll be right back, Lucas," Eugenia told him, as she started to build yet another tower of blocks.

"I have eyes, Mother. I can see," Tucker reminded her.

Eugenia smiled. "I just wanted to make sure."

Oh, yes, he had noticed the moment she stepped off that stagecoach just how much motherhood seemed to suit Sarah. She was more beautiful than even he had remembered her, and he was trying his damndest to ignore the attraction he felt simmering between them. But somehow he wasn't having much luck. And his mother was making damn sure he couldn't deny it.

Seven

Sarah watched as Tucker carried a sleeping Lucas to the wagon. Whenever she saw the two of them together, she always got a little catch in her throat. He should know the boy was his son, should be a part of his life, yet the deception had been set in motion so long that if she were to tell Tucker the truth now, he would be angry. And deep inside she couldn't blame him.

But she had made the decision not to tell Tucker about Lucas when she didn't know where he had gone or how to find him. She had been alone, pregnant and frightened when she decided not to tell Tucker about his son. It was a decision she would have to live with, even though she hated the fact that it robbed Lucas of belonging to a group of people with whom he shared a common bond.

Tucker returned from securing the sleeping boy in the back of the wagon to help Sarah. He placed his strong hands around her waist and lifted her up onto the seat as if she weighed next to nothing, then climbed up after her.

Sarah glanced behind her to make sure Lucas was safely settled and sleeping. The child lay oblivious to the world, his small body curled on a pallet she had made for him in the back of the wagon.

She returned her gaze to the porch where Eugenia stood watching their departure along with Kira, who stood gazing at her sadly.

"Kira, you'll be safe here," she reminded the girl. The girl nodded, her eyes downcast.

"I'll be back to check on Rose in a week. Or if you need me sooner, let me know," Sarah called to Mrs. Burnett.

"We will. I'll look for the two of you at the church luncheon on Sunday," the older woman said, as she waved good-bye.

Tucker snapped the reins and called to the horses, "Yeehaw."

"See you," Tucker called, as the wagon began to roll away from the family homestead.

Sarah waved and waited until they were a ways from the house before she asked her question. "What is she talking about? What luncheon?"

"Every four months the church has an auction to raise money. The women donate food they've prepared, and the church sells it to the highest bidder. If the woman is single, she has lunch with the person who purchased her basket. I'm surprised your grandfather hasn't said anything to you about it."

"He's been busy lately. He's probably forgotten."

"If you want, I'll pick you and your grandfather up. You'd see a lot of people you know."

Sarah shrugged. "I'll consider it."

The last rays of the setting sun bathed the land in an orange glow as they passed through the gate of the Bar None. Tucker flicked the reins, encouraging the horses to pick up speed, and Sarah, who felt the tension of the day catching up with her, was grateful.

When she was with Tucker she always felt on guard. Soon she could relax and unwind from the long day.

"So how did the meeting with my mother go?" he asked, glancing at her quickly before returning his gaze to the trail in front of them.

Sarah shook her head. "I now understand where the men in this family get their stubbornness. You were right, Tucker. She's convinced we are meant to be together. I don't know if I can persuade her any differently. It was like she didn't even hear me."

Tucker laughed. "So you didn't make her understand she was wrong?"

"No. I don't think I even made a dent in that woman's armor. She wants you married," Sarah exclaimed, amazed at the depth of Eugenia's convictions with regard to her son.

"I know." He looked at Sarah, his eyes twinkling with laughter. "But you thought you would change her mind, didn't you?"

"I had to try." Sarah returned his gaze, the warmth of his brown eyes touching her like flint to stone.

Odd, but in the entire time they had known each other, they had never discussed marriage. She had always known he was a wild spirit, elusive and free, but somehow she had thought the right woman would tame him, settle him down. And she had always hoped that she would be that woman.

"So why are you resisting? Why not just get married to satisfy her? Have you never wanted to marry?" Sarah asked.

"Not since you left town and went to that fancy school and left me here to fight off all the old maids who hadn't found a husband yet."

She shook her head at him. "I don't know why I try to have a serious conversation with you."

"Oh, Sarah. Why does a man have to get married and settle down? Why can't I be different?"

"You can't be different and be married, Tucker?" she asked, suddenly curious.

"No, I can't." He glanced at her. "I had this stupid notion that when I became known for being a fast draw, somehow I wouldn't be 'that Burnett boy' anymore. That it would somehow garner me more respect."

She tried to discreetly cover her mouth and hide her smile. "So becoming a fast draw, did it help you?"

He gazed at her warily as the wagon crawled up a sloping ridge, and she had to cling to the wooden railing to keep from sliding out.

"What do you think? Now I'm that Burnett boy that's known for being fast with a gun. And being known for having a lightning fast draw only tempts foolish young men into trying to make a name for themselves by getting rid of me."

"So what does all of that have to do with getting married?"

"I guess the reason I don't want to settle down is because those two words equal being tied down. Never going anywhere, never seeing new places. I guess I associate raising a family with loss of freedom and tied to responsibility."

Sarah nodded. "There is a certain amount of both when you have children. They're dependent on you for their every need, and you can't come and go as you please anymore. But the rewards far outweigh the restrictions they place on you. And they are your blood, a part of you."

Tucker shrugged. "I guess it would be exciting to see a part of yourself living on. But if I don't have anyone depending on me, I can do whatever I want.

I can travel to different parts of the country. That's the way my life was when I was younger, and I enjoyed being free."

"So what are you doing here? Why aren't you pursuing your freedom now?"

He paused a moment. "Timing, I guess. After I left Tombstone, I almost killed a kid in Santa Fe. He was barely sixteen. I could have hit him in the heart, but at the last moment I shot him in the shoulder, wounding him seriously."

They hit a bump in the road, and the wagon rattled as dust rose up through the air. "I knew that sooner or later, I was going to kill someone, and the law was not going to consider it self-defense. I would hang, and the thought of a rope tightening around my neck was enough for me to put an end to that part of my life. So I came home unsure of what to do. Only certain that I hated ranch work."

"So now you're home, but you wish you were back roaming the countryside."

"Yes. I'm hoping to get a federal marshal's position, but until then I'm here."

"So a woman and a family couldn't fit into your life living here, right now?"

"Don't want to take a chance on them getting hurt. What happens when someone faster than me shows up and challenges me to a shootout?" he asked. "What happens if I'm killed?"

"Easy. You don't participate in gunfights. You're the marshal." She stared at him questioningly. "Surely, you don't respond when someone comes into town and wants a gunfight now, do you? You have stopped that awful practice, haven't you?"

Tucker refused to meet her gaze. "Being marshal sometimes provokes them even more than just being someone with a reputation. I have to protect the town. It's my job."

Sarah shook her head. "You mean to tell me that if someone came into town and wanted to pit their speed against yours, you'd do it?"

He stared at her as if she had suffered a memory lapse. "Of course I would. If I didn't, that person would think that he could come into my town and take over."

"That's ridiculous."

He turned his attention back to the horses, his voice a deep, rich baritone sound. "I've seen it happen, Sarah. Not here, but in New Mexico, in some of the mining towns of Colorado and even in some of the smaller towns of Texas. As long as I'm the law, it is not going to happen in Fort Worth."

The wind teased wisps of blond curls about her face, and Sarah pushed a strand away from her cheeks. "But you've already been shot once, and there's no guarantee you won't be again. Next time you could be killed."

"You're right, I could be," he said, staring into her eyes. "But I'm damn good, and I enjoy being one of the best. I want to remain free."

"You are a foolish man, Tucker Burnett. You'd give up having a wife and children just because your pride wouldn't let you pass up a gunfight?" Sarah accused, her voice rising with repressed emotion.

Why should she tell him about his son if he didn't want the responsibility of being a father? How could she tell him, knowing that he could die at any moment?

"That's not what I said, Sarah."

"No, but it's the truth!" she said fiercely. "You'd rather die than let someone else possibly outgun you.

Well, guess what? Sooner or later someone is going to, and when they do, you're going to die."

He glanced over at her as if she were an irrational female who didn't know what she was saying, not the doctor who had already patched him up once.

"You don't understand. As marshal it's my job to make sure this town is safe. I deal with criminals and take chances every day."

"I understand that, and I know that there is a certain amount of danger in being the law; but you're using your position as marshal to keep your skills up as a gunfighter, not as a peacemaker," Sarah replied, her voice rising with emotion.

Tucker shrugged. "Maybe so. As a doctor do you always choose the path of a healer or do you sometimes use your social position to convey strength and power?"

Sarah sat thinking, mulling over her response. "It's different for me. Being a gunfighter does not promote healing."

"So my job as marshal is not as important as yours is of being a healer?" he asked, his voice rising.

Sarah wanted to grit her teeth, but instead she glared at him. "I didn't say that. Being a marshal is a very important and worthy job. Being a marshal who gets into gunfights just for the sake of making sure he's still the fastest is wrong."

"I'm good, Sarah. Damn good. This is my town, and no one interferes. I'll take on their challenge either as the marshal or as a gunfighter, their choice."

She stared at him in the semidarkness, the urge to hit him upside the head almost overwhelming, knowing that wasn't the answer, but tempted just the same. In so many ways, he was still the same arrogant gunfighter she had patched up and fallen in love with in Tombstone.

"So you're going to die because of your pride. You're a damn fool, Tucker Burnett, and don't expect me to piece you back together a second time."

He turned and stared at her, the anger emanating from his body, his face a tight grimace, his brown eyes sparkling with temper.

"But you would." He said it low and with such conviction she could feel the power behind his words. "I know you, Sarah. You wouldn't leave a man to die. Not a pious do-gooder like yourself."

She turned and faced the front of the wagon. He was right, and she knew it. If something were to happen to him, of course she would try to save him, but what if this time the bullet she so desperately wanted to protect him from killed him? What then?

When was he going to realize that he was one bullet away from death? One bullet from never knowing the son he knew nothing about.

Tucker angrily snapped the reins, urging the horses to go faster. Sarah didn't understand. She never had and probably never would appreciate that it wasn't the violence or even the idea of being faster than anyone else that was the attraction to a gunfight.

For those thirty seconds a man didn't know whether he was going to live or die. A man with a gun didn't know if he was going to take his next breath or find himself eating the dust in the middle of the street. And after it was all over, life seemed sweeter for the victor.

No, he didn't condone violence, but when a challenge was issued, he couldn't just ignore the demand and pretend it hadn't occurred. A man had his pride, and Tucker wouldn't be labeled a coward or afraid to face a fight. He would rather be six feet under than have people look at him and think he had backed away from a brawl.

Yes, he was older and a little more settled than the wild days of his youth; but he would never back away from a fight, and he would never walk away from a challenge. And the good doctor could take her peace-loving ways all the way back to Tombstone for all he cared.

He had never felt as though he was good enough for Sarah anyway, and today was just another example of why a gunslinger-turned-marshal and a doctor had no business trying to work together.

Once again he was sure that he was meant to be a man without ties. A man without a wife, a family or a home. A man without a reason to keep him from taking on a fight, whether it was with his fists or with his Colt Navy revolvers. He had no reason to turn the other cheek and walk away.

Except Sarah. . . .

The image of Sarah, limbs entwined with his, blond hair cascading over her shoulders, twirling about his chest, came to mind, and he almost groaned. Some memories were better left buried in the recesses of his consciousness. Especially the ones that made him think he had lost his mind for leaving the woman behind in Tombstone.

Though he wondered why that particular image kept popping into mind. Why couldn't he forget about the night they spent together and let the image of Sarah scolding him fill his mind?

Tucker pulled on the reins, slowing the horses as they entered the streets of Fort Worth. He knew who he was, and he was not a man who was going to resolve problems by talking about them. No, he was a man who settled things in the street, with his fists or a gun.

He pulled the horses to a halt in front of the hotel. The lanterns from inside cast a yellowish glow out into the street. The sound of laughter and singing drifted down Main Street, where one of the many saloons was in full swing. It was late. As soon as the wagon rolled to a stop, Sarah leaped to the ground without waiting for his help. She walked around to the back while he set the brake and looped the reins around the wooden handle.

Tucker watched as Sarah lifted the sleeping boy into her arms.

"Wait. I'll carry him in," he said.

"No need. He's my responsibility," she replied, before he could react.

He glanced at her, noticing the tight set of her mouth, the determined look in the blue irises of her eyes. "I know that, but he's heavy. Let me carry him in."

"No!" she said, in a clipped voice. "There's no need for you to walk us upstairs. And as for the church picnic, I'll meet you there. We don't need any more rumors started than the ones your mother will be busy creating."

She was angry. Well fine, he couldn't help who he was, and he was no peace-loving do-gooder like her. Never had been. But why was it this time she suddenly had trouble accepting him? Why had it never affected their friendship before?

"Sarah . . . ," he said reluctantly, not wanting to part with anger unresolved between them.

"I think it's time we said good night. I'll see you at the picnic on Sunday."

She turned and walked away, the gentle swish of

her skirts bewitching as he watched the sway of her backside. He couldn't help but stare at her in confusion. What was different about their friendship? Somehow he got the feeling that there was something he didn't understand. She had always accepted him before, so what had changed?

And damn it, why did the good doctor always manage to get under his skin and leave him still wanting her despite the fact that he knew they could only be friends?

Sarah glanced around at the people who were gathered inside the meeting hall of the small church. Children dashed through the building chasing one another while the ladies arranged the baskets and the desserts to be auctioned.

She felt foolish and almost hadn't come. But somehow she had been determined not to let her differences with Tucker frighten her away. She was not going to let a simple argument keep her from seeing people she hadn't seen in years. She also knew that there would be less speculation about her and Tucker if she was here to dispel the rumors.

Her grandfather stood beside her, carrying Lucas. Eugenia hurried toward them. "Hello, George. How are you, Lucas?" Without waiting for a reply, she turned her attention to Sarah. "Sarah, I'm so glad that you came and you brought a basket for the auction."

"I wanted to help the church," Sarah said.

"Good, the church will be pleased with your donation." Eugenia smiled. "And I'm sure that son of mine will be bidding on your basket."

Eugenia plucked the basket from Sarah's arms.

"Mrs. Burnett, Tucker will not be bidding on my basket. The only reason I came today was to see the people I haven't seen since I left."

"Don't be so certain. But there are several single young men here today who I'm sure would love a chance to eat the food you've prepared."

"Maybe," Sarah said, glancing at her grandfather.

"The rest of the family except for Travis and Rose, who decided she really didn't feel like attending, are sitting in that far corner over there." She pointed them out to Sarah. "I must help with the baskets, so why don't the three of you join our group?"

Sarah looked up and stared straight into Tucker's earthy brown eyes. He smiled at her and shrugged his shoulders. She knew without question that it was his subtle peace offering. It was his way of saying, Let's not fight. He had used it since childhood and never was one to offer an apology.

But she wasn't ready to end the war or call a truce. She wasn't even ready for a peaceful negotiation. The battle was still on-going, even though she wasn't sure what the war was about.

She returned his smile, though it didn't quite reach her heart. She should never have gotten upset with him about his propensity for gunfights. It was his life; he had made his choices, and so had she. And hers didn't include Tucker.

If there were lingering feelings for this man, she had them buried deeper than even a miner would be willing to go, and it was best they were left there.

"Do you want to sit with the Burnetts?" her grandfather asked.

"Let's wait until after the auction, to see who will be joining us for lunch," Sarah suggested, still not ready to face Tucker.

Her grandfather grinned. "Is there anyone you have in mind?"

Sarah shrugged. "Not really."

"I was hoping maybe there was someone. Maybe if you found a husband here, you'd stay in town," he said, his mouth twitching with a smile.

"We've been over this, Grandfather," she said, an edge to her voice. All she needed was for her grandfather to join forces with Eugenia. She would be on the next stage out of town regardless of her promises to Tucker.

She wanted a man who wanted her.

"I know, but you can't blame an old man for trying," he said, with a sigh.

She turned and glared at him. "Yes, I can. Now let's try to enjoy the rest of the day."

The auctioneer walked to the podium. "We're going to begin the auction. The single ladies have prepared baskets of food, while the married ladies brought cakes and pies to auction off. So let's get started. I'm sure we're all hungry."

For the next half hour Sarah watched as they auctioned off all the desserts and then began on the baskets. There were only five baskets, and it didn't take long until they reached the one she had brought.

The auctioneer held up her basket. "The food in this basket was made by Dr. Sarah James, who has recently returned from Tombstone, Arizona, and taken over Doc Wilson's practice until he heals. So what is the starting bid on this basket?"

Neville Smith stood up, his mother by his side. "I'll bid one dollar."

Sarah groaned, then whispered to her grandfather, "I'm leaving if he gets my basket."

"Now, Sarah, just wait," her grandfather replied in

a lowered voice. "There are other young men attending."

"I'll give you two dollars," Tucker called out.

Sarah glanced over at him. He was bidding on her basket to keep her from dining with Neville. It was one more attempt at reconciliation. She smiled at Tucker, unable to resist his peace offering, knowing this would only encourage his mother.

"Do I hear three?"

"Two and a quarter," Neville said.

"Four dollars," a deep masculine voice called out from the back of the room.

Sarah glanced around until she located the bidder, but didn't recognize the man.

"Five," Tucker said, never skipping a beat.

"Six dollars and that's my final offer," Neville Smith said, as he glared at Tucker.

The crowd laughed, and Sarah felt uneasy being the center of attention.

"Seven," the unknown voice called out.

She glanced around the room, grateful for the man who nodded in her direction. At over six feet, two hundred pounds, his masculine frame seemed to make Neville look like a runt. She was grateful that he had effectively silenced the man.

"Ten dollars," Tucker called.

What was he doing? Neville had dropped out; he was no longer bidding. Yet Tucker seemed intent on getting her basket. Didn't he realize that by continuing to raise the bid, he was causing more speculation about the two of them?

His mother was sitting there smiling as though she was on top of the world. And Sarah only knew she didn't need to spend more time with Tucker. They wanted different things in life. They had no future together; yet the attraction was there, and it was hard to resist.

"That's the most the church has received for any basket, Sarah," her grandfather said. "You should be proud."

"Of what? The fact that Tucker is driving the price up? I know that's what he's doing," she whispered back.

"Eleven dollars."

A gasp went through the crowd. Sarah felt tiny prickles tingle along her spine. Whoever this man was, he was serious about winning her basket of food and her company at lunch. Maybe she would be eating with him after all.

"Twelve," Tucker called.

Sarah widened her eyes, trying to signal to Tucker to stop his bidding, to let the man win.

"Fifteen dollars," the man said, and he stood up and looked at Sarah. "I hope your cooking is as good as your doctoring."

She smiled. He was nice looking with dark hair and bright green eyes. Suddenly she had mixed emotions. Part of her wanted Tucker to win her basket, and part of her knew that this man should be the one to claim her and the lunch she had prepared.

So why was Tucker continuing the bidding war? Why didn't he just let the man win?

"Twenty dollars," Tucker said, an impish grin on his face.

Sarah felt her heart plummet as the crowd applauded. The gossips would be feasting on them today. She knew there was no way that they had squelched any rumors regarding the two of them.

A quiet hush fell on the room as they waited for the other man to respond.

He shook his head, a frown on his full lips. "Maybe next time, but right now the price has gotten a little too steep, even for your cooking, darlin'."

Tucker grinned. "No hard feelings, Brad." Then he turned to Sarah.

"Sarah, I hope you brought something good," Tucker said, aloud to the crowd, drawing their laughter.

"Pigs' slop would be too good for you," she said, under her breath. The fool had done considerable damage today and given his mother's beliefs credibility. Sarah felt the urge to berate him unceasingly for acting recklessly in front of these people. For believing he was invincible to the death of a bullet. For making her feel things she had tried her best to forget.

Tucker walked across the room, his steps steady, his swagger secure as he made his way to her. She took a deep breath. He had a commanding presence in the room that seemed to fill the space and leave her breathless. Damn, why did only Tucker seem to alert her senses to the point all she could think about was the way his hands made her feel.

She wanted to forget Tucker, but he seemed ingrained in her soul.

She watched as he tweaked Lucas on the nose. The boy smiled at him with the exact same dimples before he buried his face in his grandfather's shirt.

Tucker shook hands with her grandfather. "How are you, Mr. Kincaid?"

"Doing great. Excuse me while I take Lucas over and show him off to several of my friends."

Sarah watched her grandfather walk away and felt a moment of unease at being alone with Tucker. He stared at her, a sheepish grin on his face. It had been three days since she had seen him. Three days since their argument. Three days, and his image had never once left her mind.

"Hello," he said, a smile still gracing the hard planes of his face.

"Are you crazy?" she said, and clenched her fist. "Why did you keep upping the bid? Now everyone here is speculating about the two of us," she hissed.

Tucker shrugged a careless lift of his shoulders, the gold of his eyes twinkling in merriment as he held out his arm. "I have the basket, and you owe me a lunch."

"I owe you nothing but a good kick in the pants."

He smiled at her, his mischievousness oozing from his laugh. "You know, I thought about giving up and letting Brad have your lunch basket, but then I knew this would be your reaction. And I hadn't had the pleasure of your flashing blue eyes for the last few days. I kind of missed seeing them."

"We're supposed to be squelching rumors regarding the two of us, not starting any," she said.

He leaned down close to her. "Then, I suggest you take my arm, because if you don't, I'm going to lean down and kiss those soft lips of yours, and that will really get the rumors flying."

She gasped. "Why?"

"Just because I know it would feel good," he whispered in her ear. "And your mouth has always been hard to resist."

Sarah moved away from the feel of his breath tickling her ear, sending chill bumps down her arms.

"What's gotten into you?"

He smiled. "It's spring, and I feel ornerier than a bull in a meadow full of cows."

She turned toward the door in the need to escape

the room full of people. "Good, we're having Rocky
Mountain oysters for lunch. I hope you enjoy them."

Tucker shook his head, his cheeks dimpling.
"That's what I like about you, Sarah. You always
speak openly and honestly. There's no fancy ladies'
talk coming out of your mouth even after that im-
pressive school you went away to."

She glared at the man, her mouth suddenly as dry
as the desert in a drought, her stomach fluttering at
the thought of his mouth on hers. What was it about
Tucker that always managed to trigger her senses into
overload? What aspect of this man seemed to send
her body into a state of constant awareness? It was
hopeless and could only lead to more heartache.

"I need to talk to you about candidate number two,
and I'm going to do it over lunch. Now."

Wasn't it just like Tucker to escalate her expectations and then plunge them into despair? Candidate
number two didn't have a chance.

Tucker didn't know what had gotten into him. But
when the bidding started on Sarah's basket, he
couldn't resist the urge to outbid Brad. Yes, his
mother had suggested he bid on Sarah's basket,
though he could have stopped long before the schoolteacher dropped out. But he had wanted to continue.
The urge to win that basket from Brad had taken
over, and he had been unable to resist.

Since the argument with Sarah on the ride home
three days ago, he had avoided her; but seeing her
here today with her grandfather had made him want
to rile her just a little, and the lunch basket auction
had provided the perfect opportunity.

Sarah walked beside him now, past the area where
his family was gathered and out the door.

"Where are we going?" she asked. "I have to take care of Lucas."

"Your grandfather is watching him," he replied. He refused to release her arm, and they continued on out into the courtyard and the bright Texas sunshine. "It's a pretty day, and I didn't want to eat in there with all those people staring at us."

"You should have thought about that before you made us the center of attention," she remarked.

"Why? Then the auction wouldn't have been near as much fun."

She turned toward him. "Nor would it have created the amount of speculation about the two of us."

"Relax, Sarah, we're going to take care of that little problem right now." He stopped at a table nestled behind some evergreen shrubs, set the basket on the table and seated Sarah. Then he sat down across from her and stretched out his long legs.

"Now you can serve me the lunch I bought, while I tell you about candidate number two."

"If I weren't a healer, I would serve you a dose of strychnine. Guaranteed to cure a rogue like you," she retorted.

He couldn't help but smile at her. This was exactly what he had missed these last few days. Her biting sense of humor, her scathing retorts. He watched as she leaned over the table, spreading a cloth and setting out the various plates and silverware.

Her dress dipped dangerously low, giving him a brief glance at the tops of her breasts. At the sight of her luscious mounds, he felt as if he had fallen off of his horse and had the air knocked out of him. He gasped and hid it behind a cough.

She glanced at him. "Are you all right?"

"Yes," he managed to choke out.

"There's no need to tell me about candidate number two, because I've decided I'm not going to do this again. The last man you arranged for me to meet was enough to last a lifetime."

"You can't back out now. Not after I bought your basket in there," he said, sitting straight up.

"You should have thought of that earlier," she said, setting out their lunch on the tablecloth. "Before you decided to outbid that handsome cowboy."

"Who, Brad? He just wanted to taste your cooking," Tucker replied. "We won't tell him the truth, that you're a lousy cook."

"You know, that strychnine sounds better and better. Like the perfect dessert to top off my lousy cooking." She sat down across from him, irritated at herself for letting her emotions and her dreams surface regarding Tucker. She had to quit thinking about this man. He would never settle down, though the attraction was strong between them.

He was going to have to do some fast talking to convince her to have dinner with the banker.

"Candidate number two runs the local bank, he's looking for a wife, and he has money. This is the perfect opportunity for you."

"No. There's no reason for me to do this. I'm not looking for a husband, and I don't care whether he has money or not. I have my son, my practice, what else do I need?"

"But you agreed to do this for me."

"Well, now I've changed my mind."

"Look, I know that Neville was a mistake, but just give my plan a second chance. If you don't, my mother is going to be on us like ants at a picnic since I bought your basket."

"Yes, well, if you hadn't made such a spectacle

over my basket, then we wouldn't be in this mess. Would we?" she said.

He grinned. "I aim to please."

She stared at him. "You know, I really shouldn't help you out anymore. You're obstinate and hardheaded. I should just let your mother continue with her prying. Eventually she'll give up on me."

"I know. But you're the one she's trying to fix me up with. And she's going to be bothering you just as much as me."

Sarah shook her head at him. "Maybe it's time you and your mother realized I can't be pushed. Maybe it's time you had a frank discussion with her on her interfering."

"Sarah, Mother doesn't call it interfering. She calls it matchmaking."

"I don't care what she calls it. I'm not participating." She handed him his plate.

"Come on, don't do this to me."

She shook her head. "I'm going to pass on this, Tucker. There's no reason for me to continue seeing anyone, because just as soon as Doc Wilson is feeling better, I'm going home."

Eight

Sarah looked up just as Eugenia burst through the door to the church, a panicked look on her face. "Sarah, come quickly. Something's wrong with Lucas."

Her heart almost stopped before it began a mad race as she sprang up, her legs not moving fast enough. She ran into the church searching for her son. A sense of panic sent her headlong into people who were laughing and enjoying themselves. She pushed them aside and found her grandfather sitting with the gasping child on his lap.

Lucas's breathing was raspy and shallow, as if he struggled for each breath. His face was red and splotchy. The part of her that was a trained doctor told her to evaluate the situation, while the mother in her just wanted to grab the child and make him better.

"What happened?" Sarah asked, kneeling down in front of her son, who sat so lethargic on her grandfather's lap.

The old man's face wore a worried frown. "I don't know. We were playing, and suddenly he crawled up on my lap. I thought he was tired; but then he started breathing funny, and I noticed him breaking out in a rash."

Big red welts splotched his small face and hands. Sarah knew without raising his shirt that there would be more. It appeared he was having a reaction, but from what?

Tucker came running up beside her, and she gave him a quick glance before she returned her attention to the boy.

"Where has he been? Has he gotten into something he shouldn't?" Sarah asked.

"Not that I know of," her grandfather said worriedly. "He was right here with me the entire time."

"Tucker, my medical bag is in Grandfather's wagon. Would you get it for me?" she asked.

"Sure." He ran toward the door, his boots making a hollow sound on the wooden floor.

"Momma," Lucas said, holding his arms out to her. At his desperate cry the mother in her could not resist his plea. She took him in her arms, cradling him against her chest.

Her grandfather stood, and she sat down, setting the boy on her lap. She ran her hand across his forehead, but he wasn't hot.

"What could have caused this?" she asked, as she ran her hands over the small bones in his chest, searching for any clues regarding his shallow breathing.

"He's been right here playing beside us," Eugenia said, watching the boy. "Something about this seems familiar."

Tucker came running back in with her medical bag. Unfortunately, she didn't know what to treat him for, but she felt better just having the bag nearby in case she needed it.

"Thank you," she whispered, her eyes never leaving Lucas.

His lips were beginning to swell, and she was frightened for her child. He was having some kind of reaction, and whatever triggered the event must have entered his body through his mouth.

"What did you eat, Lucas?" she asked, wishing the child were older.

"Hurts," he said.

"Did you put something in your mouth, son?" she asked, again fearing he had put some poisonous plant in his mouth.

He looked up at her, his eyes so much like Tucker's, growing wide with confusion. "Pretty berry."

Berry? What kind of berry? she wondered, her mind going over the poisonous plants with brightly colored berries that grew in this area.

Eugenia hovered around Sarah and the distressed child. "You know, Tucker used to break out like this whenever he ate strawberries."

Sarah thought her neck would pop as she jerked her gaze back toward Eugenia. "What did you just say?"

"Tucker could never eat strawberries or he would break out all over. The first time he reacted that way, it scared me to death," Eugenia said. "I didn't know what was wrong with that child."

The old man grimaced. "I gave him strawberries. Ed Green had brought some in from the hill country, and I let him have several."

"Whenever Tucker broke out like this, the only thing I could do was just wait it out. In about twenty-four hours he'd be back to normal."

Sarah felt panic gripping her throat and for a moment was afraid that *she* would break out in red welts. Lucas was having a reaction to the strawberries. While it was a serious condition that should be watched carefully, the worst was probably over. Even now his breathing seemed to be returning to normal.

But Lucas could never eat strawberries again. And she feared Eugenia or even Tucker would realize the truth of Lucas's parentage.

"Do you think it's the strawberries, Sarah?" Tucker asked.

"I don't know," she evaded, almost certain that the berries were the problem. "His symptoms are common with a food reaction."

Her son looked terrible—his face was red and splotchy, his lips were swollen wherever the berry had touched his skin—and she was afraid. If it was only a food reaction, he should start to clear up soon, but she didn't need to give Eugenia Burnett any reason to believe that the strawberries were the culprits.

"Young man, I think we need to take you home. You've had enough excitement for one day," she said, leaning over the boy.

Tucker glanced into her eyes, his earthy brown ones serious for a change. "Do you want me to help you get him home?"

"No, I think we can manage, but thanks for the offer," she said, unable to let him take her home, afraid he would finally realize the truth.

"Well, at least let me carry him out to the wagon for you." He took the boy from her arms, and the child only glanced up at him through swollen, half-lidded eyes.

She clenched her hands as she watched Tucker carrying her son. Why did she worry that he would recognize some small part of himself in the child? He had not even considered for a moment that the boy was his.

"Come on, young man, let's get you home so your momma can take care of you," Tucker said, gazing down at Lucas.

Sarah followed Tucker out the door of the church, her grandfather right behind her as they walked to the waiting wagon. She climbed up into the buckboard, and Tucker lifted Lucas and put him in her arms. She felt a sense of relief once her son was in the security of her embrace. She noticed Eugenia standing in the doorway of the church, watching them.

"Thanks, Tucker. I appreciate your help," Sarah said, suddenly wishing he knew the truth and that they were a family. She pushed the feelings aside. There was no sense spending time yearning for things that were never going to happen.

"No problem," he said, gazing at her, his brown eyes warm and concerned.

Sarah sighed. She glanced back to the door of the church where Eugenia stood studying them and then back at Tucker. He knew just how to get to her.

"And tell candidate number two that I will have dinner with him," she said, the sight of his mother watching them suddenly changing Sarah's mind. Eugenia's remembering that Tucker had reacted to strawberries could only cause trouble. Sarah had to do something to divert Eugenia's attention from Lucas.

"I'll arrange it." Tucker reached down and stroked Lucas's hair, and the child seemed to settle into a drowsy state.

He glanced back into her eyes, and for a moment she thought she saw a trace of something that looked like longing shining from them. "You better get him home. I'll talk to you tomorrow about when you should meet the banker."

Her grandfather called to the horses, and the wagon slowly rolled away. Sarah looked down at her son.

Strawberries. Tucker and Lucas shared a reaction to strawberries. What other things did they share that Sarah had yet to discover? God, that had been a close call.

Several days later the bell on the office door jingled, alerting Sarah that someone had entered. After being caught off guard when Wo Chan had entered the first time, she had decided that it was safer to put a bell on the door to alert her when patients arrived.

She walked into the office area, and there stood the Chinese man and two young men. They were dressed in the eastern fashion with loose trousers and long shirts. Her first reaction was panic, but she took a deep breath, determined to act as though everything was normal. If she appeared frightened, they would know she had information regarding Kira.

"Good morning, gentlemen. How can I help you?" she asked.

Wo Chan came forward and bowed. "Good morning. I'm still looking for my bond servant, Mrs. James."

"The one you came by and asked me about once before?" she questioned innocently.

"Yes. Kira was last seen around your office. I fear she was hurt when she fell down a flight of stairs and that her bruises were mistaken for something different."

Sarah frowned. "I don't remember treating her, Mr. Chan."

"Later she was seen at your grandfather's hotel," he informed her.

Sarah shrugged, trying to appear disinterested. "A lot of people visit my grandfather's hotel. The dining room has excellent food."

The little man stepped closer to Sarah, but she refused to back away. He stopped mere inches from her, his dark eyes hard, radiating with hatred. "I hope you're not lying to me, Mrs. James. If I find out you are, there will be serious consequences. Give her back to me so that no one gets hurt."

His English was somewhat broken, but spoken well enough to be understood. She swallowed, fear rising up until it almost consumed her. "I think it's time you left, Mr. Chan. Don't come back here again."

He nodded and started backing toward the door. "I won't return unless I find out you had something to do with Kira's disappearance. I will find her."

With that last parting shot, he and the trio of henchmen backed out the door. Sarah managed to walk over to a chair and sink down onto the soft fabric. Her hands were trembling, and her heart was beating so fast and loud, she feared anyone else who came in the door would know she was frightened.

What was she going to do? How could she live with herself if she gave the young woman back to a horrible man like Wo Chan? But what about the safety of her family?

Thank God, Tucker had convinced her to take Kira out to the ranch. But the girl couldn't stay there forever.

And she could never tell Tucker about Wo Chan's visit. If he found out that the man had threatened her, she was afraid he would call the man out or try to shut him down. She could not be the one to provoke him into an altercation with Chan's henchmen. She would not be responsible for getting Tucker into a gunfight where he could possibly be killed.

No matter what direction she turned, someone was going to get hurt. She only hoped she could hold off long enough to get herself and Kira out of town before Wo Chan realized she was responsible for the whore's disappearance.

When Doc Wilson recovered and Sarah went back to Tombstone, she would take Kira with her. Surely she would be safe in Tombstone away from the clutches of the opium dealer. But until that time, Sarah would keep this visit from Wo Chan to herself.

"By the time I'm forty, I plan to own a huge portion of this town. The bank will be expanding in the next year, and I'm going to have to hire two more tellers," Clyde Waltham III, candidate number two, informed Sarah.

She sat across from the wealthy banker, eating dinner in the Merchant's restaurant. They had been at the plush eating establishment for nearly an hour, and the entire time had been spent listening to the man brag about how much money he made, his position in the community, and the way he ran his bank.

"The way the economy is growing in Fort Worth, we could be one of the leading cities in the nation before long."

She tried to appear as though she was listening to the man, but her mind kept drifting back, like a bad dream, to the visit this morning from Wo Chan. Even when she wasn't thinking about the man, suddenly a vision of him would appear in her mind, and she would have a moment of pure terror.

She refused to let his fear tactics work. She was not going to let him affect her life, yet she worried about Lucas and had reminded the desk clerks at the hotel not to let anyone up to their suite of rooms.

Part of her wanted to hire a bodyguard for Lucas; but she knew that would raise limitless questions, and she had to believe that the man had no proof or he would have done more than just frighten her this morning.

And his threats had been very successful. She was terrified, but she refused to give in to her fears and let Wo Chan win.

Clyde cleared his throat, bringing her attention back to him. "Your grandfather has built one of the nicest hotels in the city, and soon our opera house will be completed. Then we'll have some culture in this cow town."

The banker droned on about his business while Sarah smiled and nodded, pretending to be engrossed, when in actuality she only wanted the evening to end. Maybe he was a nice man, but she was not in the least attracted to him.

He was tall with a round stomach and, if his hair had been white, could have passed for Saint Nick. Though he hardly had the manners of a saint.

"I want to leave a better place for my children. Of course, I've got to find a wife before the children can come along."

She stifled a yawn and forked a bite of steak. At least the food was good this time, even if the company was rather boring.

"So how long have you known Tucker?" Clyde asked.

"Since I was ten and came to live with my grandfather," she replied.

"Why haven't the two of you ever gotten hitched?" he asked, the question taking her by surprise.

"We're friends," she said. "Nothing more." Her insides clenched. It was a lie. They had a son together, they had shared a wonderful night of passion, and there could be so much more between them if only she could trust him again, and if only he wanted forever. But he didn't want forever, and she was unwilling to settle for anything less.

"I don't think men and women can be friends," the banker responded. "Men want only two things from a woman, and they'll do just about anything to get what they want."

Of all the asinine things to say. "What two things are you referring to, Clyde?"

He grinned. "I don't need to explain that to you. You're a woman. You know."

"I'm also a doctor, but I'd like a clarification from you because I think there are many things a man needs from a woman. So, I'd like to hear what you consider the most important two," she said, her anger simmering just beneath the cool look she bestowed upon him.

He leaned back and crossed his arms above his stomach. "Okay. Sex and children are the only two things a man needs from a woman. The rest he can get just about anywhere else."

"But you can get sex from a soiled dove and children from an orphanage. What other two things are you talking about, Clyde?" She let his name slide off her tongue and wished she could rinse out her mouth.

Clyde sat up and leaned closer to her and whispered,

"But I don't want a whore for sex, and I want my own children not someone else's."

Sarah took a sip of water from the glass sitting on the table and then picked up her napkin and wiped her mouth. Anything to give her time to cool her response.

"I have a son from a previous marriage."

"Oh. Tucker failed to mention him. Sorry, but I don't want to raise another man's son. I'm sure that there are boarding schools he'd be very happy in," Clyde replied. "No offense."

"None taken," she said, knowing that her son would never be put in a boarding school.

"And I know you're a doctor, but no wife of mine would ever hold a job where she looked at people's privates. It's just not seemly," he said, his eyes wide with outrage.

"I heal people."

He shook his head. "Men are doctors."

If the man didn't shut up soon, she was going to come unleashed on him. "My son will not be raised by strangers. And I enjoy my work. I find it very satisfying, and I'm doing a service to the community."

"As my wife, you'd be doing even more service to the community by hosting parties and catering luncheons. I need someone to run my household, bear my children and be my hostess."

"Is this an interview for the job?" she asked.

His face suddenly brightened. "You know, that's not a bad idea. I could ask for references."

Sarah stared in disbelief. She threw down her napkin, unable to finish her dinner. "I think it's time I called it a night. My son has been sick, and I need to get back to him."

He ignored her. "So what do you think? Wouldn't

you like to be the leading lady of Fort Worth? I'm giving you the opportunity to be my wife."

It was all she could do to keep from busting out laughing. They had dinner together, and he was asking her to marry him? This was crazy! How many other women had turned him down?

No more! She refused to do this again. She had originally agreed to Tucker's idea just to deter his mother's interference. In the process she had hoped that she could prove to herself and to him that she no longer cared about him—that it would show Tucker that other men did find her attractive. But instead it had backfired. She was not going to do this to herself anymore. She was through with Tucker's own matchmaking skills. They were lacking to say the least.

"Clyde, I just don't think that would be a good idea. I like my work, I love my son, and I'm not willing to part with either. We've barely met, and I just don't think I'm what you're looking for."

She watched as his chest puffed out. "I'm sorry to hear that, Sarah. I was hoping that we could join forces, get married and have several kids."

She forced a smile. "I'm honored that you asked; but my son is the most important person in my life, and we need each other. Plus I wouldn't be happy not being a doctor. I studied way too hard to get my medical degree."

"Oh," he said, stunned by her forwardness. "I understand. Let me take you home, then."

She was finding there were a lot of things Tucker failed to mention to the men he arranged for her to meet.

* * *

Several days later, Sarah was filling her medical bag with supplies, concentrating on getting ready to ride out to the Melbournes'. According to Doc Wilson's notes, Mrs. Melbourne suffered from consumption and had been doing poorly all winter. After Sarah checked on the woman, she wanted to examine her children to make sure the disease had not spread.

Lucas was back to normal, and she was counting the days until Doc Wilson returned and she went back to Tombstone, taking her son and Kira with her.

The bell above the door tinkled, and Sarah spun around, fear exploding through her. Tucker strolled in, and she exhaled in relief. "I saw the buggy tied out front. You going somewhere?"

She glanced at him irritably and closed her bag. "Hello, and in case you're interested, I'm fine."

Tucker grinned. "Good. Where are you going?"

She shook her head at him. "I'm driving the doctor's buggy out to the Melbournes' place to check on Mrs. Melbourne and her children."

His face darkened into a frown. "You shouldn't be driving out there by yourself. It's not safe for a woman to be traveling alone."

She shrugged. "I drive myself in Tombstone all the time. I refuse to live in fear. I'll be fine."

He picked up her doctor's bag. "Are you ready now? You're not going by yourself."

Sarah stared at him as he stood at the door waiting for her, his hat in one hand, her medical bag in another. His hair was the color of the prairies in winter that lay at the edge of town, golden brown. His eyes twinkled with gold flecks that seemed to call to her and tempt her just as they had three years ago in Tombstone.

What was she doing? She couldn't think of him

this way, couldn't remember the way his hands had felt on her body that night, the way his voice touched some deep inner chord in her. She couldn't remember the feeling of safety and security that seemed to envelop her each time he had held her in his arms.

Quickly she pushed the thoughts away. Unable to acknowledge that she was grateful for his company, she replied, "If you insist on going, you can't complain about what we find when we get there."

"I've been to the Melbournes' before. It's no big deal," he said, and opened the door for her. "Let's go."

"Okay, but you've been warned."

They walked out the door, and he helped her into the small vehicle, his hands warm and firm through her clothes. She watched as he walked around the buggy and climbed in, picking up the reins. "You know, you drive me places almost more than I do."

He smiled. "I like to do it."

As they rode out of town heading south, she relaxed, sat back and watched the scenery roll by, the warmth of the sun making her drowsy on this spring day. Because Tucker was with her, she wasn't nearly as worried about Wo Chan and his threats. But she could not tell Tucker about the man and his intimidation. She didn't need Tucker getting into any gun battles because of her, and soon she would be returning home.

"So how did you like Clyde?"

She looked at him and shook her head, a smile gracing her face. "You have the most incredibly bad taste when it comes to men. If you were a woman, I'd worry about you marrying poorly."

His hands flicked the reins, and the conveyance bounced over a chuckhole. "Does this mean you aren't interested in candidate number two?"

"Clyde will make some woman very unhappy, but not me," she said, suddenly realizing that she would probably find fault with any man except Tucker.

The thought shocked her. Did she still love him? Quickly she pushed the idea out of her head. He had broken her heart once, and she would be damned if she would let him have a second go at her fragile organ.

Their first encounter had left her shaken and with a son that she loved dearly. The second time around would be even more devastating when he chose wandering over staying with her.

"So who should I go to next," he asked, a frown wrinkling his forehead.

"Oh, Tucker, I just don't think this is a good idea. I'm not interested in finding a husband."

"Why not? Your son needs a father," he said.

"He has a mother and a grandfather. The boy is well taken care of," she replied, a hint of irritation in her voice.

"Yes, but he needs to be taken fishing, and when he's older, he'll need to be taught how to hunt, how to take care of a horse. There are just so many things that the boy will need to know."

"I think I can handle most of them, Tucker," she said, defensiveness edging her voice.

"If you were going to stay around here, I could teach him."

Her heart lurched into her throat at the thought of Tucker unknowingly teaching his son all the things a man needed to know.

"I can't. I'm going home to Tombstone just as soon as Doc Wilson is well. I'm going to take Kira with me."

"Yes, well, it's time I was moving on anyway. I hope to be leaving soon myself."

This was why he would always be a man on the move, never staying long in one place, with no permanent ties or commitments. She couldn't help but feel angry that once again he couldn't see that there was so much right here in Fort Worth for him. Right in front of his eyes, if only he would open them.

"What is it about wandering you enjoy so much, Tucker?" she asked, irritated. "Why do you want to leave people you care about?"

He nodded. "I've always wanted to see other parts of the country. I've told you before how I want to be different from my brothers. I want to be me."

"But didn't you get that when you were younger? Back in your gunslinging days? You have a good job. Why not stay in Fort Worth?"

He glanced at her, frowning as he shrugged. "It just doesn't seem very exciting to stay in one place the rest of my life. Everyone gets married, has children and settles down. I want to be different. I want to do unusual things. See new places."

"Why couldn't you do that with a wife and children?" she asked.

"Because then you're tied down. You have to work. You have to take care of the children and support your wife." He pulled on the reins and slowed the horse as they rounded a curve.

"So you think being a family man would become a chore, a duty?" she asked.

He turned toward her and said, "Yes, I do."

Sarah gazed out as the countryside sped by, her heart in her throat. He didn't want the accountability of taking care of a family. Even now his avoidance of responsibility seemed to drive his decisions, just as it had in Tombstone. Only this time he wasn't a wounded gunslinger, but rather a grown man with a penchant for danger and an aversion to dependability.

Once they reached the Melbournes', Sarah sighed and climbed out of the buggy. It was time to go to work and do the job she loved, but she had wanted just a few more moments alone with Tucker. Just a few more moments to point out to him his avoidance of responsibility, to point out the value of family, to share with him a cute story about his son.

Nine

Tucker watched as Sarah spoke with Mrs. Melbourne, amazed at Sarah's gentle nature, the way she listened to her patients, making them feel special. She had always had a way with people, since they were children.

"I'm going to listen to your chest, and I want you to take several deep breaths," Sarah explained. She put her stethoscope against the woman's chest, listening for the sounds of her breathing.

She repeated the process by putting the metal cup against the woman's clothed back. Sarah's face was intense as she listened to the woman's lungs. She came around to face the woman and sat down in front of her. "How have you been feeling?"

"I've been coughing a lot lately, and I'm so tired. I just can't seem to get enough rest," Mrs. Melbourne complained.

"You have fluid in your lungs, which is not good. I want you to nap every afternoon for at least two hours, plus I want you to walk every day. You need to get exercise or that fluid will continue to build."

"I don't have time to take a nap in the afternoon.

My family needs me," the woman replied, pushing back a strand of wayward hair.

Sarah took her patient's hands in hers, gazing at her as if there were no one else in the room, and explained slowly and softly, "Mrs. Melbourne, your life is at risk. You have consumption, and if you don't take care of yourself, the fluid will continue to build until your lungs are full."

"Doesn't everyone die when they get consumption?" the woman responded.

"No. Some people get well. But you have to take care of yourself, and that means rest, eating healthy foods and exercise to keep the fluid down."

"But my family . . . ," she protested.

"Your family has to understand. You could die if you don't take care of yourself. I'd be happy to wait and talk with your husband," Sarah offered, staring sympathetically at Mrs. Melbourne.

"No. I can tell him. I know you're busy."

"Now, I want you on a diet of meat, milk and vegetables. Walk each day until you feel tired, and then rest. You've got to get plenty of sleep."

"And this will cure me?" Mrs. Melbourne asked again.

"There's a chance." Sarah paused and waited expectantly, her attention focused on the woman. "Do you have any other questions?"

"No. It's just that Doc Wilson never told me I had a chance of living," she said, puzzled. "I thought I was going to die, so why even try to get better?"

"For many years we didn't think a person with consumption could survive, but now there's hope." She stood and patted Mrs. Melbourne on the back. "Now, if you don't mind, I'd like to examine your children while I'm here."

"Please do," Mrs. Melbourne said, before a coughing spell took her breath away.

"Any handkerchiefs that you spit up blood and phlegm on, don't let anyone in the family touch. My recommendation would be to burn them or wash them in boiling water with the strongest soap you have."

"Okay," Mrs. Melbourne said breathlessly.

Sarah stood and walked to the children. "Who wants to be brave and go first?"

"I do," the little girl cried. "I'm not afraid."

"Good, there's nothing to be afraid of."

Tucker sat back and watched as Sarah talked to the children and listened to their lungs. She checked their throats and looked in their ears.

She was the smartest person he had ever met, and he admired the way she did her job. For as long as he could remember she had wanted to be a doctor. But then, her father had been a physician, and she had traveled with him for awhile.

This was the life she was meant for, a country doctor caring for the townspeople. She didn't need to go back to Tombstone. These people were her family and friends. These people should be her patients, not some no-account gunslinger who'd taken a bullet.

And if she stayed, he could watch over her. But how could he do that when he was leaving? He pushed the thought away, his mind drifting back to the times when they were children growing up.

When she graduated from that fancy school, she had wound up in Tombstone of all places, patching up gunslingers, doctoring whores and trying to help Indians. She was such a do-gooder, and for years he had been just the opposite. They were like night and day, and he wondered how they had stayed friends all these years. What kept them coming back to one another, except fate?

He feared he would never be smart enough or good enough for Sarah, yet they were still friends.

He admired the way she was tough and bright. The way she listened as though the one speaking was the only other person in the world. She was genuine and caring. And he admitted she wasn't too bad on the eyes either. Motherhood had finished shaping her hips, and her curves were in all the right places. She was sharp, she was beautiful and she needed a man to marry and settle down with.

He cleared his throat, that thought suddenly making him nervous. Sarah glanced up at him, her brow furrowed in concentration. Her blue eyes were smoky and warm, and then she went back to her exam.

God, when she looked at him that way, he could feel the heat of her gaze all the way to his toes. It was a wonder there wasn't smoke coming out the tips of his boots.

As she finished looking in the young boy's throat, she reached down and tickled him, making the child laugh.

She looked up and noticed Tucker watching her, and for just a moment they stared across the room at each other. An image of them naked and in bed together came to mind, and quickly he glanced away.

The urge to cross the room and kiss her was almost overwhelming. He wanted so much to just taste her one more time. To run his hand down the velvety smoothness of her skin, to taste the honeydew sweetness of her lips. But that would be way out of line for a cowboy who was determined to remain a bachelor.

"Mrs. Melbourne, your children seem very healthy,"

Sarah said, jolting him back from his mind's exploration of her body. "I intend to come back and check on you again before Doc Wilson returns to his practice. So I should see you again in two or three weeks. If you need me before then, send word and I'll come."

"Wait here, just a minute," the woman called, and hurried out of the living quarters of the house.

They stood there waiting for about five minutes before she came running back in with a basket. "Here, I want you to have this. It's not much; but it's after lunch, and you've spent the entire morning here with us."

Sarah took the basket. "Thank you. It smells delicious."

"It's such a beautiful day outside, maybe you and the marshal could stop by Pecan Creek and have a picnic," Mrs. Melbourne said.

Tucker nodded and took Sarah by the elbow, leading her out the door. "Thanks for the basket, Mrs. Melbourne. Hope you get to feeling better."

They walked out the door, and he helped Sarah up into the buggy and then crawled in behind her. They waved to the woman and her children, who had come out to watch them leave, and Tucker called to the horse.

"Yeehaw!"

With a lurch the vehicle rolled out of the yard and back toward the road to town.

"Will she get better?" he asked.

"Depends on whether her body can fight off the disease. But without the proper food and rest, she'll be dead within the year." Her voice was calm and steady. "I hate losing patients."

He reached out and patted her on the leg, somehow

wanting to give her comfort. The feel of her leg beneath his hand was warm and arousing.

She gazed at him, one brow lifted in surprise. He pulled his hand back, flabbergasted by his comforting gesture. What was he thinking? Reaching out and touching her to console her?

But worse, he had enjoyed the feel of her thigh beneath his fingers.

The next few miles they rode in silence, Tucker trying to comprehend the feelings that watching Sarah at work this morning had stirred. What was it about this woman? They were mere friends and nothing more. Yet when he was around her, it felt like so much more.

Tucker glanced over at Sarah, who sat gazing out at the countryside, the wind teasing wisps of her blond hair about her face. She was a beautiful woman, and he had already made the error of sleeping with her in Tombstone, though at the time he had enjoyed every minute. He was not about to repeat the same mistake, but her blue eyes were sparkling, her lips were so full and tempting and dang she looked good, even better than he remembered. And if the truth were told, he wouldn't pass up the opportunity to be in her arms a second time.

Turning onto the main road back to town, Tucker noticed the sky was beginning to turn a robin's egg blue off to the west. "Looks like the clouds are starting to build."

"A little rain would be nice," she said, tightening the strings on the bonnet she was wearing. "Did you want to stop and eat the food Mrs. Melbourne prepared for us?"

"Not with the way those clouds are beginning to look. Remember, it's springtime in Texas." He slapped the reins on the back of the horse. "I think we better get back to town, before we get caught in a frog choker."

They were well over an hour from town, and the road to the Melbournes' was rough from lack of use.

"Frog choker!" she said, her voice trailing off. "I haven't heard that expression in a long time." She laughed. "You know, you always were one to come up with the silliest expressions. It was one of the things I liked about you."

She stared out at the countryside as if she had said too much.

"Why have we remained friends all these years, Sarah? We're so different," he said.

Her face turned, and she gazed at him in amazement. She laughed, the sound light and carefree. He hadn't heard her laugh like that in years, and it reminded him of when she was a young girl.

"What brought this on?" she asked. "I didn't think you were a man who did too much thinking."

He shrugged. "I don't know. Watching you this morning with Mrs. Melbourne, I realized how different we are."

"It's hard for me to imagine you thinking about our friendship." She paused and brushed back a strand of hair from her face. "Especially after . . . after you came to Tombstone."

He gave her a sheepish grin. "I guess you regret me . . . us doing what we did?"

She looked at him, her eyes wide with surprise at his question. "No. I don't regret that night." She paused, staring at him, her facial expression guarded. "I was hurt and disappointed that you left without saying good-bye. I had no expectations, but your leaving in the middle of the night made it seem cheap."

He looked away, his eyes transfixed on the road in front of him. "It wasn't cheap, Sarah. But I didn't know what to say, so I left."

"Good-bye would have been nice."

She turned her attention back to the countryside, and he felt ill at ease. Good-bye? That was all she had expected? Not "let's get married"? Live happily ever after? Have babies? Wasn't that what good women expected?

"What do you mean, 'good-bye' would have been just fine? Most women expect more, especially after you've just shared their bed with them," he said, stealing quick glances at her as he drove steadily.

"You're right. But why in the world would I expect or want to marry a man like you? At that time you were a wounded gunslinger with a thirst for vengeance. Why would I want to become involved in that kind of mess? I still don't need a man that desperately."

For a moment he sat stunned by her words. She had had sex with him, but she hadn't wanted to marry him? Seemed too good to be true, yet he was uneasy.

"So you weren't mad?" he asked.

"Sure I was. You left without saying good-bye. But did I want to marry you? No. Why would I?"

She had taken the wind right out of his sails. Somehow he had thought of her pining away for him. But instead she had gone out and married someone else.

"So why did you marry your husband?" he asked. Tucker watched as her mouth tightened and her eyes widened, as if he had offended her by even asking.

"I married Mr. James for the same reason that people have been marrying for hundreds of years. I loved him."

He shook his head. "No. I mean, what caused you to fall in love with him?"

She sighed. "He was dependable. He was there when I needed him. He was kind, considerate, loyal and trustworthy. His word stood for something. He supported my being a doctor, and he knew when to back away and leave me alone."

Tucker couldn't help but think that the man sounded more like a saint than a husband.

"You must have met him pretty quick after I left."

"Yes, I did. And we fell in love very suddenly."

He didn't say anything for a moment. The warm breeze blew briskly across his arm.

"So why have we remained friends all these years?" he asked, getting back to the original question.

"I only know that when I was growing up you were fun to be with. You made me laugh. You didn't treat me like a girl, but rather a kid. No matter what I wanted to do, you encouraged me."

"Well, you certainly grew up to look like a girl."

"Is that a compliment, Mr. Burnett?" she teased.

He glanced at her. The sun had kissed her cheeks until they were pink, the blue of her eyes matched the disappearing sky and the smile she bestowed upon him made him forget about the encroaching storm clouds. Made him forget everything but being with Sarah.

"You know it is," he said, his voice coming out deep and husky.

The trees were becoming sparse as they rode toward an area of prairie that was filled with tall grass that swayed in the wind.

"So do you believe that men and women can be friends without anything sexual between them?" she asked.

The question surprised him. How did he answer this one and stay out of trouble? Yes, they were friends. But right now he wouldn't hesitate at the least indication from her, and he would be all over her like bees on honey. He wanted her so badly he was aching with the knowledge, but they were friends. Not lovers, not a couple, just two separate people who wanted different lives. Friends attracted for all the wrong reasons.

"Yes, but for men everything is sexual."

She started laughing. "I should have known better than to ask you that question."

Thunder rumbled in the distance, and Tucker glanced up at the white cirrus clouds that were suddenly moving above them very quickly. "We'll be lucky if we don't get drenched."

"How far from town are we?" she asked.

"Almost an hour," he replied.

"How long before this storm hits?"

"Depends. But it appears to be gaining speed on us. Hang on, we're going to pick up the pace a little." Tucker took out the whip and snapped it across the back of the horse that was pulling the buggy. "Yeehaw! Let's go."

The horse lifted its head and picked up its legs, moving into a fast trot. Sarah bounced on the seat next to Tucker, occasionally bumping him with her hip, the edge of which brushed against his leg with a sensuous rub. He couldn't help but remember her long, naked limbs wrapped around him, and he wanted to groan at the image.

He watched with increasing uneasiness as the clouds grew darker, the colors changing from blue to turquoise. Thunder rumbled closer, and Tucker stared as a wicked streak of lightning met the earth. It was still miles away; but the storm was catching them, and no matter how fast he ran the poor horse, they would soon be wet.

Suddenly, the horse stumbled in a prairie dog hole, and Tucker swore beneath his breath. He watched the horse's gait and knew the animal had somehow hurt itself. Pulling on the reins, he brought the buggy to a halt.

"Why are you stopping?" Sarah asked.

"Something's wrong with the horse," he said, climbing down. He walked to the animal and knelt down beside it. Running his hand over the back of the animal's leg, he felt the muscles and tendons. The horse gave a cry of distress.

Sarah jumped down from the buggy and walked around to Tucker. "Let me feel," she said, running her hands down the animal's leg. "He's torn his muscle."

"Whose horse is it?" Tucker asked.

"He belongs to the hotel. Grandfather keeps extra horses on hand that guests can rent." She stood and glanced up at the clouds. "So now what do we do? We have no horse, a buggy that can't be pulled and a storm brewing."

Tucker began loosening the bit from the horse's mouth. They would have to leave the horse behind and continue on foot, abandoning the doctor's buggy as well.

"What kind of shoes are you wearing?" Tucker questioned.

"My boots, what else?" she said. "I know better than to wear those flimsy fashionable slippers. At least not when I'm working."

"Good. Because it looks like we'll be walking until we either find help or some place to wait out the storm."

He lifted the bridle over the horse's head, then slapped it on the rump and sent it trotting off to find grass.

"He may find his way back to town before we do," Sarah said, watching the horse limp across the field.

Tucker put the harness in the back of the buggy. After picking up the basket of food Mrs. Melbourne had given them and a blanket that was tucked underneath the seat, he turned to Sarah.

"Let's get started. This weather isn't going to hold off much longer."

"Let me get my medical bag. I'm not leaving it here." She grabbed the black bag out of the wagon.

They started walking down the dirt road just as the wind kicked up, showering them with a cool, dusty breeze.

Sarah coughed and turned her face away. "Oh, my. This should be a fun walk."

"I know we passed a line shack this morning. We'll stay there until this storm passes."

They walked along, the thunder getting closer. The skies were beginning to turn green with bubble formations in the clouds.

"I don't think I like the way these clouds are looking," Sarah commented.

"Me neither," Tucker admitted, certain they were

going to be soaked at any moment. But just as the first fat drops of rain started to fall, he spotted the building he was looking for.

"There it is," he said, pointing. "Come on, I think we better make a mad dash for it or we're going to get wet."

He grabbed her hand, encompassing her smaller one with his large fingers. He couldn't remember holding her hand before and was awed at the protective sense that overcame him. Her fingers felt so right intertwined with his own.

As the drops of rain began to pelt them, they ran across an open field to the shack Tucker had spotted.

Tucker turned the knob, and they ran inside, laughing at how they had beat the weather. The skies suddenly opened up, pounding the earth with the storm's fury. Thunder shook the shack as lightning struck nearby, and Sarah stayed next to Tucker as he gazed around the small building.

A cot, a table and two chairs were all the furniture in the one-room building. Quickly he found a match and lit a lantern sitting on the floor.

"So what do we do now?" she asked, peering out the door at the rain that fell in sheets from the sky.

"We wait," Tucker replied, setting the basket of food on the table. "We eat our lunch and we wait for the storm to blow over."

"I'm glad you remembered this shack. How could we ever walk in that?" she questioned, still watching the rain.

Tucker glanced back over his shoulder as he turned up the lamp to brighten the room.

Lightning hit a tree across the way, and Sarah jumped back from the door. "Oh my, did you see that?"

"Come away from the door, Sarah. Let's eat the food Mrs. Melbourne sent with us."

The wind whipped the rain in different directions, and a tree limb snapped off and fell to the ground. Lightning flashed, the sound crackling across the sky. The shack shook as thunder boomed, and Sarah flew into Tucker's arms.

He wrapped his arms around her, enjoying the feel of her soft womanly body snuggled against his. He gazed down into her eyes. They had darkened with fear, the color reminding him of the turquoise rocks he had seen in New Mexico.

"Are you afraid?" he asked.

"No," she said, belying her fear. "I'm just fine."

She smiled at him in such a way he knew it was bravado, and all the resistance he had been hanging on to these last few weeks suddenly melted away. Like a beaver dam washed downstream in a flash flood, the desire for Sarah he had tried to pretend didn't exist overwhelmed him. He stared at her full, luscious lips so close, so tempting, and with the rain pounding outside, he gave up resisting her any longer.

The tension had been building and building, until he thought it would near burst inside him if he didn't kiss her. He lowered his lips to hers in a kiss that had been weeks in coming. A kiss he had wanted to give her when she had stepped off that stage.

Softly he brushed his lips across hers and felt as if lightning had struck him, the burn searing all the way to his core.

This was Sarah, the sweet, tempting woman who lingered in his thoughts way too much. He crushed her lips beneath his own in a kiss that released the pent-up desire he had been withstanding these last few weeks. This kiss showed him the error of his thinking that sweet Sarah had been only one night of passion, but was rather a lifetime of regret.

At first her lips were stiff and unyielding, but then her arms wound their way around his neck. He felt the imprint of her body against his, the fullness of her breasts touching his chest, her skirts swirling about his legs, the way she fit so snug against his body.

Surrounded by the smell of lavender, his mouth plundered hers, tasting and teasing her lips with an urgency he had never felt before. He had waited so long to taste her, to feel her in his arms again. She was so soft, so pliant and he wanted her so badly.

The rain pounded against the roof of the little building, a sweet smell of clean, cool air blowing through the open door as lightning flashed and thunder boomed around them. Their kiss was anything but gentle as he plied his lips against Sarah's, his tongue tracing the outline of her mouth.

His hands moved down to her breasts, caressing them through the material of her dress. Hunger the likes of which he had never experienced before had him sweeping aside the cotton cloth of her dress, pushing her chemise out of the way, until he found the sought-after kernel of her breast. He rolled the hardened pebble between his fingers before he released her in desperation.

She moaned, the sound echoing in the little cabin, mingling with the sound of the rain.

Bending down, he put his arm beneath her legs and lifted her, setting her on the table in the middle of the small room. There he put his lips to her breast and suckled gently, laving her breast with his mouth and tongue.

He wanted her fiercely, knowing that at any moment

they would both regain their senses and realize this was the act of a crazy man. Their friendship was at stake. The tenacious agreement they had could blow up in their faces if they followed through on their desires.

But he didn't want to release her. He wanted more. He wanted to seek that level of pleasure he had experienced in her arms before. He never wanted to let go of her, regardless of what he had told her previously. He wanted Sarah naked and vulnerable beneath him.

She plied her fingers through his hair, holding his head as he lavished her nipple. Her head was thrown back, and she moved it from side to side, her eyes closed.

"Tucker," she moaned.

His hand slid down her waist, farther down her thigh, until he lifted her dress and exposed her stockings. Slowly, he slid his hand up her leg, until he reached the junction between her thighs. His hand gently rubbed her through the slit in her drawers, the slick feel of her desire coating his fingers as she gasped and arched her back, leaving her neck vulnerable and exposed.

But before Tucker could put his lips against her tempting throat, she sat up, pushing his hands away.

"Stop! We can't do this," she said breathlessly. She shoved him out of her way, yanked down her skirt and jumped off of the table. Her chest was rising and falling from her labored breathing as she straightened her chemise. "I can't do this again with you. I just can't."

She glanced out the door of the cabin where water dripped from the doorsill. The ground was wet and sparkling with raindrops. The sun was starting to peek from behind the clouds, making the land glisten like crystals dazzling and new.

Somehow the storm outside had passed while the one inside had just been getting started.

"The storm's over. I've got to get home to Lucas," she said, her voice stilted as she looked about the room wildly. "I'm leaving."

Tucker stared in disbelief as she grabbed her medical bag and ran out of the cabin, leaving him alone.

Ten

Sarah wanted to run. She felt the urge to lift her skirts and run as fast as her legs would carry her away from the line shack and the feelings that Tucker had evoked in that small cabin. He would never commit himself to her, and somehow she had let down her guard and let him kiss her. That simple action had brought up all sorts of feelings that she had thought she had long ago buried. All sorts of emotions she had tried her darndest to hide.

He had admitted all he thought about was sex. He was a man, she was a woman, and they had been trapped in that line shack, a storm raging around them. He had done nothing more than any other caged male would have done. It meant nothing to him, and she couldn't let her overly romantic, female mind make more of that kiss than just a simple case of lust brought on by a rainstorm. Tucker Burnett didn't want a future with her any more today than he had all those years ago. And if he did want her more today, it was only because he had been bored and she had been available.

No. This meant nothing. She refused to take a step back in time to where he had dumped her heart that

night in Tombstone. She refused to let her mind con-
jure up the images she had tortured herself with
while she was pregnant. Images of them together as
a family, in a little house where they lived as man
and wife, where he held the son they had made together. She refused to let this man make a fool of
her once again.

Even though she longed to be in his arms, even
though their kiss had felt like a homecoming, she
must guard her heart against Tucker. He could not
slip through her defenses again.

The kiss meant nothing.

A bird flew by, cackling in the cool, clean air.
Sarah walked in the grass that grew between the now
muddy wagon ruts, trying to keep her boots from
caking with muck from the recent rains. They were
miles from town, but she was determined not to wait
another minute in that cabin.

Ahead the storm clouds raced on, radiating
glimpses of lightning, with an occasional rumble of
thunder in the distance. She had to get away from
Tucker, back to Lucas and her grandfather. Where
her world was more grounded in reality, not the
dreamlike quality of Tucker's kisses.

"Slow down, Sarah," Tucker yelled.

She couldn't slow down. The urge to run was still
strong within her, and she didn't know if she would
stop before she reached Fort Worth.

At the sound of someone running behind her, she
turned and glimpsed Tucker hurrying toward her. He
ran up beside her and slowed to a walk. "What's the
all-fired hurry? What's gotten into you?"

The urge to laugh was strong. He knew why she
had left so abruptly; he was just trying to ignore the
obvious problem. Just like he always avoided any kind

of responsibility or commitment. Or anything that could possibly tie him down or make him deal with an uncomfortable issue.

"The storm was over. It was time to go."

"You could have waited for me."

She had to bite her tongue to keep from busting out at that statement. She felt like she had been waiting for him most of her life, and she was getting damned tired of his delays.

"It was time to leave," she said, her hands clenched as she strode down the road.

He grabbed her by the arm and pulled her to a halt. "You're mad that I kissed you, aren't you?"

She stared into the brown of his eyes, the color reminding her of leaves in fall. "No, I'm not mad, but what's the point? I'm not interested in just a quick tumble to ease the aching between your legs. You're not interested in anything that might hint at forever. What we did back there was a total waste of time, and I have responsibilities waiting for me at home."

He grinned at her and started to laugh. Anger cascaded through her, and she jerked her arm free and started walking again, leaving him standing in the road.

"Damn it, Sarah," he called out, laughing. "You know how to ruin some great kissing. It was fun."

"Good, I'm glad you enjoyed it. But I must get home." She dropped her voice to a whisper. "And I certainly know where all that kissing leads. Heartache!"

Several days later, Tucker sat trying to focus his attention on the paperwork that lay strewn on his desk.

He couldn't help but remember how Sarah had looked, her head thrown back in passion as he had explored her body years ago. The image of her naked, the moonlight shimmering on her skin like silk, returned, hitting him below the belt. He clenched his fists on top of the desk.

A rapid knock caused him to jump as he jerked his gaze in the direction of the doorway. Federal Marshal McCoy stood staring at him.

"Tucker, you awake, man?"

Tucker shook his head. "Sorry, my mind was busy thinking about something else. When did you get back in town?"

"Just today. I had to go to Dallas, so I made a special trip to come by and see you."

"Oh? Something I can do for you, Marshal?"

"Yes. Can I come in?"

"Sorry, come on in and sit down. How can I help you?"

The marshal took a seat in a chair across from Tucker, crossed his ankle over his knee and laid his hat on top of his calf.

He glanced up at Tucker. "Remember the last time I was here, I was telling you about one of my officers getting married?"

"Yes, I do."

"Well, it's official. His last day is a month from now. And I've got to find someone to replace him."

An impending sense of interest suddenly caused Tucker to pay closer attention.

"I was kind of wondering if you'd be interested in taking his place. You've been here now for a couple of years. I know you're good with a gun, and you don't have a wife and children to tie you down."

Tucker smiled. "What's the pay like?"

The man shrugged his shoulders. "It's not much more than you're earning now, but you would be working on cases that are in your territory, not just in one city."

"So do you enjoy the job?"

"Yes, I do. I get to travel, work on interesting cases and bring in men who need to be brought to justice."

"Sounds exciting," Tucker said.

He watched as the marshal picked up his broadband hat and beat it against his leg, then glanced back at Tucker. "It's not a job for just any lawman, and it's a real opportunity if you want it. You have to work long hours, and you're often far from the people you know. I haven't been home to see my sisters in over three years."

"There are always sacrifices."

"That's right." He stood. "I've got to go, but I wanted to stop by and offer you the job before I went back to Austin. Think about it, and in a couple of weeks I'll be back. We can talk some more at that time."

Tucker stood up and walked around the desk. "Thanks! I appreciate you thinking of me. I already know my answer, but I'll agree to think about it just like you said."

The man nodded and put his hat on his head. "I'll be going now." He shook Tucker's hand and then walked out the door. "I'll see you in a couple of weeks."

"Thanks again!" Tucker called as the man strode out of the Tarrant County jail. Calmly Tucker shut the door from the prying eyes of the deputies and then danced a jig across his office floor.

Finally, after over two years of being home in

Texas, he would be leaving Fort Worth. Once again he would be a roving man with few responsibilities.

Across town, the bell tinkled above the door of Doc Wilson's office, and Sarah looked up to see Eugenia Burnett stroll through the door. She wanted to groan, but resisted. Already she had felt the day was less than stellar with her continuous thoughts of Tucker, but now it was a total disaster.

"Good morning, Sarah."

"Good morning, Mrs. Burnett," she said politely.

"I just wanted to come and check on you, after I heard about you and Tucker being stranded during that terrible storm several days ago."

Sarah did her best to control the irritation she felt for being reminded of that day as she gazed at the older woman. "Thank you for your concern, Mrs. Burnett, but as you can see, I'm just fine. We had to walk for quite a few miles, but that was no problem."

"Any progress to report with my son?" Eugenia asked, taking a seat across from Sarah.

The question made the back of Sarah's neck prickle like a thousand needles cascading down her spine. The woman had a lot of gall to sit there and ask her about Tucker, especially after their trip to the Melbournes'. Sarah was trying hard to put the memory of his kiss out of her mind. That simple kiss had stirred up more reflection, more feelings of heartache and regret, than Sarah cared to remember.

"Yes, there has been some progress," Sarah replied, her voice carefully controlled. "Which part would you like for me to tell you about? The man he introduced me to that I wouldn't wish on my worst enemy, or the one who was more interested in climbing the social ladder than the care of my son?"

"Oh, my," Eugenia said, frowning.

"Yes, we made so much advancement on our little trip to visit the Melbournes' that I walked away from the line shack where we were waiting out the storm and left him."

Sarah stood and began to pace.

"But don't you see, Sarah, he's introducing you to men that are completely unsuitable because he wants you for himself," the older woman said quietly.

Ridiculous, Sarah thought. *This whole conversation is simply ludicrous.*

"Have you changed your mind yet about us marrying?" Sarah asked.

"No, Sarah, I haven't. When Tucker falls, it will be hard and it'll be everlasting. Don't give up on him just yet."

"Mrs. Burnett, your son and I will never marry. You need to accept that fact. As I told Tucker the other day, we are wasting each other's time. He doesn't want to settle down, and I have a son who I must consider. He's planning on leaving Fort Worth soon, and I won't be here when he gets back. So your matchmaking isn't going to work this time."

"But . . ."

"Forget this foolish scheme and don't come here talking to me anymore about marrying Tucker. The next time you come to visit me, I will expect that you are here for a medical reason, not one of the heart."

Eugenia stood and glanced across the room at Sarah. "I know it looks pretty hopeless to you right now; but I know my son, and you are the woman for him, whether the two of you are ready to accept that fact or not."

"Mrs. Burnett, I have been polite to you while you

have been pushing this outlandish notion of marriage to your son since I returned. I'm asking you kindly to leave before I completely lose my patience. Tucker and I will never marry."

Later that afternoon, Sarah decided she couldn't stand her own company any longer. Patients had been few and far between today, and she found her mind drifting to Tucker way more than it should. The urge to spend time with Lucas and escape the images that had plagued her all day had her flipping the sign on the door to CLOSED

After locking the door, she quickly walked down the wooden sidewalk to the hotel several blocks away. Spring seemed to have finally appeared as the sun beat upon her, and she rushed to the hotel, anxious to spend time with her son.

When she arrived at the hotel, she nodded to the desk clerk on her way up the stairs.

"Mrs. James, I have a message for you from your grandfather," he called.

She halted from going up the stairs and came back to the desk. The man handed her a small envelope that had her grandfather's handwriting on the outside. "Thank you."

Ripping open the envelope, she quickly scanned the contents.

Sarah,
   Tucker came by and took Lucas fishing. He said you'd know where. Hope you don't mind, but I had a meeting I needed to attend, so I agreed to let Lucas go. I'll be gone until tomorrow.

Sarah did mind, her heart pounding with adrenaline. Her grandfather had let her baby go with his father. A more undisciplined man she had never met. What if he didn't watch Lucas carefully? What if Lucas slipped and fell into the pond? What if he realized the child was his son?

Maybe it was illogical, but she didn't want Tucker spending time with the boy, especially time alone.

"Please have a wagon brought around for me," she informed the clerk.

"Yes, ma'am," he said.

Within fifteen minutes they brought around a small team for her to drive.

She walked out to the waiting wagon and climbed up into the wagon seat.

Sarah slapped the reins against the back of the horses and yelled, "Giddyap."

The wagon lurched, the wheels rolling down the street. How could her grandfather let Tucker take Lucas? But then again, her grandfather didn't know that Tucker was the boy's real father. He didn't know that Tucker had left her before the sun rose the morning after they had made love. Just as she had not known that she was pregnant until two months later.

The horses kicked up dust, but Sarah paid little heed as the wagon carried her to the creek where they would meet when they were younger. It took her little more than half an hour to find Tucker and her son. Yet when she did, the sight gave her a jolt for which she was unprepared.

Lucas sat in his father's lap holding a fishing pole, while Tucker's head was bent next to the child. She watched as her son giggled when they caught a small perch. He clapped his hands excitedly as his father swung the fishing line up to the bank where they sat.

Her heart suddenly shattered. What had she done? Tucker was the boy's father. Didn't he deserve to know he had a son?

A lump formed in her throat, and for the first time she doubted the decisions she had made regarding her son. He deserved to know the man whose facial features had fashioned his own. He deserved to know the man who had sired him. Lucas deserved to know his father, just as Tucker deserved to know the boy he had helped to create.

She swallowed and watched as Tucker removed the fish from the line, put it on a stringer, and then baited the hook for her son once again. He dropped the line in the water, the cork bouncing with the ripples of the pond.

Sarah sighed, set the brake and then climbed down from the wagon, carefully holding her skirt. As she started walking toward the two of them, Tucker had his arms around the boy, talking to him quietly.

How could she be angry with him for taking her son when the two of them were having such a good time? How could she continue to keep the knowledge of Lucas's parentage from Tucker and live with herself? How could she break up this party when Lucas was obviously quite contented?

"Watch your cork, Lucas. You have to sit real still and let the fish play with your bait."

Tucker put his fingers together and tried to make his hand look like a fish going after the bait and explain how it would work for Lucas.

"Here comes the fish. And when it takes a big bite of the worm, the cork will go under, and you'll pull the pole up to catch the fish."

Lucas giggled, and Sarah had to cover her mouth

as she watched Tucker showing Lucas how a fish would bite his worm.

"Tish," Lucas called.

"Yes, we're fishing," Tucker said. "Look, you're getting a bite now."

Sarah looked on as Tucker steadied the pole and then helped Lucas pull it up just as the fish let go."

"Oops, we missed. Let's try again," Tucker said to the boy, still unaware that she watched them.

Sarah felt an overwhelming tug on her heart as she stared at the two of them together, fishing, having fun. The anger she had been filled with dissipated, and she was left standing there in shock, with the realization that sooner or later she had to tell Tucker about Lucas. Sooner or later, her secret would have to be exposed. But when? And how?

"Hi," she called out weakly, suddenly afraid to be alone with her thoughts any longer.

Tucker turned around and saw her standing there. It was the first time they had seen each other since that awful trip to the Melbournes' that had ended with them snapping at each other all the way home.

She could only stare at Tucker as a compelling warmth stole over her, settling in the lower regions of her body. No matter what had happened between them before, at this moment she wanted his arms around her once again, holding her, telling her that everything would be all right.

He returned her stare, his eyes saying so many things he would never follow through on. Things she had steeled her heart against ever thinking about Tucker again.

Lucas caught sight of her and squealed with delight. He jumped up from Tucker's lap and ran as fast as his little legs would carry him. "Momma, Momma, see tish."

He wrapped his arms around her legs, almost knocking her over. She had to pry his arms loose to squat down beside him and hold him tightly in her embrace. The smell of talcum powder drifted in the air, soothing her, swelling her heart with love. "What have you been doing?"

"Tish. I tish." He pulled out of her arms, grabbed her hand and tugged on her. "Come see."

She laughed at her son and glanced up to see Tucker watching them. She let Lucas lead her over to Tucker on the bank of the stream where they had spent the afternoon together. Lucas leaned over the water, reaching for the string of fish.

Tucker grabbed him by the arm. "Whoa there, son, let me help you."

Sarah felt her heart skip a beat, and while she tried to tell herself it was because Lucas had been hanging over the water, she couldn't help but hear the echo of Tucker saying the word "son."

Tucker pulled the string of fish up out of the water and handed them to Lucas. "Show your mother what we've been doing all afternoon."

"Momma, see. Tishes. I caught tish." He jumped up and down excitedly.

"You are such a good boy. And a good fisherman, too. I'm so proud of you," she said, feeling the tears prick her eyelids, knowing it was silly, but it was one of those motherly moments. In years to come, she would look back and remember her son holding that string of fish, so proud of his accomplishment, while Tucker looked on.

For a moment she thought of Eugenia and could almost understand her interfering ways. Yet it was hard to remember the woman meant well and that she had honored Sarah by choosing her to be with Tucker.

Sarah glanced up and saw Tucker watching her, a silly grin on his face.

"Momma, I rode horse with Tuck," Lucas cried. He dropped the string of fish and ran to her.

"What did you say, son?" she asked, afraid of what he had just told her.

"I rode horse." He shook his head. "I big boy."

She sent Tucker a stern look. He had put her baby up on his horse? She glared at him.

"Did Tuck think that maybe you were a little young to be on a horse?" she asked quietly. Her son frowned, knowing from the tone of her voice that she was displeased, but not really understanding.

Tucker, who had finished putting the fish back in the water, walked up the embankment to Sarah and Lucas. "Come on, Sarah. This is Texas. Babies are born on horseback."

"Maybe, but not my son."

"I wouldn't have let anything happen to him. You must know that."

"Maybe so, but I wasn't all that happy when I found out you had him."

"Why? The boy needs to spend some time with a man. It was time he learned how to fish."

Sarah felt Lucas tug on her skirt, but she ignored him. Tucker's insinuations that she was less than a good parent, simply because her son didn't have a man, were starting to infuriate her.

"He's two and he's my son. You should have asked my permission."

Lucas tugged even harder.

"You weren't around, and your grandfather needed some help. So I volunteered."

"Momma?" Lucas said, tugging on her skirt.

She glanced down at the boy. "What?"

Lucas took her by the hand, and then he reached up and took Tucker's hand. "Tish?"

The sight of their son holding both of their hands, gazing up at her with such a soulful expression in his big brown eyes that looked so much like his father's, caused her to choke up.

Her gaze briefly went to Tucker. What was the point of arguing over what had been done? Why not enjoy what was left of the day?

Tucker stared back at her, a sheepish grin on his face. "He's quite a charmer, isn't he?"

"Yes, he is," she whispered. "Okay, Lucas, show me how to catch a fish."

Not releasing their hands, he pulled them toward the water, laughing excitedly.

She glanced at Tucker. He smiled at her, his eyes warm with a light that usually shone just before he kissed her. The thought of his lips on hers left her with a feeling that curled her insides.

She let the feelings wash over her. For just this moment she was going to enjoy this day. For just this small space of time, they were a family on an outing, teaching their son to fish.

For just this moment she wanted to pretend that Tucker loved her and would be by her side forever.

The sun had long since disappeared below the western horizon as the trio rode back into town. Tucker had tied his horse to the back of the wagon and sat driving the team with Sarah beside him, the wagon jostling her against him. The rub of her body against his had him fairly smoldering for Sarah. It was late, they were tired, but Tucker couldn't remember a more pleasant afternoon.

Lucas had kept them laughing at his silly antics, while the three of them had fished until they ran out of bait and were forced to return to town. Sarah had laughed and bantered with Tucker as she had when they were kids. It was the first time since she had been back that he felt as if the girl he knew had finally come home.

Several times he had caught her staring at him, but neither one had said anything about the afternoon of their kiss. Though he had wanted to kiss her again, he knew she would have resisted because of Lucas, and they were having too much fun for him to cause trouble.

He glanced at Lucas. He had never given children much thought. But Lucas was fun. He was bright, vivacious, and it would be exciting to watch him grow into manhood. If ever Tucker wanted a family, this was what he would want.

The thought of staying and raising children surprised him. That would mean staying forever. That would mean getting married and settling down. That would mean responsibilities and no more drifting. And he had been born never to settle down. Even the thought of putting down roots disturbed him. Yet being without Sarah left him uneasy also.

He looked over at Sarah. She held Lucas in her lap, asleep. Her cheeks and nose looked as though the sun had kissed them. Her blond hair was more down than up with wisps flying loose around her face. She was windblown, tired and had never looked more beautiful.

Tucker drove the team up to the front door of the El Paso Hotel and set the brake of the wagon. "Sarah?"

"Hmm," she said, distracted as she rubbed the back of Lucas's head with her hand.

"I really enjoyed today. It was fun."

She glanced up at him. Even in the darkness the expression in her blue eyes caused his breath to quicken.

"So did I, Tucker."

"Maybe next week on my day off we can do that again. Or better yet, we'll take Lucas out to the ranch and go horseback riding."

She smiled. "We'll see."

"You know, as much as I enjoyed Lucas, the thing that brought me the most pleasure today was you." Tucker said the words before he had a chance to stop himself.

She turned and stared at him, an astonished look on her face. He shrugged and gave a small grin. "We've always been good together, and today reminded me so much of how things used to be between us. Before Tombstone."

They sat there in front of the hotel, staring at one another, feeling awkward, the air thick with the memory of their night together in Tombstone.

Finally, after what felt like forever, Tucker cleared his throat. "I better carry Lucas upstairs for you."

She smiled. "That would be nice. He's almost too big and heavy for me to carry."

After climbing down from the wagon, he helped Sarah alight and then lifted the sleeping child in his arms and held his soft cuddly body against his own. A feeling of protectiveness overwhelmed him, and he looked up to find Sarah watching him.

"We better get him in bed," Tucker said, his voice cracking when he spoke.

"Yes," she said, and turned toward the hotel.

They walked through the front door, and Tucker waited as Sarah hurried over to the desk clerk. "The wagon I borrowed this afternoon is outside. Please take care of it. And have someone care for Mr. Burnett's horse."

"Yes, ma'am," the young man replied.

Together the two of them began to climb the stairs to her grandfather's suite of rooms. Neither one of them said anything, yet Tucker couldn't help but recall the way Sarah felt in his arms, the soft texture of her skin and the feel of her lips against his.

Sarah, who was so smart, so strong and defiant, so much more than he ever deserved in a woman. Yet she was the one woman he could never seem to erase completely from his mind. And he had tried. Lord, how he had tried.

Tucker gazed down at the boy in his arms. Sarah was a mother. What in the hell was he doing thinking about her in the biblical way?

Sarah unlocked the door, and they stepped into the living area. "Where do you want me to lay him down?"

"Let's put him in his bed. He's so tired," she said, rubbing her hand down the child's arm.

Tucker carried the boy down a short hall to a room that held a small bed and gently laid the sleeping child down, careful not to wake him. The boy rolled onto his side and curled into a ball, sinking deeper into sleep.

"He is out," Tucker whispered, as they stood there watching the boy sleep.

Sarah nodded, reached down and pulled the covers up over the child, then gently kissed him on the cheek. They tiptoed out of the room, closing the door behind them.

"I can't believe he slept through all that and didn't open his eyes once," Tucker said.

"He played hard today," she replied.

They stood in the living area, Tucker feeling anxious as he stared at Sarah. She hadn't turned on a lantern yet, and the semidarkness seemed to surround them like a cloak. The air was thick with tension, and the urge to pull her into his arms was strong, but he resisted.

"Let me turn up a lantern," she said, bustling about nervously. She struck a match, the flame flaring, radiating her face with light. Her hands were shaking as she put the match to the lantern wick and then turned the flame until the light seemed to glow about the two of them.

He glanced at her and felt as if someone had knocked his knees out from under him. She stood in the living area, the lantern light reflecting off her hair, shimmering about her, iridescent and soft. Her full lips seemed to beckon to him, and all he could do was think about the way her kiss made him forget everything but the touch of her lips.

He swallowed and tried to look away. But the very air around him seemed heavy, suppressed. Almost as if it were so thick he couldn't breathe. Yet the swish of his own breath sounded loud in the lamplight.

"Would you like something to drink?" she asked. "I know you must be tired."

Not too tired for her, he couldn't help but think.

"I better be going," he said, twirling his hat in his hands, wishing she wasn't so tempting as he stared at her, knowing he had to leave or be enticed to stay.

"Yes, it is getting late," she whispered.

He walked to the door and put his hand on the knob. The metal felt cool against his hand. As he turned to tell her good-bye, he bumped into her, their bodies pressing against each other for a brief moment of contact.

Tucker almost groaned. First the wagon ride and now this; how much more could a man take before he gave in? A man whose resistance ran like a half-dried creek, low on substance.

She was so close he could smell the lavender soap she bathed with, and he breathed deeply, trying to control the desire that filled him. She stepped back, and he wanted her closer. He wanted to touch her, feel her soft skin beneath his fingertips, and wrap his arms around her. He wanted to lose himself in her gaze and find himself in the shelter of her embrace.

"Will I see you tomorrow?" she asked, her voice whispery soft.

He couldn't speak as he stared at her lips, drawn to their fullness, to their silky sheen. He nodded and watched as his finger reached out and stroked her cheek.

That simple touch was a mistake. The feel of her skin beneath his own ignited a firestorm that flashed through him. Unable to resist a moment longer, he lowered his mouth to hers as she lifted her lips to meet his halfway.

Eleven

Blood roared in Sarah's ears as she leaned into Tucker's kiss, unable to resist the pull of his attraction any longer. The realization that she still cared for this man had left her feeling reckless. Coupled with the pleasant interlude they had shared this afternoon, she was defenseless against her unbearable need to be in his arms. And she could no longer fight the feelings she had for this man, the father of her child.

Consequences be damned, she was hungry for the feel of his body twined around hers, delirious with wanting him, desperate to be possessed by Tucker. His mouth plundered hers, and she returned his feverous kisses with a fierceness that surprised her. She placed her hands on his face and molded his lips to hers, opening to receive him. He tasted of sun-kissed days and pleasure-filled nights. Sweet, sinful sensations erupted in a delicious soft moan that escaped from the back of her throat.

His hands gripped her shoulders as though he would never let her go, his lips plundering hers, as he pushed her back until the back of her legs bumped into the wall. Her body was flat against the hard surface as he leaned into his kiss, pressing his arousal through her skirts into the vee of her legs. From the feel of his muscular thighs to the strength of his sinewy chest, she felt all of him. Every delicious, rockhard inch.

Since she had returned home, she had fought the way their bodies seemed to be drawn to each other. She had fought the need to experience being in his arms again. She had fought the memories of their one night together.

In one weak moment he had managed to overcome her defenses.

She slid her hands down his shoulders, down his muscled back, past his waist, until she gripped his buttocks, melding them even more firmly together.

She was tired of fighting these sensations. She wanted Tucker, the man who fished with her son— and kissed like the devil. The only man she had ever given her heart to.

He moaned, his tongue tracing the ridges of her lips, his kiss turning savage as she held him tight against her, intoxicating her with desire. Nothing mattered at this moment except this man, this kiss and the feel of his body taut with need for her, only her.

The rational part of her mind that refused to be quiet warned her to step away, that it wasn't too late to stop this crazy risk she was taking with Tucker. But she knew she was past the point of control. Nothing could stop her from being with this man, not even the risk of losing her heart to him again. Not even the chance of him walking away and leaving her behind again.

Tucker made her feel alive, he made her feel things

she tried to resist, and he made her feel like a woman.

His lips moved to her throat, pushing the soft fabric of her dress out of the way as he slid his hands down the front of her dress, skimming her curves like a man reading braille.

"When will your grandfather be home?" he asked, his voice husky.

"Not until tomorrow morning," she said, tugging on his shirt, pulling the material free of his pants.

She wanted to feel his naked flesh, run her fingertips over his muscles, down the wisps of fur on his solid chest. She wanted to touch him, make him as giddy with passion as she felt. She wanted Tucker, and she wanted him now.

The past be damned, the future was tomorrow, but tonight she needed to experience the gratification they had found in each other's arms so long ago. She needed Tucker. She was tired of fighting this thing between them; she was tired of denying the attraction she felt for him.

With a final tug, his shirt came free of his pants, and she slipped her hands beneath the material, needing to feel his naked flesh. She ran her fingertips lightly up the hardened muscles of his chest, touching every solid ridge.

Why couldn't she put him out of her mind instead of craving his touch? Why couldn't she just give up and walk away from the gunslinger turned marshal and give her heart to someone else?

Because no matter what, he made her feel alive. With just one smoldering glance her senses were quivering with anticipation. No other man intrigued her like Tucker.

"Sarah," he moaned, his lips covering hers once

more. As their kiss deepened, his fingers deftly worked at the buttons on the back of her dress until she felt him sliding the sleeves over her shoulders, down her arms. The cool night air brushed her skin, and she felt a moment of panic. What was she doing?

And then his lips touched the sensuous part of her neck, causing her to shiver. Their previous coupling had been spontaneous, primitive and so pleasurable it could only be described as sinful. Was it just a fanciful memory or would their lovemaking tonight offer the same stunning experience.

His lips trailed the material down her neck, nipping her in the curvature of her shoulder. A shudder went through her as his lips seared a path down her chest. With a final swish her dress landed in a pool around her feet.

She leaned her head back against the wall. She was crazy. But she wanted him, and at this moment nothing else mattered. Her breathing was fast and shallow as her fingers fumbled with the buttons on his shirt. Clumsily she made her way down the front of the garment, resisting the urge to stop and let her fingers explore.

As she undid the last button, she yanked the shirt off of his back and tossed it to the floor with the other clothes. A shiver of need ran through her as she reached for the buttons on his pants.

How was this any different from the last time they had made love? There were no promises for tomorrow. There were no declarations of love. There was only this need to feel his arms around her once again.

"Wait, Sarah," he whispered, as he reached down and tugged his boots off, kicking them across the room. He stood, and she leaned into him and kissed his naked flesh, gently running her tongue along his chest, his skin rippling from the effect.

He grabbed her shoulders and pushed her back. Quickly he untied the front of her chemise and pulled the cotton garment over her head, throwing the material in a haphazard way. She stood before him, bare from the waist up.

She stepped away from the wall, grabbed his hand and tugged on his arm. Maybe she was crazy, but her son was asleep in the other room, and though she doubted he would waken, she would feel more comfortable with another door between them.

Halfway to her bedroom, she stopped and kissed Tucker, leaning into his embrace, unable to bear their bodies being separated. Her lips expressed what her heart knew and her voice could not say as he pulled the string on her drawers. They dropped to her feet, leaving her naked and exposed. He stepped out of her kiss, his eyes raking her with a warmth that was visible even in the dim light.

Suddenly, standing there naked before him, all the doubts she had held at bay slammed into her with the realization that they had promised each other nothing. Just like last time, they had spoken no words of love, only the secret language of their bodies clamoring for each other.

He had walked away from her once before; there was no guarantee he would stay this time. "Tucker, maybe we shouldn't. . . ."

"Like hell," he said, his lips covering hers, his belt rubbing against her naked skin.

Maybe she worried too much, but the feel of his lips covering hers pushed aside her remaining doubts. There were no promises for tomorrow, but there was the pleasure of tonight.

Reluctantly he released her lips, and she felt bereft at the loss of pleasure. He stepped out of her embrace and quickly finished unbuttoning his pants, shucking them and tossing the unwanted garment to the floor.

He stood naked, all male before her. His manhood protruded before him, smooth and long and hard. The moonlight streaming through the window cast an iridescent glow about him. She had lost her head over him once before. What was to stop her from losing it again? Or had she already?

With a cry, she reached out and touched his face, her hand caressing his cheek and pulling him toward her. "I want you, Tucker."

His lips covered her mouth as he backed her toward the bed. She felt the wooden frame touch the backs of her legs and found herself being laid gently down on the bed. The mattress sagged when he joined her on the bed, and she knew soon she would give herself to him again.

Though this night was different, with the memory of Tombstone hovering like a pleasant ghost, shimmering like that night so long ago when they first made love.

"Thank God you do," he whispered, nipping the curvature of her neck.

His lips trailed down until he reached her breasts, and his mouth closed over her nipple, laving the bud until she gripped his head, her breathing harsh.

His hands skimmed her body, sending shivers through her, while his fingers delved into the soft curls that covered her femininity. She jerked at the unexpected jolt of pleasure that rippled through her. Only Tucker seemed to make her act like a wanton. Only he could break down her barriers and release the lustful woman inside. She wanted him desperately, yet she was afraid.

"I'm going to tease you until you beg me to stop," he gasped, breathing hard to fill his lungs.

Sarah moaned, the sound loud and voracious in the darkened room. She arched against his hand, gripping the sheets against the raging need his hand was building with his caresses.

"Tucker!" she cried, as she tensed, trying to hold on to the sweeping pleasure that ascended on her as she disintegrated beneath his hand.

For a moment she lay there, her breathing shallow and fast, her eyes closed, while she slowly collected herself. Until the feel of Tucker thoroughly aroused, lying beside her, caught her attention.

She opened her eyes and gazed at him, his eyes dark, hungry and so beautiful she had to resist the urge to kiss each one.

She didn't want to love him, didn't want to experience these emotions. But there was no denying he made her feel wonderful. He made her laugh and he made her cry, but most of all he made her feel so alive. And there was no denying she still loved him.

Her hand slid past his waist, teasing him, getting just close enough to brush her fingers across the tip of his manhood. She gazed up at him and watched as anticipation rippled across his face.

"Now who will be doing the begging?" she quipped.

Finally she wrapped her hand around his rock-hard shaft. She gently slid her palm over the tip, then wrapped her fingers around him. She stroked the hot and smooth length of him gripping him until he grabbed her hand.

Rolling himself on top of her, he caught and held both her hands high above her head.

She writhed beneath him, teasing him with her body, when her hands could not do the job.

Slowly he slid his body down her breasts, her thighs, still holding her hands captive in his own. His knees nudged open her thighs.

"Enough, Sarah," he whispered, his husky voice sending tremors down her spine. "It's past time for me to feel you wrapped around me."

"Wait," she gasped, jerking her hands free. She wanted only to feel him inside her. She had been waiting so long for this moment. But she couldn't. One reckless night of passion had given her Lucas. She had to be cautious.

Sarah reached beside the bed for her doctor's bag and opened it quickly, finding what she was looking for.

She pulled out the condom and slipped it on Tucker, quickly tying it into place before he could protest, not quite meeting his gaze.

"What's that?" he questioned.

"It'll keep me from getting pregnant," she said, glancing up at him.

Again, she thought silently. Though she loved Lucas, she didn't need a second child by this irresponsible man.

He gazed at her questioningly but didn't refute her comment. When she was finished, his knees nudged open her thighs, his hands gripped her waist as he brought her hips up to meet him and he entered her in a single thrust.

She moaned, the sound loud in the small room as he thrust into her welcoming body.

"Tucker," she cried, unable to contain the passion their bodies were creating.

"Do you want me to stop?" he asked, staring at her, his gaze hard and unwavering.

"Not until I die," she said, as she rose to meet each thrust.

He delved into her rhythmically, filling her, melding her to him while she clutched him, relishing in the feel of his flesh to hers.

With each recurring thrust, his moans filled someplace deep within her heart that had been empty for so very long. Sweat glistened on his brow, and Sarah reached up to caress his face with her hand. He opened his eyes, staring at her, filling her soul as well as her body with sweetness, with a contentment that had long been denied. A pleasure that even now was rushing toward her, unstoppable.

Sarah moaned with satisfaction as her body went rigid, spasms of desire surrounding Tucker. Cascading shivers of delight left her clinging to Tucker while he reached his own climax, shuddering, gripping her, as he found pleasure.

Sarah breathed deeply the musky scent of Tucker and pressed her lips to the inside of his neck between gasps for air. She was completely spent as she lay relaxed, sated and more confused than ever by the sensations Tucker seemed to generate.

Tucker's breathing was fast and shallow as he leaned against her. For several minutes they lay in each other's arms, their breathing slowly returning to normal.

"Damn, Sarah," he said softly. "How in the hell can a man top that?"

She laughed, amazed their thoughts were so closely related.

"It's not right for a man to compare, but being with you, Sarah, is the best."

Shock rippled through her, dousing her like a cup of cold water.

He sighed and rolled to his side, pulling her close to him. "We've always been good together. At school, as friends, even as bedmates. No wonder I keep coming back for more."

"All you can say is that we're good as bedmates?" she asked, a feeling of disbelief steeling through her.

Just sex. Good sex, but suddenly all of the doubts she had pushed aside came rushing to the forefront. Why had she thought that this time would be different? Why had she believed that she could just accept passion from him and expect nothing more?

Her heart was seriously involved with this man, being with him, with sharing the most intimate act between a man and a woman, and all he could say was, "You're the best"?

She was a damn fool. He probably thought she was just some woman to pass the time with. He probably was thinking how fortunate she should be feeling right now that he had spent his time with her, not someone else.

Why had she lied to herself and believed that he had changed? No, he was still the same man who had deserted her in Tombstone. A little older, none the wiser.

She sat up in bed, suddenly feeling the need to be alone. Suddenly wanting him out of her grandfather's suite of rooms.

"It's getting late. You better go," she said, anxious to get him out before her barely controlled emotions were unleashed.

Tucker rolled over beside her, pulled her back

down in the bed and tried to take her into his arms, settling in for some cozy cuddling. "I thought maybe you'd give me a chance to do better? Who knows how good the next time will be."

She pulled out of his arms, stood and went in search of her robe. Wrapping it around her nude body, she picked up his clothes, her stance rigid. God, she just wanted him out of here, so she could cry. So she could cleanse her soul from the hurt and pain of letting him back in again only to realize he was still the same fool. And she had given him a second chance to break her heart.

"Come back to bed, Sarah."

She dumped his clothes on the foot of the bed at his feet. "It's time for you to leave, Tucker."

Sarah stared as the door closed behind Tucker. She had let herself be fooled once again. She had taken a tremendous risk, and though this time he had not snuck away in the middle of the night, he had cheapened their joining by telling her how good they were together, as if she was his favorite whore.

She picked up a vase sitting on the table and flung it at the closed door, the glass shattering in the darkness. "Damn you!"

And if the baby hadn't been asleep, she would have thrown a second one and maybe even a third.

But the possibility of waking Lucas halted her destructive quest.

Tears rolled unchecked down her face, and she collapsed to the floor, sobbing as she relinquished the hold she had placed on her emotions. Tucker was gone, the dreams of being together again were dashed and it was time she realized that no matter what, he was incapable of giving his heart to anyone permanently.

He was good for a quick tumble in her bed; but anything more serious was beyond his scope, and that was what hurt most of all. The death of her dreams, no matter how unrealistic they possibly were, was like a searing pain deep within her.

She loved Tucker. Had probably loved him for years. But until she had returned to Fort Worth, she had managed to lock those feelings away. Now she was back, and Tucker was still the same selfish, rambling man. And Sarah had a child to think about. Tucker's son.

Sarah swiped the back of her hand against her eyes. She was a fool for thinking that somehow he would fall in love with her. She was a fool for thinking that he would realize his mother was right that they belonged together. She was a fool for holding tight to her dreams of them married. But most of all she was a fool for thinking of telling him that Lucas was his son.

She was through with Tucker. She had given up on finding happiness with that man.

Tucker pushed his hat on his head as he closed the door behind him. He stood there for a moment wondering about what had just happened. One moment they had been having the best sex of his life, and then she was asking him to leave.

She had been angry when he left her in Tombstone, yet here she had all but thrown him out the door? He couldn't win.

Just as he turned to walk down the hall, he heard

her curse him. Then glass shattered against the door behind him, and he jumped as if he had been shot.

"What the hell?" he said, putting his hand on the doorknob to reenter the suite of rooms. And that was when he heard the gut-wrenching sobs.

He almost kicked the door open, he wanted so badly to get to Sarah. The sound tore at him, causing him to ache for her. Had he physically hurt her? How had he upset her?

But instead he stood there listening through the door, debating whether to demand she let him back in or to continue on his way to his own quarters.

Soon the sound had quieted to hiccupping little sounds that though they still tore at him, didn't seem to leave his insides shredded.

Okay, he would let her have her way tonight, but in the morning he wanted some explanations. He wanted to know why she had suddenly jumped up and asked him to go. He wanted to know what had caused her to cry.

She had said she didn't expect marriage, but then she threw things and cried after he left. Could Sarah be lying when she said she didn't want to marry? Could she really want the two of them to be together?

Tucker stood outside the doctor's practice, anxious about going in to visit Sarah. How would she treat him after last night? He had slept very little as he lay there wondering about her, what she was doing, how she looked in her sleep.

Good women like Sarah normally expected a marriage proposal the next morning. Most women would expect him to be over there promising them the world. While Tucker admitted they had been good together, he wasn't ready to send out the wedding announcements. But if marriage wasn't the reason Sarah had been with Tucker, why had she risked her reputation to have sex with him?

What was in it for her besides the pleasure? And could this be the reason for her tears?

Puzzled, he continued walking, trying to figure out what made a woman like Sarah function. She was different from any woman he had ever met, which was probably why they were still friends after all these years.

Yesterday had been more fun than he could ever remember having with a woman. But then again, he always seemed to enjoy spending time with Sarah. With Sarah he could let down his guard. He could play. And yesterday he had played like a kid once again.

So what had happened while they were having great sex? Why had she suddenly reacted so negatively? He recalled their conversation and went over it word for word for the thousandth time. What had he said that upset her so?

He thought he had even complimented her, when he had said she was the best. He had tried to put his pleasure into words, but somehow his language didn't express how he had really felt. But then, he had never been good at expressing his feelings, and Sarah knew that.

There was no other way to find out what was troubling her than to see her. He walked the last few steps to the doctor's door and pushed it open. The bell tinkling above announced his arrival.

She was standing at the window, watching him from the street. As he entered the door, she turned and glanced at him. Her eyes appeared dull and life-less. There were dark circles beneath them.

"Good morning," he said, trying to judge her mood.

"Good morning," she replied, her tone brisk and all business.

"I trust you slept well," he said, taking his hat off and twirling it in his hands nervously.

"Fine."

There was an awkward silence that seemed to stretch into forever as he tried to think of anything to say that would give him a clue as to what he had done wrong.

"Did you break something after I left last night?" he asked. "I heard a crash, and I came running back to check on you; but the door was locked."

She shrugged and then smiled, the emotion not quite reaching her eyes, which weren't the vibrant blue of yesterday.

"I broke a vase." She turned her attention back to the window, dismissing him.

She would hardly look at him, and when she did it was almost as if she looked right through him. The passionate woman from the night before was gone. And his fear that her reaction would be for them to marry appeared totally wrong. Even though he should be feeling relieved that she didn't insist on marriage this morning, he felt oddly insulted.

"Are you mad at me about last night, Sarah?" The words were out. He had to know.

She walked from the window and picked up a stethoscope lying on the desk, polishing the metal. "No. If you're worried I would be expecting promises this morning, you're in the clear. You're still free to wander the countryside with no ties or commitments."

"Then, what's wrong? I can tell something is wrong."

Her eyes would hardly meet his. Finally she glanced up at him. "I don't think we need to repeat what we did last night, knowing how we both feel regarding a permanent commitment. I thought I could just have sex with you, but I can't."

"Oh. I was kind of hoping . . ." He cleared his throat. "I enjoyed last night and was hoping that we could . . . we could maybe do it again?"

Her head jerked up, and her eyes appeared to flash with annoyance. "Why? Because the sex was good? You found a good woman who doesn't expect anything from you, so why not visit between her sheets on a regular basis?"

He ran his hand through his hair nervously. Yes, the sex had been great, but he also had enjoyed being with her yesterday. And he certainly didn't regret being with her last night. "Yes, the sex was good. Why not? You're my friend and I like spending time with you."

She bristled as if he had insulted her, but he didn't mean it that way. He was torn. Sarah represented everything he had never wanted, yet he wanted her. He wanted both Sarah and his freedom. And after last night he had been hoping that maybe he could have Sarah without a commitment. But if he wasn't careful, he was going to lose both the woman and her friendship.

"Like you said, last night was the best. I think we should leave it at that," she said, her voice tightening. "We both know that you don't want forever, and I'm not willing to be your mistress."

"Sarah." His voice was wistful. She was right, he knew it, and yet he didn't want what they had discovered to end. He didn't know what he wanted anymore. He was about to take a new job. He would be gone, and he certainly didn't need a woman, any woman, attached to him. But this was Sarah.

He twirled his hat in his hand. An awkward silence filled the room. She began to pick up things, tidying the room as if he weren't even there. And he got the distinct feeling she didn't want him here.

"I guess I better go. Tell Lucas I said hello," he said, not wanting to leave her, knowing she was upset.

From outside, the sound of gunshots blasting in the street sent him scurrying to the window.

"What is it?" Sarah asked, following closely behind him.

He looked out and saw a single man on horseback riding through the streets, firing his pistol in the air as people scurried to get into a building off of the street.

The man was laughing as he sent people running for cover.

Tucker opened the door, once again mindful of his job. Sarah ran out behind him.

"Get back inside," he said, motioning with his hand.

"Oh, my God," Sarah said, her hand going to her mouth, clearly ignoring his command.

Tucker glanced up straight into the eyes of Kid Lansky, the only man to ever outgun him. The man who had almost killed him in Tombstone.

"Well, well, well." The man leaned over the saddle horn of his horse. "Look who's the marshal, and if it ain't the doctor. Looks like we're going to have us a reunion."

Twelve

Tucker laid his hand on the handle of his short-barrel Colt Peacemaker .45. "Get back inside, Sarah."

"No," she said, the tone of her voice emphatic.

Damn! Of all times for Sarah to suddenly show she could be not only stubborn, but completely disagreeable. He stepped in between Sarah and the Kid, his eyes never wavering from the gunfighter's face as he tried to shield her with his body.

Though the man sat casually on horseback, his hands were not far from his own guns, his appearance relaxed yet alert.

"Marshal Tucker, you ain't being very friendly. I thought you'd be glad to see an old friend."

People walked up and down the street, staring at the two men and the scene playing out before them. Tucker focused on the gunfighter who sat before him.

"You're not my friend," Tucker said, his voice deep and rough. His blood pounded fiercely through his veins.

"You're wrong, Tucker. We were friends right up until the day I shot you in Tombstone. You've never gotten over the fact that I outdrew you that day," he said, tossing back his head, his jet-black hair peeking from beneath the wide brim of his stained cowboy hat.

Tucker stared at the man hard. The years had not been kind, and the evidence of his hard living lined the outlaw's rugged face.

"I don't draw on my friends." Tucker wiped his hands on his pants and flexed his fingers.

The gunfighter laughed, his voice mocking, his eyes dark and cold.

"Why are you here?" Tucker asked bluntly. "I know it's not our friendship that brought you to town."

"Got a job, Tucker. Right here in your little piece of the world," he said, shifting in the saddle, causing it to creak.

Tucker frowned, not happy with this news at all. "Doing what?"

"That's my business, not yours." The gunfighter sent Tucker a knowing smirk. His clothes wore the dirt of a man who had ridden hard and fast to reach his destination.

"Since I'm the marshal, I'm making it my business. Whatever it is, Lansky, I don't want to see you in town. The sooner you leave, the longer you'll live." The gun handle felt smooth beneath his touch as he let his fingers glide over the cool metal.

"Ooh, is that a threat, Marshal?"

"I don't make threats."

"I haven't done anything wrong, so I'll stay as long as I like."

Tucker shrugged. "Go ahead, but I'll be watching your every move. You won't be able to take a breath without me telling you you don't know how to inhale."

"I don't mind," Lansky said, leaning even closer, dropping his voice. "Might even give me the opportunity to show you you're still too slow."

The man was trying to bait him into pulling his gun, but it wouldn't work. He would never get into a draw with Lansky as long as Sarah stood at his side. Tucker stared at the gunslinger for a long moment. "That's just a chance I'll have to take. This is my town, and no one comes in here and threatens me or the people who live here."

"I didn't threaten," Lansky replied, his irritation slipping into his clipped words.

"You didn't have to," Tucker said. "Just your being here is a threat to the people in my town."

The man grinned and shrugged, his hands not far from his guns. "That's a chance you'll have to take. I'm here to stay until the job is done." He paused and glanced over at Sarah, his eyes giving her a quick perusal. "Haven't seen you in a while, Doc. You're looking good, real nice. Heard you had a son."

Sarah glared at the gunfighter and stepped from behind Tucker. "Who told you about my boy?"

He smiled and leaned back on his horse. "Just heard it from a friend. You might even know him. Wo Chan."

Tucker heard Sarah's deep intake of air. It wasn't quite a gasp, but enough that he knew the words had frightened her. He resisted the urge to glance at Sarah. He didn't dare take his eyes off the gunfighter. Not while the gunfighter's hands were within easy reach of his Starr Army revolvers.

"He's who you're working for," she concluded.

The gunfighter shrugged. "Maybe."

"Why did he hire you?" she asked, her voice startled.

"He wanted a fast gun and a man who had beaten the marshal here." Lansky grinned. "I'm both."

Tucker had an uneasy feeling in his midsection.

Lansky was here to kill him. And unfortunately, he had ridden into town without Tucker even knowing he was here, until he had made his presence known by shooting off his firearm.

God, Tucker felt like an idiot. He had become too laid back in his job, and that could only get him killed. He was too obsessed with Sarah.

The thought completely stunned him, and he had to force himself to pay attention.

"You may have shot me the first time, but you're older and you're naturally slower. There's no guarantee that you won't die this time," Tucker said calmly.

"No, there's not. That's just one of the hazards of the job. But I'm not afraid. I almost killed you that first time. If not for the good doctor here, you would have died."

Tucker shrugged. "You're right. But you're not the first gunslinger to ride in here and think that I'm sitting in a rocking chair. When you think you want to meet me in the street, set the time and place."

"Whoa!" the gunslinger said, leaning away from Tucker, his hands still close to his sides. "You may be anxious to die; but I have a job I've been hired to do, and I aim to get it done before I leave town."

"Just what has Wo Chan hired you to do?" Sarah asked. Her voice brooked no argument. "It's obvious you want us to know."

He grinned at her. "I always thought you were a smart lady. And you're right, I want you to know what I'm here for."

"Just spit it out, Lansky. You've played your games long enough," Tucker said, wishing he could just go ahead and draw on the man now and get it over with. But Sarah was beside him, and he wouldn't risk her life.

The Kid laughed. "Though it's been fun chatting with the two of you, I think you know why I'm here."

Tucker didn't reply, but just stared, determined to outwait the man. Horses clopped down the street, and people continued on unaware a shooting could erupt any moment.

"Mr. Chan hired me because one of his girls is missing. A pretty little Chinese whore about sixteen years old. She was one of his favorites. Earned him a lot of money, and he thinks that maybe the doctor here had something to do with her disappearance."

"You're wasting your time. You can go back and tell Mr. Chan that nothing's changed since the last time he visited my office regarding that young girl," Sarah said. "I still don't know where she is."

Wo Chan had gone to Sarah's office more than the one time she had told him about? When? Why hadn't Sarah said anything? Damn! How was he supposed to protect her if she didn't confide in him and tell him when the man was bothering her?

"What about you, Tucker?" Lansky asked.

The man was not stupid, and something in Tucker's face must have come to his attention. "I haven't seen the girl since she disappeared."

The gunfighter smiled. "Well, I just thought I would mention it to the two of you. Let you know that I'm in town for a short visit and some quick cash. I will find the girl."

"Let us know when you do. I've been worried about her," Sarah said, with a relaxed shrug. "In the meantime, we need to get going, Tucker, if we're going to check on Rose."

Tucker frowned. They weren't going to the ranch today. What in the hell was she talking about?

"Lansky, if you know what's good for you, you'll be gone by sundown."

"I'll still be here long after dark."

"I just bet you will."

Tucker waited until Lansky pulled the reins on his horse, heading the animal down the street at a slow, leisurely pace, as though this was his town, his place.

Damn, but Tucker didn't need this complication. Not now! Not with Sarah involved.

Sarah watched as Tucker drove the wagon around to the front of the building, past the mercantile, the bank and the café. The urge to take her reticule and bounce it off his skull was strong, but she resisted. Violence of any kind never solved problems, but sometimes it was tempting just to get his attention. Just to see if he would notice there was a problem.

He had practically issued the challenge himself while he was standing there talking to Kid Lansky. He must have some sadistic death wish to continue to put himself at risk by taking chances. Did he think that she could piece him back together again and again? That he was invincible?

He pulled the wagon to a halt in front of her, and before he could help her, she climbed in and plopped down on the hard bench. She deliberately ignored him as she gazed at the people bustling down the street, oblivious that the marshal was a fool.

With a flip of the reins, the wagon began to roll down the street. Dust kicked up by the animals' hooves floated behind the horses. Sarah grabbed on to the side to keep from falling out as Tucker snapped the reins and urged the horses to a faster clip, the wheels taking them closer to the edge of town.

Finally, he turned and gave her a questioning look. "I didn't know you were going to the ranch today."

"I wasn't going to tell you. I must check on Rose," she said, her voice short and clipped.

"So what changed your mind about asking me to go? Our little run-in with Lansky?" he questioned.

The frustration and anger that had simmered just beneath the surface since last night, when he had openly admitted they were good bed partners, but never acknowledged it could be anything more, exploded. She faced him, the air in her lungs rushing out in a hissing sound.

"Do you want to die? I was afraid to leave you in town with Lansky for fear I'd come back to a corpse," she said, venting her anger.

He laughed, the sound of his voice loud and confidant, irritating Sarah even more. Death wasn't funny, and neither was a man who couldn't face his feelings or admit that something more existed between them than sex.

"Oh, Sarah, I thought after last night, I was just another pretty face, but you really do care about me."

Why did she get the feeling he was deliberately pushing her away, putting as much distance as he could between the two of them. And why did comments like that hurt so much?

"Damn you, Tucker Burnett. I've already patched up your sorry hide once. Next time you may not be as lucky."

He smiled, and she wanted to swipe it from his face.

"I don't want to die; but I'm the law, and I know his kind. He's not welcome in my town. The sooner he leaves, the better."

"Understood, but what were you thinking? You

practically issued him a challenge," she said, her voice rising, while he appeared so calm, so collected.

"Don't be so dramatic, Doc. We haven't met yet," Tucker said, frowning for the first time.

"Tucker, you've as much as admitted to me that you enjoy meeting gunslingers. This is just another chance for you to continue living out your past. You still haven't given up the danger, the excitement. I watched you while you spoke with Lansky, and you were intrigued. I could see the challenge reflected in your eyes, your stance. You were excited."

He glanced over at her, an irritated expression on his face. "Yes, I'm a man! This is my job. No one gets away with disturbing the peace in my town. But especially not Kid Lansky."

"Is it worth dying over, Tucker?" she asked.

"If it's my time, then yes, I'll die. But I'll die doing my job, protecting the town," he said.

"Your pride is not involved in this at all, then. You're doing this strictly for the town and not to avenge the fact that he almost killed you three years ago?" she said, knowing the answer before he uttered a word.

"Hell yes, my pride's involved. But I'm doing my job, Sarah," he said.

The scenery rolled by, and she paid little heed to the few bluebonnets that were starting to open their flowers to the spring sunshine. Sarah knew that no matter what she said, he was not going to heed her warnings; she knew she was wasting her breath, and that frightened her.

She turned and glared at him, taking a deep breath. "Damn you, Tucker Burnett. You'd better not die, because hell isn't ready for you. And I'm not ready to say good-bye."

He laughed, while Sarah sat beside him rigid with anger.

"Don't you think you're getting all worked up for nothing? All we did today was talk. This may never come to pass."

She glared at him. "I know you too well. If he remains in town, you'll meet him. You'll tell yourself you're just doing your job, but you'll be glad."

He turned and stared at her as the wagon bumped along the road to his mother's. His voice became serious, and his eyes darkened with fury. "I promise you I won't meet him unless I have no choice."

"Is that supposed to make me feel better? Surely there's some crime you can pin on him, or if you'll just give him some time, I'm sure he'll commit one."

"No, Sarah. I don't arrest a man for a crime unless he deserves the punishment."

Sarah turned away. She couldn't look at him right now for fear he would see the tears that were gathered in the corners of her eyes. She was so angry with him. She was so afraid for him. She was so scared.

"So when did Wo Chan ask you about Kira?"

She wiped her hands across her eyes and then turned to face him. "What are you talking about?"

His muscular hands controlled the reins of the horses, gripping the leather firmly but not too tightly.

"Today when we were standing there, you mentioned Wo Chan coming to your office. He's been there more than once, hasn't he? Did he threaten you, Sarah?"

Sarah glanced at him and then looked away. "It was nothing."

Tucker cursed. "You should have told me. I can't protect you if you don't help me. I'll post a deputy over there until this is over."

"Maybe I don't need your help dealing with Mr. Chan," she said, her voice rising. "If you can take a chance on getting shot, I can take a chance on Wo Chan coming back."

There was silence. Sarah wished she could take the words back. She hadn't meant them to sound so harsh. But fear threatened to overwhelm her at the thought of Tucker meeting that gunfighter again. Last time she had saved him, but could she do it again?

"You know, Tucker, I didn't tell you because I didn't want you to overreact. I kept hoping that he would just accept that Kira was gone and leave us alone. I can't depend on you or come to need you, because you're not always going to be around. And I couldn't take it if you were hurt because of me."

He glanced at her, his brown eyes confused and hurt. "You're not responsible for me, Doc."

She felt tears welling up behind her eyes, and she blinked them rapidly away. So much had changed in the last twenty-four hours. She had learned once again that Tucker was still capable of breaking her heart. And now the gunfighter who had almost killed him was back in town.

"No, but if you were to get into a gunfight because of me and get hurt . . . I'd have a hard time living with myself. It's just better if I don't depend on you or anyone else to fight my battles. I have to make it on my own. I don't need . . . you."

"I'll remember that." Tucker shook his head and snapped the reins. "Damn it, Sarah, just once I'd like to hear you say 'I need you.' "

"Why? You wouldn't be there. You'd be off traveling the country, and I'd be alone."

* * *

Tucker watched as Sarah ushered everyone out of the room, leaving her alone with Rose.

The poor woman looked as though the baby she was carrying was sitting on her knees, and Tucker couldn't help but feel sorry for her. In some ways he was envious of Travis having a child; but he also knew what went with being a father, and the responsibility just didn't fit with the life he had chosen. A federal marshal traveling the countryside had no need for a wife and family.

Somehow, though, the thought of living such a nomadic lifestyle just wasn't quite as exciting as before. But once he left Fort Worth, once he was on the road, the thrill would return, he was certain.

"Come on, Travis, let's go outside and talk," Tucker said, leading his brother through the front door. "Where's Tanner?"

"He and Beth are working on their new home down the road a ways. I try to go out and help them as much as I can, but I don't want to be too far from Rose right now."

"That's understandable," Tucker said, pacing the wooden porch, his boots rapping in steady rhythm.

"I'm so ready for this baby to get here. I want my wife back," Travis said. "I guess I'm more nervous than I want Rose to know."

Tucker nodded. "I'd think that was normal, especially with the first."

Travis nodded and sighed. "So tell me what's been going on with you? We haven't seen much of you since Sarah came back to town."

Tucker shrugged. "That's what I wanted to talk to you about. Several things have come up."

Travis glanced at him, a worried expression on his face. "Like what?"

"Like a federal marshal's position working with Marshal McCoy."

"That's great." Travis smiled at him. "You'll be good at that."

"Yes, it is. I'll be doing a lot of traveling and won't get home much. But then, I've always liked traveling and seeing new country."

"And you've enjoyed being a lawman."

"Yes."

"So when are you going to tell Mother?"

"Well, I haven't accepted the position yet. And then I need to give the city council my resignation. Could be a while."

"Does Sarah know?" Travis asked.

"You're the only person I've told so far. I've been waiting."

Travis's forehead drew together in a frown. "For what?"

"I don't know. I just haven't done it yet," Tucker said with a shrug.

"What's holding you back?"

"Nothing."

"Are you certain this is what you want?" Travis asked.

"It's a great job for me. Like you said, I enjoy being a lawman. I like to travel and see new places. I'll be working on interesting cases. It's everything I could have ever wanted."

"So why do I get the feeling there's a big 'but' in here somewhere?" Travis asked, staring at Tucker.

For a moment Tucker was shocked at the question. He wanted this position. He had been waiting forever for just the right job, and this was exactly as he had dreamed.

"No, really it's what I want. I'm going to take the job. I just have one minor complication," he said.

"What's that?" Travis asked.

"Remember me telling you about a gunfighter named Kid Lansky?"

"Yes, the one who shot and almost killed you in Tombstone."

"He's here in Fort Worth, and he's gone to work for Wo Chan."

"What's he doing for him?" Travis asked.

"Wo Chan wanted to hire someone faster with a gun than me, who could find Kira. That man just doesn't give up when he loses a whore."

Travis swore. "The timing really stinks. Is Sarah still planning on taking her to Tombstone?"

"As far as I know. Don't let Kira leave the ranch. In fact, don't let her out of the house. They could be watching the ranch even now."

"I'll put out some extra watchmen at night. We'll keep an eye out for this character."

"Sorry to bring this on you at such a bad time, but I thought you needed to know."

Travis shrugged. "So how are you and Sarah getting along? Things seemed a little tense between the two of you when you arrived."

Tucker shook his head. "That woman could drive a preacher to drink. She's afraid I'm going to get into a gunfight with Lansky, and she was angry the entire trip here. And you know, she just might be right. He oversteps his rights, and I'm going to be right there. And this time he won't be walking away."

"Sounds to me like she cares about you. If he's the one who almost killed you last time, she's just concerned you're going to get hurt."

"No, I don't think so. We're friends, nothing more. She proved that last night."

"Should I even ask about that statement?"

"Don't." Tucker pushed his hat back away from his face. "And to think that Mother wants me to marry this woman. She can sure pick them."

Travis laughed. "That she can. Maybe the reason you've told none of us about this job is you're afraid you've changed and aren't the man you once thought you were. And maybe that's because of Sarah."

Sarah watched as the Burnett brothers and their wives gathered in the family parlor. A loveseat, a rocking chair and a sofa filled the room. Rose was seated in the rocking chair, while the women took the couches and the men reclined on the floor.

Eugenia was visiting a friend this afternoon, and Sarah had felt relief that the woman wasn't here to witness the tension between Tucker and herself.

Not only had they argued the entire way here, but even now there was a feeling of opposition between them that seemed almost tangible. Of course, the fact that she felt the urge to reach out and knock some sense into his prideful, male brain had nothing to do with the friction.

"Rose, what did Sarah say about the baby?" Beth Burnett, who had returned with her husband, asked, jerking Sarah back to the present.

Rose glanced at Sarah, frowned, and patted her stomach. "She said this baby and I still have three weeks of sharing the same living space."

"It'll pass real fast, I promise," Travis said.

The extremely round woman glared at him in a way that made him visibly cringe. "Don't placate me.

I'm hot, I'm tired, and Travis, honey, *you* can have the next one."

He smiled at his wife. "Would you like another pillow for your back? Or a cool glass of water?"

The frown on Rose's face reluctantly turned into a smile. "A pillow would be nice."

Travis left the room to fetch his wife a pillow.

Beth glanced around the parlor. "Hey, you know this is the first time we've all been together without Mother being present since the last time we discussed her matchmaking ways."

Tucker groaned. "Oh, no. Here it comes. Sarah, I'll apologize now for my family."

Sarah ignored him.

"Well, we all thought it was a good idea, and you agreed to it, baby brother," Tanner acknowledged.

"I had a weak moment. She's actually left me alone recently." Tucker glanced over at Sarah. "Then again, I think she was trying a new method. She sent Sarah her wedding veil."

Beth gasped. "She did what?"

Sarah smiled. "Actually, now it's funny. But when it happened, I wasn't too happy that she had chosen me to send her wedding veil to. She wanted to show me how much she thinks that Tucker and I are meant to be together."

"Who'd want to marry Tucker? He's the least favorable of the men in this bunch," Beth said, winking at her brother-in-law.

"Watch it. If you remember right, you were engaged to marry me because of my mother."

"That's why I can tease you," Beth said, smiling.

"You should join us in setting up Eugenia. We're trying to figure out someone to match her up with,"

Rose said. "You've just been touched by the Burnett curse or blessing. We've yet to decide which."

"Who would want to marry our mother?" Tanner asked. "The thought of our mother and a stranger is creepy."

Travis stepped back into the room and slipped a pillow behind Rose's back. "Is that better, honey?"

"Yes, thank you."

Travis sat down on the braided rug by his wife.

"We should make a list of men who are suitable," Beth said. "Men that you boys think would go well with your mother."

"You know this has been a great joke, but I just don't think I could carry through with finding her a husband. I mean, after all, our mother nearly drove us crazy when we met our wives," Travis said, laughing.

Tanner grinned. "I kind of like the idea. It's funny. At least if we choose our new stepfather, then we're bound to get someone we like."

Tucker shook his head. "The only man I'd like to see marry our mother would be the one who could keep her out of our business."

"That's the whole point," Rose said, crossing her hands over her large belly.

Travis frowned. "Okay, let's get a list together, and I'll agree to look it over; but that doesn't mean I'm going to participate in introducing her to anyone."

"We could do this just like she does: 'I'm not pushing you into it. I just want you to get to know him,' " Tucker mimicked his mother. " 'I just want you to be happy.' "

They all chuckled.

Travis glanced over at his wife. "Actually, I hate to admit this, but if Mother hadn't pushed me, I probably would still be unmarried. And marriage has been the best thing that's ever happened to me."

Rose leaned over and kissed her husband on the cheek. "Thank you."

Tucker watched his older brother and Rose and felt a twinge of envy. Travis was a much happier man. He seemed more settled, content and at peace. And he had resisted tying the knot for so long. But Travis had never wanted to leave the ranch. He had always been happy right here at home.

"So are we serious? Are we going to try to find someone for Eugenia?" Beth asked.

Tanner shrugged. "She definitely deserves for us to give her a taste of her own medicine, yet I, too, can't help but be grateful she answered Beth's ad. My wife may have been meant for Tucker, but I'm glad she married me."

Beth squeezed her husband's hand, which Tucker had noticed was never far from touching his wife somewhere.

"How about you, Tucker? You're the only one she hasn't managed to maneuver to the altar," Travis said.

Tucker glanced at Sarah, who waited for his reply. And when it came, it was all she could do to keep a smile on her face.

"And I intend on remaining unattached," he acknowledged. "I'll help, just because maybe she'll leave me alone if she has her own romantic involvement."

Thirteen

Tucker helped Sarah up into the wagon and then went around to the side where he climbed up beside her and picked up the reins.

"Rose, remember what we talked about," Sarah gently reminded the pregnant woman. "Travis, you come and get me at the first sign this baby is coming."

Travis put his arm around his very pregnant wife. "Don't worry, Sarah. I will."

"Well then, I'll see you in a couple of weeks when the baby is on the way." She waved at them. "Until then, take good care of Rose, Travis.

"I will, Doc. See you soon."

"Bye."

Tucker snapped the reins, and the horses pulled the wagon out of the yard of the big house. Since his brothers had married, he enjoyed spending more time with them than he could ever remember. Both of their wives had taken the hard edge off of his siblings and added genteel warmth to the family gatherings.

Would a woman do the same for him?

He pushed the thought out of his mind, refusing to think of how Sarah seemed to always have a calming, soothing effect on him. How well she blended in with his brothers and their wives. That was no reason to consider marriage, even if Sarah seemed to be constantly in his thoughts.

The afternoon had been pleasant. He would miss them all when he took the marshal's job. Since he and Tanner had returned home, Tucker had enjoyed being with family. He would miss watching the new baby change and grow.

"So is Rose going to be okay?" Tucker asked, worried about his sister-in-law.

"She's having a baby, Tucker. All women run the risk of having complications, and we won't know about Rose until she goes into labor. I prefer to be positive and say she'll be just fine," Sarah said, not looking at him, her tone precise.

Obviously she was still peeved with him over his response to Kid Lansky. The tension that had enveloped them on the way out to the ranch had returned, making it a somber ride.

But Tucker was glad he had taken this unexpected journey to the ranch with Sarah. He had gotten to spend some time talking with his brother, and Travis had a way of making him think about things from a different perspective.

"I just don't want anything to happen to Rose and that baby. Travis would be devastated," he said, trying to get Sarah to talk to him. He sighed and pushed his hat back from his scalp. "I've never been around a woman having a baby before, and Rose looks miserable. I hope this child comes soon."

"Believe me, she does, too." She turned and gave him a puzzled look. "You know, for a man who doesn't want to be tied down with a wife and children, you seem almost curious about this whole process. Aren't you ever afraid you're making the wrong choice? That you'll hate being alone?"

The question took Tucker back for a moment. Hadn't he been asking himself this same question lately? Even Travis was questioning his decision about being a federal marshal.

"I enjoyed it when I was younger. Why wouldn't I now?" he snapped, not liking the fact that Sarah and Travis were both questioning his decision.

The memory of his days chasing the fastest draw filled his mind, and the feeling of conquest and being the absolute best returned with startling clarity. He had been good. Damn good. And he liked that feeling. And until then he had never experienced the satisfaction or gratification that came from a job well done. His two older brothers' accomplishments had always seemed larger in comparison to his.

Not that he didn't love them, but sometimes being the youngest he had been the follower. Until his gunfighting days, he had never felt he could be the best at anything.

"We all change. I'm not the same girl who left Fort Worth and went to medical school. And you're not the same man who was shot in Tombstone," Sarah said.

Her voice still had an edge to it and she was sitting on the farthest end of the wagon seat, griping the side.

"No. I'm not that kid anymore. But I still like the same things. Hopefully age has only made me better."

She shook her head.

"You'll get back into gunfighting if you wander aimlessly from town to town," Sarah said. Her blue eyes flashed with an iciness he had seldom seen from Sarah. "Even now you haven't given it up totally. You're just itching to get into a draw with Lansky."

He didn't want to mention the federal marshal job offer just yet. Being a federal marshal would keep him busy and out of trouble. He was deliberately refraining from telling her about the job until the situation with Lansky was settled. But the urge to prove her wrong and how he had already thought of that possibility was tempting.

"No, I won't," he said with confidence. "Before, I was a renegade kid just looking for trouble. But not now."

Sarah shook her head. "I don't understand why you would give up being close to your brothers and their wives, your mother, the possibility of a good woman and a family of your own to wander in a meaningless way. Knowing that no good woman is going to show interest in you because you're unstable." She took a deep breath, her voice angry. "Why, Tucker? Help me to understand, because it seems so foolish."

Why was Sarah so angry that he had decided to live his life this way, unless she really had wanted the two of them to be together? He pushed the thought out of his mind. No, she would tell him if she felt that way. This was just because Lansky had returned and she was afraid for him.

"Why do women always seem to think that if a man wants to be alone, he's unstable?" he asked, irritated. "Why is it foolish because I've chosen a different kind of life?"

Sarah shrugged. "I don't understand."

"In a town where no one knows who I am, I'm not seen as Thomas Burnett's son, or Travis Burnett's brother or even Tanner's brother. I'm not that younger Burnett kid. I'm me." He turned and glanced at Sarah. "You don't have any brothers or sisters whose footsteps you have to follow."

"I have my father's. He was a doctor, and as a woman most folks think I can never be as good as he. I don't like the attitude, but I don't run from it."

"I'm not running. I'm just going where I can be me."

"But you're *you* here," Sarah argued. "People associate you with your family, and you're known as that youngest Burnett boy. The one who runs this town. The one who keeps us safe and has cleaned up Fort Worth. The one who jokes and has fun. The friendliest of all the Burnett boys. You're known for your generosity, outgoingness and good-natured spirit. You're known for you. Not just your brothers."

She turned away from him as if she had said too much.

Tucker frowned as he gazed at the road in front of him. Everything she said made sense, but he still had this itch to explore new country, see new things, that had never been resolved. When he had come home, he was only going to stay a few weeks, but then the death of his father and his job as marshal had extended his short visit into years. Now he had a chance to leave once again and experience this vast country.

"I'm not trying to stop you. Life should be spent doing the things you love, with the people you love," she said with a wistful sigh, not looking at him.

"Is that what you're doing, Sarah? Doing what you love? Spending time with the people you love?"

"I love my work," she said softly.

"What about your time? Do you spend it with people—"

"Yes, I spend as much of my time as possible with Lucas and my grandfather," she said, her voice catching at the end. Her face was blocked from his view. She hadn't mentioned Tucker. She hadn't said that she enjoyed being with him, and he knew without question that he took pleasure from being with her. Most mornings he awoke with Sarah on his mind, and every night was spent dreaming of the feel of her in his arms.

Didn't she like being with him?

But more importantly, he never wanted to cause her pain, to hurt her in some inexcusable way. And he had worried that somehow that was exactly what he had done. Hurt her. Did she really want marriage, and he had failed to see that their friendship could possibly be more?

Tucker cleared his throat. "Sarah, I do enjoy being with you."

She turned and faced him, her blue eyes filled with pain, the wind whipping her blond curls around her face.

"Maybe that's why we've remained friends for so many years, because we enjoy each other's company," she said, the words sounding wistful.

Tucker felt them reverberate inside of him. He enjoyed being with Sarah more than with any other person he had ever met.

"Sarah, I know I can be a selfish bastard sometimes, but I never meant to hurt you."

She turned toward him, her eyes filled with tears. "In our culture it's not often that men and women can be friends like we have all these years. I don't understand why we're still close. We certainly have tested the strengths of our friendship to the point of breaking, but it always seems to rebound. I know I was harsh with you on the trip out, but I don't want anything to happen to you."

She took a deep breath, glanced out at the edge of town that was quickly approaching. "But no matter how good we are as friends, it can never be anything more, never again."

Several days passed, and though Tucker had been by, he hadn't been in the best of moods. She knew he was busy trying to resolve the situation with Kid Lansky, and after their discussion on the way home, maybe it was for the best that he stayed away more.

For so long she had held hope that someday he would come to the realization that they were meant to be together. Though she knew it would never be easy, she would tell him about his son, and they would live together as man and wife. For so long she had dreamed that he would realize she loved him and that he would love her in return. But her aspirations were quickly dying.

Sooner or later she was going to have to give up on Tucker and pursue her own life. Soon she would leave Fort Worth, return to Tombstone and her own practice. And maybe that was for the best. Maybe it was time she put behind her all thoughts of a life with Tucker and the dream she had built of a family with Tucker and their son.

The bell above the door to the clinic tinkled and for a moment her pulse leaped. Since the day that Wo Chan had come into the doctor's office unannounced, she had been nervous. She stepped from the examining room, determined to face whoever had just walked in the door, and was surprised to see Brad Riley, the man who had bid so high on her basket of food at the church auction.

"Hello," he said, smiling shyly at her, the emerald green of his eyes twinkling. "I hurt my hand mending a fence the other day on my ranch and thought maybe you could take a look at it."

She returned his smile, a pleasant feeling of awareness coming over her. "Sure, come back into the examining room where I can look at it in the light."

"It's not bad, but it's irritating the fool out of me," he said, as his boots echoed on the wooden floor of the front room.

He walked down the hall, and she followed him into a private exam room. "Sit down if you don't mind on the stool there by the window."

The tall, dark man sat down and held out his hand. "It's barely more than a scratch."

Sarah picked up his hand, the warm, rough texture surprising her. "You don't want to get blood poisoning."

"No, I don't." He paused nervously. "I hope I didn't embarrass you too much at the church auction a couple of weeks ago. I've been meaning to come over and apologize for my behavior, but just haven't been in town."

She gazed at the splinter in his hand and reached for the small tongs that were good for getting finite pieces of debris from skin tissue. "No need to apologize. I was flattered."

Taking the tongs, she started to pick at the sliver of wood with the pointed end. She tried to be gentle as she plucked at the wood chip.

Sarah finally managed to snag the irritating splinter. She held up the sliver of wood in the tongs. "Here is the problem. Let me pour some iodine over the wound and you should be good as new."

"So how's your son, Lucas? Has he recovered from his reaction to food that day?"

Sarah smiled at the mention of Lucas. "Thank you

for asking. He's doing fine. He's completely recovered, and I don't allow him anywhere near strawberries."

"He's a cute boy. If I had a son who had food reactions like that, I'd be extremely careful about what he's around."

She gazed at Brad, noticing he appeared ill at ease. "Yes, I am. This is going to sting a bit."

Tipping the bottle, she poured the iodine on his hand. He flinched, but never took his eyes off her.

"I was wondering, Doc, since you don't appear to be upset with me over the basket bidding war, if you'd have dinner with me some night. When you're not busy."

Sarah felt her cheeks flame. She was old enough not to react this way to his invitation, but still a flush spread across her cheeks. Slowly she turned her head and gave him a smile of encouragement. "I'd like that very much."

The man relaxed visibly before her eyes. "Great! How about tomorrow night? If you don't already have plans."

"Tomorrow night would be fine."

"So it'll be me, you and Lucas," he responded. "Unless you'd like to ask your grandfather to join us."

She had been bandaging the small wound on his hand. She raised her eyes to his. "I was thinking more of just the two of us having dinner. My grandfather will take care of Lucas."

He nodded. "That would be really nice, but in case you wish to bring the two of them, it's fine with me."

"Thanks. I appreciate your being so thoughtful, but I'd like an evening without them," she said.

"What time should I pick you up and where would you like to go?" he asked.

Sarah felt a ripple of pleasure. The man was asking her what she wanted. He was secure enough in his own masculinity not to have to show his power by making all the plans himself.

"I'd like to go to the Merchant restaurant down on Main Street."

"What time?"

"How about seven."

"I'll pick you up at the hotel."

"Well, I think you're all patched up," she said, knowing that the hand hadn't been bothering him near as much as he let on.

"If it turns red and puffy, soak it in warm salt water. But I think it's going to be fine."

"Oh, I think it will be just dandy," the man said, gazing at her. "How much do I owe you?"

"A steak dinner," she said.

He grinned. "Guaranteed."

"I'll see you then tomorrow night."

"Promptly," he said, picking up his hat that he had laid down on the small table in the room. He walked out of the examining room and out the door of the clinic.

Sarah smiled. Brad Riley was a nice man. Maybe he was just the man to show her that there was life after Tucker.

Tucker watched as Kid Lansky sat in the Trinity Saloon. He had followed him as much as time permitted these last few days, hoping to catch the gunfighter at something that he could throw him in jail for. But the man was wily, and so far he had been discreet in his dealings with Wo Chan.

The Chinaman ran an opium parlor and a whorehouse on the edge of the Acre. As long as the law wasn't out there breaking up fights every night, the city council pretty much turned a blind eye to the establishment, regardless of how sadistic his trade was.

One slipup, though, and Tucker would have Wo Chan and Kid Lansky looking through bars.

Tucker sat on a stool watching the room from the bar, a drink in his hand as he surreptitiously observed the gunfighter.

"How you doing, Marshal?" Charlie, the bartender, asked. He had known Tucker since he was a kid.

Tucker turned on his seat. "Not too bad, Charlie. Looks like you've got a pretty good crowd tonight."

"Not bad. Business has been slow. Will be until the herds hit town."

"Spring's almost here, so it won't be too much longer."

"Hey, Marshal, rumors say you're trying to shut down the Chinaman's business. Is that true?"

"Rumors are just gossip. I'd love to shut him down, but the council has told me to leave him be." Tucker took a swig of whiskey. "Drinking is one thing, but opium is against the law."

"So who is this gunfighter the Chinaman hired?"

"Kid Lansky. He's the tall guy sitting at that table playing poker."

"Him? He's been in here the last several nights."

"Yes, I know."

Tucker watched a billiards game from across the room and sipped his whiskey.

"So how's your mother doing now that she's got two of you boys married?" the man behind the bar asked.

Tucker frowned, set his glass down and poured from the bottle again. "She's all right. She's pretty busy getting ready for the first grandchild."

"Good thing for you, huh?" The man laughed.

"She's leaving me alone, and that's all I care about," Tucker said.

The bartender smiled. "You know, several of us got together after the last wedding, and we've got a pool going on how much longer before your mother finds you a woman, Marshal."

"What?" Tucker asked, shocked at the news. People were gambling on if and when his mother would manage to drag him to the altar?

"You want to bet against us? The one closest to the date of your wedding wins the money."

"So what are my odds?" he asked, irritated.

"Not good, I'm afraid."

Tucker cursed. "A man can't even get a drink in this town without people pestering him about getting married. What happens if I never marry?"

"We've put a six-month time limit on it. If you're not married in six months, then we donate the money to some charity."

"Do I get to choose the charity?"

"Depends. Who do you want it to go to?" Charlie asked, wiping down the bar.

"To start a retired lawman's association. Any man who could do this job day after day, putting up with stuff like this, deserves to get some kind of reward."

"If you don't marry, maybe we should just give it to your mother." The bartender laughed. "She'll never rest until you do settle down."

"Don't give her any more ideas," Tucker insisted, thinking that this little joke had gone far enough.

The bartender looked out at the crowd and frowned. "You following that gunman, Marshal?"

"Like fur on a bear's behind."

"Well, you better drink up, because he's heading toward the door."

Tucker downed his drink and slid off the barstool. "Thanks, Charlie."

"Anytime, Marshal."

He pulled the brim of his hat down as he walked out the door of the Trinity Saloon.

Sarah dabbed a drop of lavender-scented water on her wrist, feeling nervous. What did she really know about this man named Brad, other than he was a rancher who had bid on her basket at the church social. He was handsome, and he seemed more of a gentleman than any man she had met recently. But that little bit of information meant nothing.

He was obviously attracted to her, but would dinner with Brad be any different from her previous engagements?

The sound of a knock echoed through her grandfather's suite of rooms, and she knew he was here. He had insisted on escorting her to and from the restaurant where they would be having dinner, and she appreciated his thoughtfulness.

She heard her grandfather open the door and knew the moment for her to greet him had come. A brief thought of Tucker flashed through her mind, and she quickly blocked the memory of his laughing face and teasing brown eyes. The time had come for her to put him out of her thoughts and her life.

She pinched her cheeks, opened the door and stepped into the sitting room.

Brad Riley stood there in a western-cut suit, a bolo tie, and his hat in his hand, looking uneasy. He smiled at her as she walked into the room, relaxing a bit as she returned his smile.

"Good evening. You look mighty pretty tonight," he said, his eyes glowing as he gazed at her.

"Thanks," she replied. "You look very dashing yourself."

The man blushed at her compliment before turning to her grandfather. "Are you sure you don't mind watching Lucas. We can take the boy with us if it causes you any inconvenience."

Sarah felt herself melting as he offered to take Lucas again with them to dinner. Of the men who had escorted her recently, he was the first to offer for Lucas to tag along, and she could feel her barriers melting.

Her grandfather shook his head. "I don't mind watching the boy at all. But I do recommend you kids leave before he realizes his mother's going and starts to wail."

Brad nodded and glanced at Sarah, his green eyes warm. "Are you ready?"

Sarah picked up her favorite lace shawl and wrapped it around her shoulders. "Let's go."

He opened the door, and she told her grandfather, "We won't be late."

Then he ushered her out the wooden portal, taking her by the elbow and gently guiding her through the door. He closed it with a firm click behind him.

"If you don't mind, I thought we'd just walk down to the restaurant. I brought the buggy; but it's not far and it's such a gorgeous night."

"That would be nice."

They left the hotel and crossed Third Street, walking down the wooden sidewalk. He took her arm and placed her hand in the crook of his elbow, patting her gently.

"You know, Doc, I've wanted to ask you to dinner for quite sometime, but thought that Tucker had already claimed you."

"Well, he hasn't. Tucker and I are good friends from way back, but that's all."

"I guess I was mistaken, then. I had some crazy notion that the two of you were sweet on each other."

"No, and in fact, Tucker has been introducing me to some men in the community since I returned." She laughed. "I let him talk me into the crazy arrangement, and all I can say is he has extremely bad taste in men."

Brad looked at her as if she had lost her mind. "Doc, I don't think you need anyone introducing you to men. I'd say you could attract your own without any help."

"I did it as a favor to him. His mother has this outlandish idea that we're meant to be together, so Tucker decided if I was seeing other men, she would back off and leave us both alone."

"And did it work?"

"I don't think so. But she has been a little quieter lately."

A curious look crossed Brad's face. "If you don't mind me asking, who did Tucker introduce you to?"

"They were both nice men, just not my type at all. One was a local schoolteacher, and the other was a banker."

Brad started to chuckle, and he shook his head. "Are you certain Tucker didn't play a joke on you?"

Sarah glanced at him, stunned for a moment. "No, why?"

"I know exactly who you're referring to, and you haven't even told me their names. They're both renowned bachelors who say they're looking for wives, but never manage to snare a woman. This has been going on for several years now."

Why would Tucker introduce her to men that were really not interested in marriage if he was seriously trying to find someone for her? Could Eugenia be right?

"If he knew they were not interested in marriage, why would he introduce me to them?"

"Maybe he felt that you were safe with them," Brad said, laughing.

She looked at him, her mind whirling with questions. "What do you mean, safe?"

They halted on the sidewalk, just the two of them on this quiet little side street. Brad reached down and tilted her chin up with his fingers. His touch was warm and comforting, not heady and exciting like Tucker's.

"Sometimes when a man isn't ready to face his feelings, he tries to keep what he wants safe until he's prepared. Maybe Tucker isn't willing to face what he's feeling for you."

Sarah calmly gazed up into Brad's emerald eyes. "I think we better keep going to the restaurant."

He smiled down at her. "Let's go."

They walked the remaining blocks, chattering about small stuff, laughing and talking. Within minutes they entered the restaurant and were promptly seated.

Brad pulled out her chair and seated her before moving around to his own. It was such a simple gesture; but it left her feeling special, and she couldn't help but compare him to Tucker. And Tucker wasn't faring well.

Once Tucker was outside, he noticed the night air had chilled considerably. The weather was still confused between winter and spring, so the nights fluc-tuated in temperature. He shivered deeper into his jacket.

Lansky stepped out of the shadows and fell into step beside him. "Marshal, I didn't quite believe you when you said you were going to follow my every move, but now I'm a believer."

"Good. Let me escort you to the edge of town, and we'll forget all about seeing one another again."

"But it's been so enjoyable. Me taking you to all the best saloons in town, while you follow so close you almost have your nose up my ass." The man rested his hand on the gun that was strapped to his thigh. "You know, why don't we just settle this right now. Let's just go ahead and get it over with. In five min-utes, you'll be dead, and I'll be taking over this town."

"That's not going to happen," Tucker said firmly.

"You're still going to have to face me in the street, Tucker. There's no way around it, because sooner or later you're going to try to arrest me, and it's not going to happen."

"I'm warning you, Lansky. If I'm there, I'm going to kill you. Do you understand? This time we end it forever."

Lansky laughed. "I'm not afraid of dying. How about you, Marshal?"

"Everyone dies. Some of us just sooner than the others." Tucker shrugged. "If you want to meet me, then meet me down at the county jail and I'll be happy to give you a cell."

"No. You know there's a full moon out tonight. Spring is close at hand, and I'm feeling feisty. There are more saloons to visit and more ladies to try. See you at the White Elephant Saloon."

The man looked over his shoulder and grinned at

Tucker, who cursed beneath his breath. Why couldn't he just arrest the gunfighter and be done with it. But his conscience wouldn't allow him to take care of the problem that easily. And he had to admit that part of him wanted to meet Lansky in the street, but the other part was determined to do this Sarah's way. Though why he felt so strong-minded to please her, he didn't know.

He knew only that he was trying, though frankly he would just as soon get it over with, like Lansky wanted.

Tucker followed him into yet another bar, walked in and leaned relaxing against the bar, his boot resting on the footrest.

"May I have your attention?" the Kid called, bringing the piano to a jangling halt. "Shut up everyone and listen to me."

An uneasy feeling crawled up Tucker's spine. He was not going to like what was about to happen whatever the Kid had planned.

"I'm sure you all know Marshal Tucker Burnett. But what you don't know about him is that I almost killed him several years ago down in Tombstone, Arizona. He lived only because Doc Sarah James managed to stitch him back together."

"You'll shut up, Lansky, if you know what's good for you," Tucker said, his voice low and steely.

Lansky smiled and pointed to him. "But now the marshal has turned yellow. He's afraid. He's afraid I'm going to kill him, so he's refusing to meet me." The gunfighter laughed. "I never thought I would see the day, that Marshal Tucker Burnett feared dying."

Tucker stepped rapidly the few steps to the Kid,

then grabbed his shirt, pulling the outlaw to within inches of him.

"I'm the law, Lansky. I don't kill people; I arrest them. And you're pushing your damn luck."

The gunfighter swung his fist at Tucker, hitting him in the jaw, knocking him back. But he didn't let go of the man's shirt. "Damn you!"

Tucker threw a right punch to the man's stomach. He ducked when Lansky blocked his next swing, and the two men grappled with each other, staggering. Locked in combat, they stumbled.

Suddenly they fell to the side, crashing through the window of the saloon, landing on the sidewalk outside.

Tucker shook the glass from his face and hair and looked around for Lansky, who lay semiconscious on the wooden sidewalk, moaning. It was then that the smell of lavender in bloom tickled his nose, and he glanced at a pair of female slippers before him.

He frowned, a feeling of apprehension overwhelming him as his gaze traveled up the skirt of the female before him.

He wanted to groan when his eyes met and held the flashing blue orbs of Dr. Sarah James.

"Keeping the peace, Marshal?" she said, her voice tightly controlled—her hand tucked in the crook of Brad Riley's elbow.

Fourteen

Tucker stared into Sarah's blue eyes.

"Your lip is bleeding, there's a cut above your right eye that needs stitches, and it looks like you're going to have a beauty of a shiner." She took a deep breath. "Are you having trouble breathing?"

"No."

"Too bad, I was really looking forward to binding your ribs." She sighed. "I better check on the other man."

Sarah walked over to the gunfighter, her back straight, her steps slow and methodical.

Tucker heard her asking Lansky questions, but his gaze was fixed on the rancher. Slowly he sat up, letting the fog clear from his brain, and then rose to his feet.

"What are you doing with Sarah?" Tucker couldn't refrain from asking Brad.

Brad smiled at him. "We were just returning from dinner, when you fell at her feet."

"Dinner?"

"Yes, I took Sarah to the Merchant restaurant."

"Why?"

"Because I happen to enjoy her company and find her attractive."

"I know, but why would she go out with a cow-puncher like you?"

Brad laughed, stuck his thumbs in his belt loops, shrugged and stared at Tucker. "Because she likes me."

Tucker beat at the dust that clung to his clothes, before he looked into the face of the man who had gotten into a bidding war with him over Sarah's basket at the church dinner. He didn't like Brad's response or the ugly feelings he suddenly was very aware of.

Sarah walked back over. "He's okay. Said he was going back to his hotel room. But you're going to need stitches. I'd say you lost this round, Marshal."

Tucker tensed. He had already lost one fight to Lansky; he would be damned if he was going to lose again. "It was a draw. If we hadn't crashed through that pane of glass, it would have ended differently."

Sarah shook her head. "Meet me at the office and I'll clean up that head wound."

"No."

She frowned, her irritation clearly showing. "Fine, get gangrene, have your face rot off, but don't come running to me."

"Doc, you're being dramatic."

"That's why I went to medical school instead of going into acting," she retorted.

He frowned. "All right, let's go, then."

"I'll meet you there," Sarah said.

"No," Tucker responded, realizing that here was his opportunity to send Brad on his way. "It's not safe for you to walk alone."

"I'll walk her, Tucker," Brad said, his hand on Sarah's arm.

Tucker felt an overwhelming sense of irrational anger seeing the rancher's hand lay so possessively on Sarah. "No. There's no need for you to go, too."

Sarah turned to Tucker and gave him a harsh glare. "Did that fall affect your thinking? What's wrong with you?"

"I don't need an audience watching while you doctor on me," he said, knowing it was just an excuse to get rid of the rancher.

Sarah started to laugh. "A minute ago you were going to let your face rot off; now you're complaining about an audience."

"Well . . ."

Brad placed his hand on Sarah's shoulder and gently turned her to him. "Look, you need to take care of him. I'll see you tomorrow."

Sarah glanced up at the rancher, her gaze soft and pretty. An urge to smash the cowboy's face filled Tucker, and he quickly pushed the feeling aside.

"All right. I really enjoyed dinner tonight," Sarah said. "I'm sorry it ended this way."

"Me, too."

A feeling of nausea overcame Tucker, and he rolled his eyes and turned away from the couple. If Brad kissed Sarah, his fist would connect with the rancher's face.

"Tucker, I can count on you to walk Sarah home, can't I?" Brad asked, interrupting Tucker's thoughts of retaliation.

Tucker turned around and faced the man. All it was going to take was one more stupid comment like that one and the smiling cowboy would find his backside in the dirt.

"Of course."

"Okay." He picked up Sarah's hand and kissed the

back of it. "Thanks for having dinner with me. I'll talk to you tomorrow."

"Bye, Brad," Sarah said, as she watched him walk away, a sappy look on her face that Tucker was eager to erase.

After the man walked far enough away he could no longer hear them, Tucker said, "You know, it's rumored he got some girl with child and then refused to marry her."

Sarah glanced at him as if he were an idiot. "Wouldn't be the first man I've known to do that."

Tucker frowned and then shrugged his shoulders. "Guess you see a lot of that in your line of work."

"All the time." She glared at him. "Now, if you don't behave yourself, I'm going to stitch my initials in that cut above your eye."

"Like hell!" he said, fitting his mood to her response. "Let's go."

They started walking down the street. "What were you thinking, getting into a fight with Lansky?"

"I've followed him for the last several nights. Every night I've tried to do this your way. Not pick a fight with the man, not get into a gun battle with him. Then tonight he stands up in a bar and tells everyone I'm yellow. What did you expect me to do?"

"I expected you to stand up and say if you believe this man, then I have a jail cell with your name on it." She shook her head. "He certainly knew the right words to get you riled, didn't he?"

"And just how did you think I was going to get them to the jail?" Tucker mimicked. "Come along nicely now or you won't get any supper."

"You expect me to believe that you tried this my way and it didn't work, so that I will say go ahead, get into a fight with Lansky. He almost killed you last time. I'm not frightened that you'll be injured and I'll be unable to heal you. Go ahead. I'm not scared that you're going to die."

Tucker stopped on the street and stared at her, his anger seeming to dissipate. "Are you scared for me?"

Sarah started walking again, her steps quick and businesslike. "Let me say it again! Of course I am."

He grasped her elbow and turned her around to face him. "Doc, I'm used to being in tough situations. I can handle this one."

"Just like you 'handled' the last one with this man."

They reached the office, and with a jerk Sarah pulled the key from her bag, stuck it in the lock and turned the doorknob. She walked through the darkened room, her back straight and her body rigid. In the darkness, he heard her strike a match against flint. A small sliver of flame showed in the gloom, and then the lantern was filling the room with a soft glow.

She turned to face him, the light in her hand shimmering across her face. "Come into the next room and I'll stitch up that cut and put iodine on your other cuts."

He followed her down the hall to a small examining room.

"Sit on the stool."

"Yes, ma'am," he said, smiling, hoping to lighten the mood, hoping to talk her out of seeing "Goodguy" Brad.

She took out a small needle and threaded it. Then she poured alcohol on a rag and held the pad up to the cut above his eye.

He sucked in air when the cloth touched the wound. "Damn, Sarah, could you find anything that would hurt more?"

"Don't think I didn't try. Now shut up or the stitches could leave you with an ugly scar."

"Does this mean you're still mad at me?" he asked, noticing for the first time that her breasts were right at eye level. It was tempting to lean into her and put his lips on the bare skin above her dress.

"Why would I be mad? I'm out with one of the nicest men I've been around in a long time and suddenly there you are at my feet bleeding," she said, her voice taut.

She stuck the needle in.

"Ouch!"

She pulled the thread and tied it off. She repeated the process, her touch, normally so gentle, quick and jerky as she rapidly stitched him up.

"Now close your eyes while I put iodine on this wound. This could hurt."

The stuff stung like fire.

"Damn, Sarah!"

"You're all set," she said, putting everything in a metal bowl. "But you might want to put a cold rag on that eye tonight. It's kind of swollen and probably will get worse."

He slipped his arms around her, unable to resist her nearness any longer. He wanted to feel her soft, tempting body up close against his. He laid his head on her chest.

Her body stiffened.

"Thanks," he said, placing his lips on the swells of her breasts.

She gasped, her breath halting. "Don't, Tucker."

He moved his lips up the exposed skin of her chest, up the curve of her neck, around to the apex of her neck and shoulder. She shivered, her breathing coming a little more rapidly. Maybe she enjoyed the rancher's company, but Tucker still could make her quiver with desire.

But they were friends, nothing more. Why couldn't he be glad that she had found someone she enjoyed being with?

He pushed the question out of his mind, not wanting to think about his response to seeing her with Brad, not now while he held her in his arms. His lips continued their path up her neck to her ear, his hands molding her body to his. His tongue traced the outline of her ear, and she gasped, while his lips continued to the corner of her mouth. He leaned back and gazed into her eyes. Then his lips found hers.

He covered her mouth, greedily consuming her lips with a hunger that surprised him. God, he wanted her. She made him feel alive, made him feel strong and manly. He wanted to protect her, wanted to take care of her and Lucas, wanted his arms to be the ones she longed to hold her. Reluctantly, her arms wound their way around his back.

Sarah made him feel more a man than he had ever felt, and suddenly he doubted his decision to accept the federal marshal's job.

Suddenly she shoved him away. "Stop it! Stop it now!"

She stepped out of his embrace and walked across the room, her breathing rapid as she drew in deep breaths. She crossed her arms over her chest and bowed her head, her hair falling to cover her face. For a moment it looked as if she was crying, but when she raised her head, he could see the anger that radiated from her gaze.

"Damn you, Tucker Burnett. You don't know what you want. You kiss me, you have sex with me, but you can't—you *won't* commit to me. I'm tired of being yanked around by you. Here for your convenience."

"But—"

"You don't want me. Yet the moment I find a man that's interesting, you come back around kissing me. You call yourself my friend, but you don't want anyone else to have me either."

"That's not—"

"Oh, yeah, I know what you're going to say. You set me up with men to take me to dinner. You set me up with the town's confirmed bachelors. You set me up with men you knew would never be a threat to you."

"But—"

"Damn you, Tucker. You don't want me because you're afraid of commitment, but you don't want anyone else to have me either," she said, her voice rising in volume. "You use the term 'friend' loosely. Friends don't kiss or have sex. I'm tired of your games. Get out. Get out now!"

"Sarah, wait."

She was shaking, she was so angry. "Just go, Tucker."

"You haven't given me a chance to explain."

"That's because I don't want to hear your explanations. I'm tired of being a pawn in your games. Get out."

Tucker picked up his hat from the table. "I should walk you home. It's not safe."

"Go. At this point I dare anyone to bother me."

He moved slowly, reluctant to leave. He had never seen her so angry or so upset. He regretted his kiss had caused her pain. "I didn't mean to hurt you, Sarah, honestly."

"Please, just go."

He stepped to the door of the room, his boots sounding loud in the shadows of the clinic. "I'll come by and check on you tomorrow. I do care about you, Sarah."

As he walked out of the room and through the halls of the clinic, he listened intently for the sounds of sobbing or the breaking of glass. This time he would refuse to leave if he heard any of those noises. But it was eerily quiet as he shut the door.

Had he done all those things she said? Had he really used her for his convenience and then, when another man found her attractive, come back around kissing her?

He swallowed. Maybe.

And he *had* set her up with the town's bachelors, knowing instinctively that the matches would never work.

Did he really not want anyone else to have her? They had always been friends, and he wanted her to find someone here in town and stay on as the doctor, didn't he?

Why did he feel so guilty? Why did he feel as though her accusations were somewhat true?

The cool spring air bit at him as Tucker glanced around at the shadows of the darkened night. The sounds of revelry came from several blocks over as the saloons cranked out the noise. He couldn't just let her walk alone, but he also knew that she would never accept his company.

He melted into the shadows behind the clinic and waited for Sarah to leave. Once he saw her, he followed her all the way back to the hotel, making sure she made it home safely, always staying hidden so she would never know he followed her.

* * *

The next morning found Tucker sitting in his office, his eye swollen, his pride bruised and his ego completely deflated. Over and over his mind had replayed her comments regarding his behavior, wondering if her accusations were true.

And he couldn't help but remember seeing her happy last night, her hand intimately tucked into the crook of Brad's elbow.

Damn! They had looked happy. They looked like they belonged together. And Brad had been smiling as if he was the luckiest man in town.

The door to Tucker's office opened and in stepped his mother. His stomach sank. He didn't think that he could take her manipulating ways today. He wasn't in the mood to hear a speech on the benefits of being married.

"Hello, son," she said cheerfully, pulling the door closed behind her. She turned to face him and gasped. "Good Lord, what happened to you?"

No, his swollen face wasn't a pretty sight, just a painful reminder of one swing too many from the gunfighter the night before.

"I'm fine, Mother."

"I heard that Lansky character was here in town. Was he the one who did this to you?" she asked.

"Yes, but there's nothing to worry about."

His mother threw up her arms. "You sit there and tell me not to worry, while your face is so bruised and swollen."

"Thanks, Mother," he said, choosing to ignore her remarks, suddenly remembering that his sister-in-law was very pregnant and due soon. "Is everything okay with Rose? I don't need to get Sarah, do I?"

"Not that I know of," Eugenia said, as she paused

and stared at him. "Aren't you going to ask me to be seated?"

"Sorry, please, sit down. Would you like something to drink?"

"Thank you, but no," she said, smiling at him graciously, pleased now that she had reminded him of his manners.

He watched as his mother took a seat and spread her skirts, settling in. It looked as though she was hunkering in, preparing for battle, which left him feeling slightly uneasy.

All it would take was one tiny opening and his mother would be on him like an ant on a stinkbug. She would circle the wagons and gather recruitments, and soon Tucker would find himself facing a preacher.

"Did Sarah put those stitches in above your eye?" she asked.

"Yes," he said curtly, remembering her none-too-gentle ministrations.

"You know, Tucker, since the fiasco with Beth and Tanner, I've really tried to do better. Since the veil incident, I've kept my word and not bothered you recently concerning Sarah. I've tried to accept your decision not to marry."

"Mother, nothing has changed. I'm not getting married," he blurted out.

She flipped her wrist at her son. "I completely understand, son, but I saw that Brad Riley fellow coming out of the clinic early this morning, and well . . . Sarah looked happy. And the two of them," she laughed. "They looked downright cozy together."

"So?" he said, a flash of irritation creeping into his voice.

"Well, I know that the two of you are such good friends, and you know Brad is *very* good husband material." She smiled at her son. "He'd be an excellent catch for Sarah and that precious little boy of hers."

"So you rushed right over here to tell me?" he asked. "Don't you think I already knew?"

Damn it! Did she think that he wanted to hear about Sarah and Brad? The rancher and the doctor were friends, nothing more! Just like Sarah and he were friends. Weren't they?

Yet why did he feel as though something that belonged to him was slipping away? And though he didn't understand why he felt so much frustration and anger at the mention of Brad, the man just irritated him. Sarah deserved better than a rancher who owned a sizable chunk of land and could take good care of her. Didn't she?

"Well, I didn't know if you knew about the two of them, but I guess if you saw Sarah last night, she must have told you all about her and Brad." His mother leaned closer. "Has she told her grandfather yet?"

"How the hell would I know?" he asked irritably.

"Well, you just said you knew about the two of them," she said innocently. "Are you feeling all right, son? I guess that's a silly question with your face all swollen like it is."

"Hell no, I'm not feeling all right. My head is throbbing, my eye hurts and you're asking me all sorts of questions I don't know."

Eugenia leaned back in her chair. "Sorry. I just thought that maybe you would know if they had mentioned setting a date yet."

"You're getting ahead of yourself, Mother. She had dinner with the man once. That's all."

"This morning when I saw her, she had a bouquet of flowers in her hand, and he was standing outside on the porch of the clinic. It looked like they had breakfast together."

Tucker took a calming breath and released it slowly. The image of Sarah naked in his arms, her head thrown back in passion, came to mind, sending a pleasant ache through his body. Had he ever given her flowers?

Brad's face swam before his eyes, and he saw red. If Brad had snuck back to spend the night with Sarah, there would be hell to pay.

But he had no right to object. And Sarah's grandfather would have been at the hotel. Sarah could make her own decisions, and after Tucker's behavior last night, their friendship could be in peril.

"I'm going to pretend you didn't say that," he told his mother, shifting uncomfortably in his chair.

"Why? They could have had breakfast together in the hotel dining room this morning. He could have met her downstairs and then walked her over to the clinic," his mother said.

He sent Eugenia a look that even a blind man would have known meant go away and leave me alone. But no, his mother didn't take a hint.

"Besides, Brad Riley is a very nice man compared to some of those other men you introduced her to. Did you set her up with Brad?" she asked innocently.

"No, they met at the auction," he said, almost gritting his teeth.

"Oh, that's right. He got into that bidding war over Sarah's basket with you." She laughed. "Now it's all coming back."

Sarah's words regarding setting her up with some of the worst bachelors in town came back to haunt him. His insides clenched at the memory. Had he really set Sarah up with men that he knew would never work out? Was that why he disliked Brad so much, because he knew the man would be good for Sarah. And if they were only friends, why was he objecting to the cowboy so much?

"Well, dear. I know you're busy, and I don't want to keep you. But I was just so excited to talk with someone about Sarah, and I knew you would know more than anyone."

His mother stood, smoothed her long skirts and picked up her parasol. "I better get along, dear. Rose is sitting at home miserable, and I don't want to be gone too long.

He frowned and nodded, frustration keeping him silent as he watched his mother walking toward the door.

Opening the door, she turned and faced him. "When you see Sarah, give her my best."

With a click she shut the door behind her and like a whirlwind departed his office, her destructive winds leaving behind a battered Tucker. God, how had his father lived with the woman for nearly thirty years?

He placed his face gingerly in his hands, then leaned his elbows on his desk. But more important, what if Sarah did marry Brad Riley? What if she fell in love with him, too?

Sarah sat in her office trying to work while Lucas took a nap, unable to concentrate as she thought of Brad Riley and Tucker. She glanced over at the bouquet of roses and wisteria blossoms. They were the early bloomers heralding the arrival of spring, and Brad had picked the sweet-smelling flowers from his ranch and brought them to her.

But the nicest compliment he had given her was telling her he couldn't sleep last night for thinking of her. She had suffered a hard time herself falling asleep. Brad had been part of the reason her eyes had refused to shut, while Tucker Burnett had charged through her mind, repeatedly falling through that window to come crashing down at her feet.

It seemed every time she closed her eyes, the sound of shattering glass had jarred her awake. And while she had lain there and tried to count sheep, the only thing she had managed was to count the faults of each of the two men who filled her dreams. One of whom seemed to jump over the fence in a steady rhythm.

She closed her eyes, determined to put the image of Tucker out of her mind, to erase him from her heart. No matter what had transpired between them in the past, she had to move on with her life. No matter that he was Lucas's father, she had to give up on him. Regardless that she had loved him for years and tried before to put him out of her heart, this time she was going to succeed if for no other reason than her son.

She glanced over at the boy, who lay sleeping soundly on the pallet she had made for him. Her grandfather had been unable to keep him today, so she had brought him to the office, determined to make it fun for both of them.

Finally, he had worn out from playing and had gone down for his afternoon nap.

She picked up her quill pen, determined to concentrate on the notes she was making for Dr. Wilson. This morning she had called on the doctor, who was recovering quite nicely. In two weeks he would be coming back to work, and she would be free to go home to Tombstone or decide to stay in Fort Worth.

And while she had arrived under the false pretense that her grandfather was ill, determined to leave at the earliest convenience, she suddenly was loath to depart. No matter what happened between her and Tucker, or her and Brad, she had found a new sense of belonging by working in the clinic with patients who needed her. A sense of rightness.

But she didn't know if she could stay here and work in the same town as Tucker and fall in love with Brad. And though she was trying, falling in love with Brad would be impossible if she didn't get over loving Tucker.

The back door opened and slammed shut. Sarah turned around in her chair, frightened by the sound of footsteps running toward her. She jumped up, determined to put herself in the path of whoever was coming in the clinic.

A tiny woman, her face covered by a big, floppy hat, came down the hall. It took Sarah just a moment to realize that Kira was hurrying toward her. Her ashen face framed her dark eyes which were wide with fright.

"Kira, what are you doing here? Did anyone see you enter the clinic?"

"I don't think so," she said breathlessly. "Dr. Sarah, you must come."

Sarah stepped toward the girl. "What's wrong?"

"Baby comes. Mrs. Rose baby come now. She all alone," Kira said.

"Let me get my bag," Sarah said, walking toward the table and picking up the satchel that carried her supplies. She opened the bag and did a quick routine check to make sure she had everything she could possibly need.

Then she glanced down at Lucas sleeping soundly on the floor and back at Kira.

She couldn't leave them here alone, with the threat of danger that they would be found.

"Kira, tell me all you can about Rose. Is the baby coming right now?" Sarah asked, hoping she had more time.

"Mrs. Rose standing in kitchen when water gushed from between her legs. She cry and clutch her belly. No one home but me and her. She send me for you. Husband gone. Should be home soon."

"Dear God, they left the two of you alone? And her water has broken." She did a mental rundown of estimated time until most first babies came. Usually they were late in showing up, but occasionally one would make an unexpected appearance. "Okay. You have to stay here with Lucas. I can't take him with me. But I want the two of you at Grandfather's hotel. You'll be safer there. I'll get the wagon; you get Lucas."

Sarah took two steps toward the back door and sighed. "We walked over from the hotel, with Brad. I don't have the wagon." She glanced at Kira. "How did you get here?"

"Horse out back." She touched Sarah's arm. "I stay here with boy. We be safe till you get back."

Sarah glanced at Kira. "I really don't have much choice. Promise me you'll stay here. Don't go outside. Don't open the door for anyone. I'll send word to my grandfather to help you as soon as he can."

Quickly Sarah penned two notes that she would give to a messenger boy she knew. One for her grandfather and one for Tucker.

She flipped the sign to CLOSED and locked the door. Then she pulled the shades so that hopefully no one could see in.

"Go. Take care of Mrs. Rose," Kira insisted.

Sarah took one more glance at Lucas. She walked over and kissed him on the cheek, not waking the child. She didn't like this. She felt uneasy, but Rose needed her. And her grandfather would be back soon.

"Okay, I'm leaving. Don't open the door for anyone, Kira. My grandfather has the key."

Kira shook her head. "No one get in. Go."

Sarah backed out the door, her bag in her hand, before she ran to the horse and climbed into the saddle, her skirts in the way.

Fifteen

Sarah rode the horse as fast as she could while still feeling in control of the animal. It would do no good for her to have an accident and hurt herself on the way, though babies generally came whether the doctor was there or not.

Judging by the time Kira arrived at the clinic, once Sarah appeared at Rose's side, it would be close to four hours since the woman had gone into labor. While most first babies took hours to be born, there was always the chance that this child would be different.

Sarah rode through the gates of the Bar None, anxious to see Rose. She pulled the horse to a halt in front of the big house. Travis came running down the steps.

"God, am I glad to see you!" he said, as Sarah swung down from the saddle. She untied her medical bag from the saddle string.

"I left as soon as Kira found me," Sarah replied. "How is she?"

They walked up the steps of the house, past the rose bushes in full bloom.

"I don't know, Doc." He ran his hand through his

hair nervously. "She seems okay until a pain hits her. And then she's hurting."

"How far apart are her pains?"

"About every twenty minutes."

Sarah laid her hand on Travis, pausing before they went into the house. "You know, Travis, we could be in for a long night. First babies are usually slow to arrive."

"Yeah, I figure it's a lot like a foal being born or a calf, except it's my wife and my baby," he said, his face turning white.

"Babies are born every day," Sarah reassured him, entering the house. "Is Rose upstairs?"

"Yes," he replied, pacing the entryway of the house, glancing up the stairs.

Sarah patted him on the hand. "I'm here now. When the rest of the family arrives, you're going to need to tell them what's going on."

"I never should have left Rose. I had to ride out and check on a fence that had been blown down. Mother was gone, but Rose assured me she would be okay. She told me she was feeling fine, and then this happens. I should never have left her."

"Maybe she wasn't feeling any pains at the time," Sarah reassured, trying to calm him down.

"Can I come up and be with Rose?" he asked.

"You can come up for a few minutes, but then it's better if the husband waits downstairs. Tucker should be here soon."

"I sent word to Tanner and Beth. They're working on their new home," Travis said, running a hand through his hair.

"Sarah, I really appreciate your coming for Rose. Please don't let anything happen to her," Travis said fretfully.

"I'll do everything I can to help her," Sarah replied. "Now I better get up there and see my patient."

"Okay. I'll give you a few moments alone with her before I come up."

"Thanks."

Sarah hurried up the stairs and down the hallway to Travis and Rose's bedroom. She opened the door just as Rose had a contraction.

"Oh, Sarah, I thought you'd never get here," Rose said, grasping onto the bed sheets until her knuckles turned white.

"Don't hold your breath, Rose. Pant until the pain passes," Sarah instructed. Dropping her medical bag in a nearby rocker and coming around the bed, she took Rose's hand. The woman squeezed her hand.

After the contraction had passed, Sarah asked Rose, "When did the pains start?"

"I don't know. My back has been hurting since yesterday, but the hard pains didn't start until after my water broke."

"Lie back and let me examine you, Rose," Sarah instructed. When Rose complied, she quickly examined the young woman. "Looks like we'll have a baby before morning."

"It'll take that long?"

"I don't know for certain; but you're not ready, and first babies generally are slow in making their appearance." Sarah washed her hands in a bowl of water, dried them quickly and then came around to the side of the bed.

"Let's get you up and walking. Not only will that speed up the baby coming, but it's better for you. When you feel a pain coming on, grab the bedpost and hang on. Tell me so that I can help you. We're going to do this together. Okay?"

"Yes. Travis was the one who insisted I get into bed."

Sarah shook her head and smiled. "Goes to show you how much men know about babies. But I must admit your husband is pretty nervous."

"It's because he has no control over the situation." Rose gave a nervous laugh just as another contraction hit her. "Oh, my God. What have I done? I'm about to become a mother. I've never even been around babies much."

Sarah shook her head, laughing at the woman. "It's a little late to back out now. You'll do fine. Come on, let's start walking."

The closer they got to the ranch, the more Tucker yelled at the horses, pushing them to their limits. After he received Sarah's note, he had found his mother shopping at Pearl's, and together they were hurrying to the ranch.

"Son, slow this wagon down before you kill us both," Eugenia cried. "I'm just as anxious to get there as you are, but I doubt this baby will be born in the next hour. Believe me, I've waited a long time for this child. Nothing is going to stop me from being there when it's born."

Reluctantly, Tucker pulled on the reins, slowing the animals. "I just want to make sure that Rose and Travis are okay and that Sarah got there all right. I worry about her riding to the ranch by herself."

"Sarah knows how to take care of herself. She'll be fine. Travis is a concern. After all, this is his first child." Eugenia sighed. "I remember your father was beside himself until Travis was born. Actually, he was frightened during all three deliveries, until each one of you kids was born. I do miss him, especially at times like these."

Tucker sent his mother a fleeting look, surprised at this sudden insight into his father. "I never thought Papa got excited about much of anything."

"Your father was not one for showing his emotions—kind of like you boys are—but he loved each and every one of you. And he was excited about each baby that came along."

"I guess I never saw that side of him since I was the youngest."

"No. But he was more excited when you were born than probably all the rest." She paused. "I lost two babies before we had you, and we were afraid there weren't going to be any more children for us."

Tucker turned and stared at his mother, seeing tears in the corners of her eyes.

"It just about killed your father to have to bury those babies. Your papa was a loving father, who made you kids mind because he wanted you to grow up to be strong-minded adults who are honest and hard-working men he could be proud of."

Cottonwood trees lined the road, their new spring leaves bright and shiny in the late afternoon sun. Tucker paid them little mind as he thought of his father burying two babies. He shuddered as he realized that all three of them had become strong-minded, stubborn adults who worked hard to take care of each other.

Yet his father had never accepted him not working on the ranch. He had always wanted him to be more like Travis, handier with a rope and branding iron than a gun.

"I guess I was a disappointment to him, since I ran off and became a gunfighter. But I wanted to see the world. I didn't want to work on a ranch all my life, like my brothers. I wanted some independence."

Eugenia laughed. "Oh, Tucker, you were never a disappointment to him. In fact, you are probably more like him than the other two. Your papa wasn't always a rancher. Before I met him, he didn't want to settle down. He dreamed of coming to Texas and starting the ranch, but not with a wife. He wasn't going to marry."

Tucker chuckled. "I guess his boys aren't much different, are they, Mother?"

"Not in the least."

The ranch came into view, and Tucker couldn't help but feel a sigh of relief at the sight of the old homestead sitting on the hill.

The sun was setting low on the horizon, casting shadows in the yard of the big house as they pulled up front. Tanner and Beth's wagon was parked out front along with one of the stock horses that he knew was used around the ranch.

Eugenia scrambled out of the wagon and up the steps of the front porch before Tucker could stop her. He secured the brake on the wagon and then jumped down. Glancing up, he saw Sarah standing at the window of Rose and Travis's bedroom.

She was here. Somehow just looking at her, knowing what she was doing for his brother and Rose, gave Tucker a warm feeling. Sarah was a fine woman in every sense. She was smart, kindhearted and loving, responsive and fun.

And he could marry her if he could just release his heart and give up his dreams.

But his dreams had been his for so very long, and though at times he wanted to give in and give her his name, he couldn't let go of everything he had ever wanted. And those plans didn't include a wife and child.

Travis slowly opened the door and watched his wife pacing the length of the bedroom in her nightgown. Her big belly preceded her as she walked the floor, her hand on her back.

Sarah stood at the window, glancing out at the countryside.

"Tucker and Eugenia just arrived," she said.

"You know, Eugenia really likes you, Sarah," Rose said, her facial expression suddenly changing. "Here comes another one."

"Grab on to the bedpost. Don't forget to breathe."

Travis stepped into the bedroom. "Shouldn't she be in bed?" he asked, going to Rose's side, slipping his arm around Rose as she clutched the bedpost, her face tightening with pain.

"She's doing just fine, Travis," Sarah reassured him. "Breathe, Rose."

"I am," she said between gritted teeth.

Travis felt almost faint as he watched his wife and saw her belly contracting beneath her nightgown.

"Don't you want to lie down, honey?" he asked nervously.

She turned and gave him a look that was clearly irritated. "Travis, I feel better up walking, rather than lying there in that damn bed hurting. Why don't you go downstairs and tell your mother and Tucker what's going on?"

"But I'd rather be here with you," he said.

Rose gasped as the pain intensified. *"Mon Cul."*

"Oh honey, don't start cursing in French."

"Couillion!" Rose said, between gritted teeth. "I'll talk any way I want to. Now—go—downstairs."

Sarah walked to Rose's side and put her hand on her belly. "It's okay, Rose. Travis, I think it would be a good idea for you to see to your mother and Tucker."

Rose gripped the bedpost, her face turning red.

"Breathe, Rose," Sarah admonished, as she laid her hand on Travis's arm and gently led him to the bedroom door. "I'll call you if anything new develops. Births can take twelve to twenty-four hours, and we're just getting started, so don't panic. It's probably going to be a long night."

Travis watched as Sarah shut the door in his face, the image of Rose breathing hard and panting frozen in his mind. He was scared as he slowly walked down the stairs. His baby was about to be born, and suddenly he was frightened for his wife and child.

Dear God, please don't let anything happen to her, he prayed. How could she take this for twelve to twenty-four hours?

At the bottom of the steps he glanced up to see his entire family awaiting him. His mother stepped forward and took his hands in hers.

"How's Rose?" she asked.

He shrugged. "She's in pain, but Sarah seems to think it's going to be a while."

"Babies come when they're ready and not before," his mother reassured. "Just think of when your mares foal. It usually takes a while."

"Yeah, but it's different. This is Rose," he said, worried.

"Come on," Tanner said. "Our job as your brothers is to take you into the parlor and get you drunk."

"I don't want to drink," Travis said, glancing back

up the stairs. "I have to be alert in case Rose needs me."

"Well, I'll fix us some coffee at the very least," Beth said, going into the kitchen. "If it's going to be a long night, we're going to need something to keep us awake."

"Come on, son, let's all sit in the parlor and wait for Sarah to let us know what's going on. Once an hour, one of us women will go up there and check on Rose."

"Thanks, Mother," Travis said, sort of stumbling toward the parlor in a state of shock.

He was about to become a father. The woman who had disrupted his orderly world, changed his life for the better and shown him the real meaning of the word "love," her life was in danger all because of him.

For the second time that night, Travis sent up a prayer. *Please don't let anything happen to Rose.*

Midnight had come and gone. Lucas had been in bed for a long time now, and Sarah missed kissing him good night. She stretched, tired, knowing that Rose was exhausted, worry beginning to nag at her. Rose's labor had been long and hard, and Sarah didn't know how much longer her strength could hold out. The pains were getting closer and closer.

Time seemed suspended, and the world was centered in this room, waiting for this child to be born.

Rose groaned, the sound eerie in the night. "Sarah, I've got to push."

"Wait."

Sarah lifted up the sheet and checked Rose again. She gave the woman a smile of relief. "We're almost there, Rose. You're ready."

"Thank God," Rose said in a low whisper, drawing shallow breaths, getting ready for the next pain.

"You should start feeling the need to push. At the next pain—"

"I've—got—to—push—now."

"Chin down. Go ahead, push, Rose."

Sarah sat at Rose's bottom, waiting for the appearance of the baby's head. Rose strained as hard as she could, but nothing happened.

Sarah jumped up and ran to the bedroom door. She yelled down the stairs. "Eugenia, I need your assistance."

Eugenia bounded up the stairs. "What's wrong?"

Rose was panting when Eugenia came into the room. She started to cry. "I can't do this anymore, Sarah. I just can't."

"I need you to help Rose. Hold her up in a sitting position so that when she pushes, the baby will come out."

Sarah tried to soothe her patient's fears. "Yes, you can. We're almost there. In just a few moments your baby is going to be born. Eugenia's going to lift you up in the bed and help you. Together we'll help this baby be born."

Eugenia got behind her daughter-in-law and crooned softly to her. "Come on, you can do this. I'm going to help you."

"Okay, on the next pain . . ."

"Oh, God, here it comes. . . ."

"Push, Rose," Sarah demanded.

"I am—"

Sarah felt a thrill as she saw the crown of the tiny head. "Push, Rose. I can see the head."

Rose took a deep breath and then gave a mighty push that turned her face a brilliant red.

Sarah saw something around the neck of the baby. "Stop pushing. Pant," Sarah cried. Sarah gently unwound the cord from around the infant's head. "Okay, now push."

In a matter of moments she pulled the infant from Rose's body.

"It's a girl!" Sarah cried excitedly.

She wiped the mucus from the child's mouth and nose and checked on the little girl's breathing. The baby lay limply in her arms, her skin a bluish gray, not kicking or crying, not even breathing.

Fear shot through Sarah, and she wiped the infant's face and mouth once again and patted the baby's back.

Nothing. No response from the child.

"What's wrong?" Eugenia asked, her voice strained.

"Sarah?" Rose questioned, her voice cracking.

Sarah didn't reply, but now pounded on the baby's back. She put her lips on the infant's mouth and forced air into the baby's lungs and then pounded again on the child's back. The infant drew a deep breath and gave a wail of protest. Sarah released a sigh of relief.

She wanted to laugh; she wanted to cry at the sight of the little girl's face scrunched up in a wail, furious at her entrance to the world.

The baby began to move her arms and feet as if suddenly realizing she was no longer cramped. She screamed and wailed, her eyes tightly shut, her fists curled, and with relief Sarah watched the color of her skin change from blue to pink.

Sarah turned to Rose and held up the crying infant. "Rose, you have a daughter."

Rose, who had been lying spent, turned her face toward the wailing infant and held out her arms. "A girl? Let me see her."

Sarah tied off the umbilical cord and then with a snip cut the link between mother and child and then handed the wet, slippery infant to her mother. The baby stopped crying and opened her eyes, blinking them rapidly in the dim lantern light.

Eugenia started to cry as she reached out and ran her finger down the infant's skin. "A little girl. Oh, my. I always wanted a daughter, and now I have a granddaughter. My first grandchild."

Sarah couldn't look at the woman. Eugenia had a grandson she knew nothing about.

While Rose and her daughter were getting acquainted, Sarah delivered the afterbirth and cleaned up the new mother. She covered the tired woman and tidied up the room. "I better go get your husband. I know he's worried."

She stepped to the door.

"Sarah?" Rose called. "Thank you."

"My pleasure," Sarah said, and stepped outside.

The shakes began the moment she stepped out of room and started down the stairs. By the time she had reached the parlor, her knees were knocking so badly she could hardly stand. This always happened after a birth, especially a dramatic one where the baby was in danger. No matter how many times she delivered a baby, each birth was unique, and she knew she would soon fall apart.

She pulled herself together just as Travis spotted her and ran to her. "What's wrong?"

"Nothing's wrong. Rose is resting. Your mother is with her and the baby."

"She had the baby?" he asked, shocked. "It's over?"

Sarah smiled and patted him on the arm. "Go up and see your wife and child."

"What did she have?"

"Go up and see your wife. I'll let her show you your child."

"Is Rose okay?"

"Rose is tired, but she's fine. Now go see the two of them."

Travis ran out of the room and raced up the stairs, taking them two at a time. When Sarah heard the bedroom door close, she turned to the waiting group of people in the parlor.

"Rose delivered a little girl about fifteen minutes ago. Mother and baby are both fine."

There was a collective sigh at her announcement, and then everyone started talking at once. It was as if they had been silently waiting for the news for hours and only now were allowed to talk.

A few minutes later, Eugenia came down the stairs, wiping her eyes, and joined the family in the parlor. "I wanted to give the three of them some time alone. She's just beautiful."

"How's Travis?" Tanner asked. "I was worried he wasn't going to make it through the night."

Eugenia laughed. "He came in asking about his son, and Rose said, 'I told you it was a girl.' But he wasn't disappointed in the least. Just happy they were both fine."

"And Rose?" Beth asked. "Sarah told us she's tired, but she's okay?"

"She's exhausted. But Sarah is a great doctor. I was so afraid when the baby wouldn't start breathing. But Sarah saved her. She kept working on her, even breathing in the baby's mouth trying to get her to take her first breath. And she did. She finally started crying, and I swear that was the most blessed sound I've ever heard."

Eugenia gave Sarah a quick hug and had to wipe her eyes again. "Thank you, Sarah."

Sarah shook her head. "We were lucky. It could easily have been so much worse. Now, if you'll excuse me for a moment, it's been a long night. I'd like a breath of fresh air."

Sarah walked through the house and out the front door, needing some time alone to calm her shattered nerves. No matter how many babies she delivered, they always filled her with awe, leaving her completely drained both physically and emotionally whenever the birth was over.

But this time she had been frightened when the child wouldn't breathe. She walked over to the swing, sat down, put her face in her hands and let the tears fall. Barely a minute had passed before the swing rocked, and she felt a pair of strong arms wrap around her as Tucker gently pulled her into his arms.

"Shh! It's okay. Rose is safe, and the baby is going to be fine."

"I know," she cried into his shoulder. "It's . . . just . . . I was . . . so frightened when she wouldn't breathe."

Her tears came faster and harder, and she laid her head against his shoulder while he gently patted her back in small, round circles.

"I've only lost two babies . . . Both were stillborn." She sniffed and wiped the tears from her eyes. "I'm sorry for crying on you. I'm tired, and this birth scared me. Delivering a baby is such an emotional event, and even though I'm a doctor, I can't help but get involved with my patients."

He rubbed her back, holding her close, as the swing gently rocked them back and forth in a soothing pattern.

Tucker stopped the swing, placed his fingers beneath her chin and tilted her face up to gaze in her teary eyes. "I'm so proud of you, Sarah. You're brave and smart. You saved the life of a baby tonight, and nothing could be more important than that."

His lips touched her forehead in a gentle kiss, and he leaned back against the swing, pressing her head on his shoulder, holding her in his arms.

"It's my job, Tucker. Just like protecting life is yours. I love it, but at times it can be draining. Especially when someone's life is at stake."

Tucker nodded, his feet moving the swing back and forth. "Rose was lucky. She had the entire family waiting for the birth of this baby. She had the love and support of people who care about her. If anything had gone wrong, she would have immediately been surrounded by the people who love her."

Sarah nodded. "I know, but carrying a baby for nine months, feeling that tiny person inside of you and awaiting their arrival only to have something go terribly wrong and have the child die is the absolute worst. I pray my patients will never experience such heartache."

"But that didn't happen, Sarah. You saved her," he soothed, still holding her as the swing gently rocked. "Tell me about Lucas's birth. Who was there for you when Lucas was born?"

She became still in his arms. Why was he suddenly interested in her and Lucas? Why would he care?

"I was alone except for the midwife I had chosen to deliver my son. There was no one waiting," she said, her voice soft in the darkness, the memory of the pain of being unaided as fresh as if it were yesterday.

The memory of the night Lucas had been born was like a distant dream. "I had it pretty easy right up until the end. When Lucas came out screaming at the top of his lungs, I knew immediately he was healthy."

"That must have been hard on you, not having anyone you know around you. Not having your husband there."

"It was the hardest time of my life. I was all alone except for the midwife."

The words were on the edge of her tongue to tell Tucker the truth, but she hesitated, wondering how he would react. She wanted to share with him the knowledge that he had a son, but fear and exhaustion held her back.

He shook his head. "You're so brave. I wouldn't know what to do with a small child. To have someone depend on you for everything. I don't know if I could have done as good a job as you've done with Lucas. I guess that's why I'll probably never have a child of my own."

She took a deep breath. She could not tell him the truth regarding his son now. The knowledge would be like an anchor weighing him down, restricting him from moving around the country like he wanted. Maybe someday . . . but not now.

They sat in the swing, the predawn breeze drifting over them. A faint glow could be seen lightening the eastern sky, just as the rooster began to crow.

"I wish I had been there for you. If I had known you were alone, I would have been there for you, Sarah."

Sarah sighed. No, he wouldn't have come when Lucas was born. The person he had been back then would never have come just to be with her. He had been too interested in pursuing his own interests.

But the man today—the man who sat holding her in his arms—he might have come to her rescue. But if he had and he learned the truth about his son, he would only leave again.

No! I can't tell him the truth about Lucas. Not now! Maybe never.

Sixteen

The next morning everyone but Eugenia and Rose piled into the wagon to take Sarah back to town and pick up a few more baby supplies they suddenly discovered were needed.

"Are you sure you want to leave Rose?" Sarah asked Travis, feeling anxious about him being gone from Rose so soon.

"Well, Rose and the baby are sleeping, and Tanner and Beth have promised me we'll come right back as soon we pick up the supplies." He lowered his voice. "And I want to get Rose something special to celebrate the birth of little Desiree Rose."

"I love that name," Beth said, sighing as she climbed up into the wagon with the help of her husband. He sat her down in the inside of the wagon.

"Are you comfortable, dear?" Tanner asked.

She smiled at him. "I'll be fine."

"Let's get going," Tucker said.

Yes, Sarah felt suddenly anxious to see Lucas. She hated being gone overnight from him and couldn't wait to get back and cuddle him in her arms. She missed him.

Tucker snapped the reins, and the wagon rolled out

of the yard with a lurch. Sarah sat next to Tucker as the wagon went through the gates of the Bar None.

"So, Travis, how did you do changing your first diaper this morning?" Tanner teased his older brother.

He grinned. "Better than you'll do the first time."

"I'm not changing diapers."

"You'll reconsider when your wife is asleep, the baby is fussing and Mother has stepped from the room. I didn't want the baby waking Rose. So I changed the diaper, and then Rose woke up."

Sarah smiled at Travis. "I think your wife is pretty smart. She slept long enough that she didn't have to change the baby."

Travis gave Sarah a quick frown. "Well, at least it wasn't a stinky one. And I did change her."

"That's true," Tucker said. "Wonder what the baby thought of your diapering. How many times did you stick her with the pin?"

"I didn't! She would have cried, but instead she drifted back to sleep. If you weren't running off, I'd say let's see you try to change a squirming slippery baby's bottom," he taunted.

An awkward silence fell on the wagon. What did Travis mean if Tucker weren't running off? Was he going somewhere?

"What are you talking about?" Sarah asked, confused.

Tucker shot Sarah a guarded glance that only irritated her even more. There was something he hadn't told her.

"Sorry, Tucker, your news sort of slipped out," Travis said. "Unless, of course, you've changed your mind."

"No, I haven't," Tucker said to his brother. "I was

going to tell everyone after things settled down from Desiree being born. But I guess I'll tell you all now."

Sarah knew before the words ever left his mouth, he was leaving. She tensed as he said exactly what she had been expecting, what she had been dreading.

"I'm taking a job as federal marshal, and I'll probably be leaving within the next two weeks."

"Why haven't you said something before now," she responded, with more hostility than she intended.

Tucker glanced at her, his expression full of concern. "There hasn't been a good time to tell everyone. I've been waiting."

She swallowed, trying hard to push away the anger she could feel swelling within her.

"Where will you be going?" she asked.

"Oklahoma Territory for a while. Every case will be different, so I'll be in various towns. The job is exactly what I've been wanting."

"We'll miss you, Tucker," Beth said. "You won't be here when our baby is born."

"I'll come home often," Tucker said, a wistful note in his voice.

Sarah gazed straight ahead. "Be sure to take warm clothes. It gets cool there at night."

Her voice sounded wooden and cold, even to her ears.

"You know you can always come home if this is not what you want," Tanner said quietly from the back of the wagon.

"Yes, I know," Tucker said, with a quick glance at Sarah.

She knew he was gazing at her, but she refused to meet his eyes. She couldn't look at him without her whole face revealing the turmoil whirring within her.

The rest of the ride into town, she stared straight

ahead, not looking at Tucker, whose gaze touched her occasionally. But it was all she could do to control the tears that threatened to slip down her cheeks.

When they reached the hotel, Travis helped Sarah alight from the wagon. She was anxious to get as far away as she could from Tucker. She needed to rest and be with her son.

"Keep Kira hidden until we're ready to leave town, and then we'll come back by to pick her up," Travis said.

She nodded. "Come to Grandfather's rooms when you're ready to leave."

"Okay." Travis stood there a moment, his hat in his hands. "Thanks, Sarah. Thanks for everything. We couldn't have done this without you."

"Delivering babies is the best part of my job. Let me know if you need anything, Travis."

"I will."

Travis climbed back up into the wagon, and Sarah watched as the group drove off, heading toward the jail where they would drop Tucker off.

He was leaving town. He was finally going to pursue his dreams, and they didn't include her.

She had known that sooner or later this day might come, and now that it was here, dismay swelled up inside of Sarah. He would never understand; he would never acknowledge that she loved him.

Sarah stepped into the hotel, not really conscious of the people around her. It was time she gave up on her dreams of the two of them. She had his son, and that had to be enough. Suddenly she was anxious to see Lucas and her grandfather. It wasn't often she was away from her son, and she had missed tucking him into bed last night and being there first thing this morning to wake him.

Sarah climbed the flight of stairs to her grandfather's suite of rooms, anxious to spend time with Lucas and maybe catch a nap this afternoon.

When she reached the door, she turned the knob and found it locked. She rustled around in her reticule until she found the key she seldom used and stuck it in the door lock. Turning the knob, she opened the door and entered the room.

"Hello, is anyone here?" she asked, a sudden uneasiness crawling down her spine.

Silence greeted her. She glanced around the empty rooms, at the made beds, the orderly tidiness of her grandfather's suite. Lucas's room looked just like she had left it the day before. His favorite toy, his wooden soldiers, lay in the same position. Sarah knew because she had put them there.

Icy tentacles of fear seized her heart.

Where was Kira? She would not have gone out, would she? The girl knew her life was in danger and would not have ventured from the hotel.

A trickle of fear ran down her spine as she closed the door and hurried downstairs. She all but ran up to the desk clerk.

"Excuse me, but have you seen my grandfather today?" she asked the man on duty.

"No, ma'am, can't say that I have."

"Did you see him yesterday?" she asked, knowing her grandfather would have left word for her, knowing she would worry if they weren't home when she came back.

"Sorry, I didn't work yesterday."

She turned away from the counter, her uneasiness growing, panic hovering on the fringes. She walked out of the hotel, not sure exactly where she was going, but certain she had to find her grandfather. She hurried down the street, her fear intensifying as she thought of her sweet little boy.

Sarah found herself at the clinic, only because this was the last place she had seen Lucas and Kira. This was where her grandfather was going to pick them up. The fear that maybe they had waited here all night for her grandfather and he had never shown up caused her to run the last block to Dr. Wilson's office.

From the outside the clinic appeared the same, nothing out of the ordinary. She put her hand on the doorknob, and the wooden portal swung open. There was no question in her mind that she had locked the door before she left yesterday.

Fear flowed through her veins like a cascading river, causing her to shake. Cautiously she stepped into the clinic. Everything was as she left it, but an unusual silence prevailed. There was no rambunctious child, no soft-spoken woman. It was quiet, too quiet. She walked past the desk and into the waiting room. The shades were pulled down, streaks of sunlight casting eerie patterns in the semidarkness. Her eyes squinted in the dimly lit room as she tried to see through the darkness.

She almost stumbled over her grandfather's legs where he sat on the floor, his wrists and ankles tied with rope, a gag in his mouth. He made a cry at the sight of her, and she felt her heart lurch into her throat.

"Grandfather!" She rushed to untie the aging man's feet and hands. She yanked the handkerchief from his mouth. He tried to speak, but his mouth was too dry. He coughed.

"Water," he croaked.

Sarah jumped up and ran for the water pitcher. She poured a small glass and handed it to her grandfather, who gulped the liquid.

"Sarah, thank God you're here."

"Are you okay? Where's Lucas, Grandpa?"

"I'm all right. But they took Lucas and Kira."

"Who?" she asked, though knowing the answer to that question.

"That gunfighter and Wo Chan."

"Oh, God," she cried. Opium dealers had her baby. He shook his hands and moved his feet slowly. "I'm sorry, Sarah. I left the door unlocked when I came in, and they followed me. They tied me up and took Kira and Lucas."

"When?"

"Yesterday afternoon, late."

Sarah started to cry. Her baby must be so frightened. She had to believe he was okay. No one would hurt a child, would they?

"Come on, Sarah, you can't fall apart on me now. We've got to go get the marshal."

She wiped her eyes. "You're right. I've got to get Tucker."

"I'm a slow old man, and my joints are really stiff. You go ahead without me, and I'll catch up to you," he said, pushing her toward the door. "Hurry!"

"You're okay?" she asked.

"I'm fine. Now go."

Sarah didn't need any other prodding. She was out the door. She lifted her skirts and ran as fast as she could.

The two blocks to the county jail seemed to take forever as she hurried past the saloons, the brothels, tears streaming down her face. She was so afraid.

Her feet were running as fast as possible, but they felt leaden, though she knew it could only have taken her minutes to reach the county jail.

She pushed open the door, almost hitting a deputy. "Tucker," she screamed. "Tucker!"

Breathing hard, she burst into his office where Travis, Beth and Tanner sat. Tucker jumped up and came around his desk.

"Sarah? What's wrong?"

"Lucas!" She breathed hard, feeling faint, knowing she couldn't pass out. "He's gone. They took him."

Gasps filled the room, and Beth said, "Dear God! Who took him?"

"What are you talking about?" Tucker asked in shock.

She gasped for air, the tears streaming down her face. "Lucas!" Her anger flared. "Wo Chan took Lucas and Kira."

"That bastard!" Tucker said, as he reached out and took her into his arms. The comforting gesture was her undoing. She sobbed.

"It'll be okay. We'll get him back, I promise."

The tears rolled down her cheeks even faster. She was so worried about her son. "Please, Tucker, don't let anything happen to him. You've got to save him; he's your son."

Sarah felt his body tense. Tucker leaned back in her arms and gazed down at her, a stricken look on his face. "My son?"

Dear God, she hadn't meant to tell him this way. She hadn't meant to let the words slip out in a room full of people.

"Yes," she said softly, her tears still flowing. "Lucas is your son. Please find him."

Shocked silence filled the room as everyone stared at the two of them. Sarah could feel the tension reverberate through the air. The secret was out, and the anger she expected was slowly building.

Tucker's eyes flared wide, and he ran his hand through his hair. "My son . . . you never told me."

He stepped out of her embrace, gazing at her in shock, his face hardening. That one night in Tombstone all those years ago and she had never told him. He stared at her, hurt and anger filling him. Then suddenly he was moving. He scurried around the desk, yanked open a drawer and pulled out a key. He unlocked the gun cabinet behind him and took out the six-shooters he had had made during his gunfighting days.

Tanner stood, walked to the desk and picked up several of the guns that Tucker laid out. "What's the plan?"

"Kill the bastard!"

"I know that. But how are we going to do that?" Tanner asked quietly.

"I'm going alone."

"Oh, no, you're not," Tanner replied.

"He's right, little brother. You're not going off by yourself. We stick together," Travis said, picking up one of the rifles.

Tucker gazed at his brothers. "You're a new father, and you're going to be a father in several months. It's too dangerous. I can't let either one of you help me."

"And you just found out you're a father. There's no way we're going to let you do this alone," Tanner replied.

"This man has kidnapped a Burnett. That could be our son or daughter, and you know you'd be there for us," Travis said.

They were right, but that didn't mean that he liked what was about to happen. Tucker looked at his brothers for just a second. "Okay, but Lansky is mine. Do we understand?"

"Yes," they chorused.

Tucker finished strapping on his holster and pushed the revolvers in place. He grabbed his hat and started for the door.

Sarah still stood by the door, and right now he was so angry with her, he didn't know if he could trust himself to speak. But he stopped at seeing the expression on her face.

"Please bring him back to me," she said, crying.

Part of him wanted to reach out and comfort her, but part of him was so angry with her for keeping this knowledge to herself that he couldn't touch her right now.

"Wait here," he said. "It'll be okay. I'll bring him back."

She gazed up at him. "I'm sorry, Tucker. Be careful."

Tucker couldn't respond. His anger was intense as he strode out the door, letting the fury flow through him. Lucas was his boy, not that of some man he had never met, but his own flesh and blood. Fear for the child shook him. Lansky, the ruthless son of a bitch, who had almost killed him, had his son!

The Chinese had several boardinghouses, a saloon, and an opium den just south of Houston and Fourteenth streets. Tucker had tried to shut the opium den down several times, only to be told to leave them alone. But not this time. This time they had crossed the line and would soon be out of business.

So many prostitutes used the opium that was readily available either at the local drugstore or from an opium den. But after today there would be one less source of the deadly opiate to supply their habit. Kidnapping a child for revenge was not something the outlaws would get away with, regardless of who the child belonged to. There were certain laws that weren't to be broken, and this was one of them.

But the part that scared Tucker the most was that Lansky had known what he was doing when he had taken Lucas.

He knew that Tucker and Sarah were friends and that Tucker would come after him. What he hadn't known was that when he had kidnapped Lucas, he had taken Tucker's son. And now the knowledge the gunfighter had his child infuriated Tucker.

This feud between him and Kid Lansky would end today. No longer would he let Lansky threaten him.

Yes, he was afraid. After all, the man had nearly killed him last time, but Lansky had gone too far. This time Tucker knew he had to kill the man or be killed. There was no going forward until this problem was resolved.

The three brothers stepped out of the jail and started down the street, walking in the very center so they could watch the rooftops.

People stopped and stared at the three heavily armed men as they made their way down Rusk Street, past the saloons, the cribs and shacks, and into the city's slum district.

The wind whistled down the street, kicking up dust, a shutter banged in the distance and a dog howled his distress. At the corner of Rusk and Fourteenth Street, Tucker slowed down as he saw Lansky standing outside waiting for him.

"Looks like they're expecting us," Travis said, shifting his gun.

"Let me handle this," Tucker said quietly.

"It's your show," Tanner said, cocking his rifle.

Kid Lansky reached through a nearby door and yanked Lucas out by the arm.

Tucker's heart stopped. Dear God, he was going to pull the boy out into the street with them. The man had no conscience, no heart, and Tucker knew at that moment that there was no way he could meet the gunfighter if Lucas was present.

"Marshal, I thought we'd be seeing you this morning. In fact, I'm surprised it took you this long to get here. The doc must have worn you out last night for you to be this slow." He smiled an evil grin. "It'll be that much easier to kill you."

Lucas started to cry and hold his arms out to Tucker. Tanner cursed beneath his breath, and Tucker steeled his expression, while his heart was slowly ripped from his chest. The child was crying, his little arms opened wide, and Tucker couldn't go to him.

"Let the boy go, Lansky. This is between you and me."

"Why should I? If I let him go, then you'll turn yellow and refuse to meet me again."

"No, I'll meet you in the street. I'm anxious to put this behind us. I'll make a deal with you and the Chinaman. If you kill me, you get to live, you have Kira and the Chinaman's business will remain open." He paused. "But if I kill you, the Chinaman loses everything. Do you hear me, Wo Chan? The business, Kira, everything. And you'll spend as many days as I can get you in jail."

"It's not good enough," Lansky said. "I'm not handing the boy over to you."

Tucker took a deep breath. "Why?"

"Because I know the doctor and the boy mean a lot to you."

Tucker felt hot and flushed and nervous and more

scared than he had ever been before. It was up to Tucker to save them. Could he outgun Lansky this time?

"Just let me shoot him," Tanner whispered. "I can get him."

"No," Tucker said to his brother. "I have to end this, but if I die, kill him."

Travis swore.

"It's a deal, Lansky, if you'll let Kira take Lucas back inside. I don't want him watching this."

Tucker was not about to let his son witness his death if that was how it ended. He didn't want the boy's only memory of his father to be of him lying in the street with blood oozing from a bullet wound.

Lansky laughed. "We'll make that your last request. And when you're gone, I'll have the doctor, the city and everything else of yours that I can find. But before I kill you, have your brothers drop their weapons in the street and walk away."

"No," Travis shouted at Lansky. "We're not leaving."

Kira had just about reached Lucas when Lansky grabbed the boy by the arm and yanked him back in front of him. He pointed his gun toward the child's head, but out of the boy's sight.

Tucker held his breath, fear paralyzing him.

"Don't do this, Lansky. You'll be dead by the time the gun goes off. My brothers will do as you say," Tucker promised.

Travis and Tanner threw their rifles in the street.

"Holsters, too," Lansky yelled.

Reluctantly they unbuckled their gun belts. Lansky laughed as they hit the dirt.

Tucker twisted toward Tanner and Travis, not completely turning his back on Lansky. "Take care of yourselves. Get behind a building, because if he kills me, he's going to go gunning for you. Promise me if anything happens, you'll get Lucas free and protect Sarah."

"Damn it, Tucker, I don't like this one bit," Tanner replied. "I can kill him."

"I know you can. But would you have liked it if I had killed Sam Bass?" Tucker asked.

Tanner shook his head. "Okay. I promise that your son and Sarah will be taken care of. But I guarantee Lansky is not leaving this street alive."

"You know I'll take care of them." Travis glanced at his youngest brother. "Be careful. You've got the fastest arm of anyone I know, and if anyone can kill this joker, it's you. So I expect to see you walking away."

"Thanks, Travis. Now get out of here."

The two brothers looked long and hard at each other.

"Be careful," Travis said, and walked up the street.

"Okay, Marshal, it's just you and me," Lansky cried.

A quick glance confirmed the streets had emptied and Kira had taken Lucas back inside. Tucker started walking toward Lansky, trying not to think about what was at stake, concentrating on his draw, picturing the gun smoothly leaving his holster.

They met up in the street. "Well, Marshal Burnett, this is it. Hope you're prepared to meet your Maker today."

Tucker nodded. "Let's do it."

He widened his stance, his hands out to the side, flexing his fingers. The familiar movements started to come back in a rhythm. He watched Lansky's eyes, and when the man's pupils widened, he knew.

Tucker yanked his pistol out of his holster, fired,

spun to the right and fired again. Lansky's first bullet whirred by his head so close, he felt as if it parted his hair. The second one went through his shirtsleeve, ripping the material, but missing the flesh.

Tucker started to shake. He was still alive. His knees felt weak, and he gazed down the street. The Kid was lying in the dirt, blood pouring from his chest.

Tucker ran to him and kicked his gun away from his hand. He knelt down beside the gunfighter. Blood gurgled each time he took a breath, and Tucker knew he was dying.

Lansky gazed up at Tucker. "I guess—we're even—Marshal."

He closed his eyes, sighed and never took another breath.

For a moment, Tucker remained kneeling by the man's side, trying to collect himself. It was over.

The sound of a second gunshot had him jumping to his feet and spinning around as he yanked his six-shooter from his holster. His brother Tanner stood with a smoking gun in his hand. Tucker turned and saw that Wo Chan lay dead in the street, a pistol in his hand.

"He was going to shoot you in the back. I guess he didn't know Travis and I were right around the corner."

Tucker shook his head. "Thanks, saves me from having to haul him off to jail. Now I'm going to collect my son."

Seventeen

Tucker went inside the opium den where Kira was holding Lucas. As soon as the child saw him, he held out his tiny arms, crying. It wouldn't have mattered that the boy was his son; his heart would have melted at the sight of any child in this situation. But the fact that this child was his boy left his heart aching, and he had to swallow the lump that suddenly rose up in his throat.

"Momma," Lucas cried, tears running down his cheeks. "I want Momma."

Tucker picked him up and held him in his arms, hugging his small frame securely. He blinked away the moisture that was gathering in his own eyes. "It's over, boy. You're safe. I'll take you to your momma."

Tucker glanced at Kira. "You okay?"

She nodded, watching him with Lucas.

"Thanks, Kira. You're free," Tucker informed her.

"I watch over Mrs. Sarah's child. I sorry this happen," she said with a small bow.

"It's okay," Tucker said, his hand caressing the small of Lucas's back. The child clung to him, his tiny arms wrapped around Tucker's neck, his legs grasping his waist, his crying now small hiccups. "I've got to get him to Sarah. She's worried sick."

Kira nodded. "Okay. I come see her later."

Tucker walked out the door with Lucas still in his arms. "You were a brave boy. Now let's get you back to your momma."

"Momma! I want Momma!" Lucas said with a hiccupping sob.

Tucker's brothers fell into step as they walked back up the street where only minutes before he had faced the biggest crisis of his life and won.

He had killed the man who had tried to kill him, not once, but twice, and who had kidnapped his son. And he felt no remorse, only relief it was over.

"Is the boy okay?" Travis asked.

"I think so. We'll let his momma check him out."

Lucas raised his head and looked at Tucker. "Bad man. Bad man scary."

"It's over, son. He won't ever bother you again," Tucker reassured the boy.

Lucas laid his head down on Tucker's shoulder as if he believed and trusted him. The gesture filled him with so many emotions at once, leaving him overwhelmed. Funny, how the days went along with nothing happening, and then suddenly, in one short span, his entire life changed and left him reeling in shock.

Today was that day.

Tanner opened the door, and they walked into the county jail. He had hurried, knowing Sarah worried.

"Good shootin', Marshal!" one of his deputies exclaimed. If he knew, Sarah must know Lansky was dead. Probably the news of what had happened on Rusk Street was all over town by now.

Tucker opened the door to his office, and Sarah

stopped her pacing. At the sight of Lucas, she ran to Tucker, tears streaming down her face.

"Momma!" Lucas cried.

"Baby, oh, baby! Are you all right?"

Lucas launched himself into her arms. She held him tightly, rocking the child, sobbing. "I'm so sorry, baby. I'm so sorry. I shouldn't have left you."

"Bad man, Momma. Bad man, hurt Papaw."

"I'm fine, boy. I'm right here," Kincaid said, as he ruffled his grandson's hair.

"Are you okay, honey?" Sarah asked, checking him while holding him close.

"I think he's just scared, Sarah. I don't think he's hurt physically," Tucker said, his voice choking as he watched their reunion.

He had never given much thought to how much a child depended on its mother or father. Suddenly he was very aware of how dependent a child was on its parents from the time it was an infant.

"I was big boy, Momma," Lucas exclaimed. "I cried for you. Tuck went pow pow."

"Oh, son, you're my brave little boy," Sarah said tearfully.

She glanced up at Tucker, the tears glistening on her blue eyes. "Thank you. Thank you for saving him. Did you ki—"

"He won't be bothering anyone anymore."

"Thank you," she repeated, staring at him.

"You're welcome. I don't particularly enjoy that part of this job, but I do what I have to."

She nodded. "I want to get Lucas home and back into familiar surroundings. I know we need to talk, but I can't. Not now."

Tucker ran his hand through his hair. She was right; now was not the time. He was exhausted, he wasn't thinking straight and certainly she couldn't be thinking very clearly, either.

"We'll talk another time—soon."

He watched as she relaxed visibly, and he knew she had thought that he was going to force the issue; but he wasn't ready. Since Lucas was his son, perhaps he needed to rethink his plans.

"Thanks, Tucker. Thanks for bringing Lucas home safe." She glanced at her grandfather. "Come on, I want to go home."

Mr. Kincaid glanced at his granddaughter and then at Tucker. He frowned, nodded and held the door open.

"Bye-bye, Tuck," Lucas said, and waved at him as his mother carried him through the door.

Tucker felt more confused than he had ever felt before. One small boy had managed to suddenly disrupt his life. One small boy whose mother continually kept his world unsettled. The two of them had left him reeling and unsure of what to do.

The room was quiet for a moment as Tucker tried to gather his scattered thoughts.

"Well, it looks like there are two new Burnett family members," Travis said. "Desiree and Lucas."

Tucker shook his head. "I had no idea. There was only one night . . . and I left town that same night."

He sat down in the chair behind his desk. "Oh, God, what do I do now? I need to marry Sarah and give him my name."

"Do you love Sarah?" Tanner asked.

"What does love feel like?" Tucker asked. "I care about Sarah a lot, but I'm not certain I know what love is."

"Then, don't marry her," Beth said. "Not unless you're absolutely certain."

"But he's my son!"

"But if you don't love Sarah, then you'll only make her angry if you ask her to marry you. No woman wants to be married out of necessity or for a child."

"That's no help," Tucker said dejectedly. "What about you, Travis? When did you know that you loved Rose?"

"I was stubborn as they come. I didn't realize I loved her until after she left me. Then I suddenly noticed how very lonely and dull my life was without her. I couldn't quit thinking about her after she was gone, and I realized that nothing else mattered but being with Rose."

Travis walked over to stand close to Tucker. "You need some time to think things through. Give it a few days and then see how you feel. A few days will help your perspective."

"Okay, guys, but do me a favor. Please don't tell Mother. I'm not ready to deal with her."

They all laughed.

"Speaking of, I have a new baby at home and a wife I'd like to see," Travis said, scratching his head. "Our short trip into town has lasted most of the day."

"Let's go," Tanner said.

They walked to the door of the office. Beth hugged Tucker's neck. "I know you'll make the right decision. Just remember, love that makes you happy is the most important thing in life. I hope you find it."

Travis slapped him on the back. "Take care, little brother. If you need us, you know where we are."

Tucker closed the door behind them, feeling completely drained. The image of Sarah came to mind. She had remained in town for almost two months now and had not told him the truth about his child.

His son. Those two words thrilled him, scared him and angered him all at once.

Tucker felt nervous as he knocked on the door to Mr. Kincaid's suite of rooms. He had waited two days and could no longer wait to speak with Sarah.

He had worried about the boy, afraid that somehow this mishap had scarred or scared him somehow. He had worried about Sarah and wanted to come see her, but felt that they both needed some time to sort out their feelings. But he was still uncertain.

She opened the door, and for a moment they stood there staring at each other. God, she looked beautiful, and for a moment he thought he was crazy if he let her go.

"Hello."

"May I come in?" he asked.

She nodded. "Sure."

He walked in the room, feeling awkward and out of place, where before he had always felt at home when he visited her.

"Tuck!" Lucas cried, and ran to his arms.

"Hi, boy," he said gruffly. God, this was hard. He looked at the boy closely, trying to see any resemblance of himself in the child.

"Papaw take me fishing. You go, too?"

Tucker smiled. "I wish I could, but your momma and I have some things we need to talk about."

He released the boy, just as Mr. Kincaid walked into the room.

"Hello, Tucker. I guess you're here to talk with Sarah. I hope you two come to your senses and work things out." He shook his head at Tucker and Sarah, and then took Lucas by the hand. "Come on, boy, let's go. The fish are awaiting."

"Bye, Momma."

"Bye, sweetheart." She leaned down and kissed the boy on his cheek. "Catch a big one."

They walked out the door, closing it behind them, leaving a tense silence. Tucker felt awkward standing there. Never before had he been aware of this discomfort between them. This sense of "How do we look at each other now?"

"Sorry about my grandfather. He's a little upset with both me and you."

"I guess that's understandable."

"Let's sit down. There's no reason we can't be civil about this," Sarah said.

Tucker didn't know how she expected him to react, but if what she had said was true, if Lucas was really his son, then he was damn angry. The more he had thought about how she had kept Lucas's parentage a secret, the angrier he had become. She had withheld the knowledge from him for the last three years and would have continued to keep this information from him if Lansky hadn't kidnapped the boy.

He set his hat down on a table beside him and ran his hand through his hair. This was hard, damn hard. But he wanted some answers, and he wanted the truth.

"I just want to make sure I heard you correctly the other day. Is Lucas really my son?"

Sarah bristled. "Yes, he's your son. Why wouldn't the boy be yours?"

"You were married, Sarah. Why wouldn't I doubt the boy was mine? I was led to believe he was your husband's son, never even considering for a moment that he was mine," he replied, angered that she had reacted so to his questioning her.

"The marriage was a ruse. I married Walter Scott James right before he died. He knew I was pregnant and unmarried. He helped me out. Otherwise your son would have been a bastard."

Tucker stood up and began to pace. "Why in the hell didn't you just get in touch with me? Let me know you were expecting my baby? Didn't you think I would want to know?"

Sarah stood and followed Tucker on the other side of the room. "You didn't want to know. You left me in the middle of the night. You didn't even have the courtesy to say good-bye, and then you wonder why I didn't contact you when I discovered myself pregnant?"

She took a deep breath. "How would I have found you? You were wandering the countryside. You didn't want to be tied down. You were a gunslinger who had almost died once. And you thought I would contact you and say 'Let's get married, we're having a baby!' "

"Don't you think as the father, I should have at least been given the chance to decide how much I wanted to be involved with my child? Don't you think I should have at least been told I had a son?"

He stared at her. Sarah glared back, eyes flashing with anger.

"When were you going to tell me? You've been in town now for almost two months. What were you waiting for?"

"Why would I tell you that Lucas is your son, when all you've talked about since I've returned is how you can't wait to leave town, how you didn't want to be tied down?" She poked her finger in his chest. "And now you're leaving town, just like you wanted. When were you going to tell me?" Her gaze challenged him.

"You still aren't ready to be a father. You're still the same irresponsible man who doesn't want to settle down, who left me pregnant in Tombstone."

"That's not fair!" he said. "I have changed. And if I had had all the information, I would have been willing to consider settling down. I could do it if I wanted to. We could get married."

"Why?" Sarah asked, her voice strained. "Why do you want to marry me, Tucker?"

"Well . . ." Too late Beth's warning came to mind, and he knew he was in trouble; but he had to offer to marry her. "If we were married, I could be an active part of Lucas's life. I could be a father to him. And we are good together, Sarah."

For a moment she said absolutely nothing. Then her face suffused with a red flush. "Damn you, Tucker. You would marry me just to be near your son? Not because you love me and you think we could be happy. Damn you, because in a few years you'd begin to hate me and wish you were a wandering man again. I want you to take the job, leave town and have a great life. I don't need you. Lucas doesn't need you. Don't come around me again."

"Sarah . . . I didn't mean it the way it sounded. We're friends."

"And don't call me your friend. We've been more than friends for a long time, but you've been too damn blind to see it. Well, let me open your eyes for you. We are no longer friends."

All the way back to the county jail, Tucker stewed over the events of the past hour. He had gone over to Sarah's to make things right, and somehow they were worse now than ever before. He had been willing to marry her. He had been willing to stay here and make them a family, but just as Beth had warned, Sarah wanted no part of his offer.

Women could be so stubborn. What was this feeling called love that was so important to them? He had been willing to give up his dream of being a federal marshal, all for Sarah and Lucas, but she wanted no part of his offer. She had thrown him out of her grandfather's suite and out of her life.

And the part about being more than friends. True, most friends didn't share a bed together. But their friendship had always been special, hadn't it?

Tucker started to empty the drawers of his desk. She had told him to get out of town, to take the job. Well, he was going to. He didn't need any more prodding from her or anyone else. He had made up his mind.

Thinking of Sarah, he packed his personal belongings in his saddlebags, thrusting them into the leather bags. Damn her! He had offered her marriage. He had wanted to be with her and Lucas, but he had been unable to say those three little words.

Why couldn't she just accept the fact that he wanted to do the right thing?

He turned in his badge and told the mayor that he had taken a new job. He walked out of the office that had been his for the last two years.

He would go by the ranch to say good-bye to his family, and then he would be on his way, to a new job, seeing new country, fulfilling his dreams. But somehow his heart felt heavy when he should feel glad. But Sarah had ended their friendship, and the thought of never seeing her again left him feeling emptier than he had ever imagined.

* * *

A week later Sarah looked up from her desk in time to see Brad strolling into the doctor's clinic. She was finishing the last notes on patients, busy packing her gear and getting prepared to turn the clinic back over to the doctor, who would be returning on Monday.

"Hello," she said, glancing up at him. "How's your hand?"

He smiled. "It's better. How are you?"

"I'm good."

"I heard about Lucas being kidnapped. I'm sorry, you must have been so frightened."

"I was, but he's okay. Scared him, but he's a tough little boy." She paused. "You know, Brad, I've wanted to talk with you, but just haven't gotten in touch with you."

"I also must confess I've been avoiding you."

Sarah glanced at him, shocked. "Why?"

"Because I think you're in love with someone else."

The muscles in her chest seemed to tighten and ache. She sighed and knew that it was true, but instead of being joyous, she felt only heartache. "Is it that noticeable?"

He smiled. "No. But you're always aware of Tucker, and you watch him whenever he's around. I guess I would be the luckiest man alive if you felt that way toward me; but I know you don't, and I'm smart enough to know when to back off."

Sarah sighed. "I'm sorry, Brad. I wish it were you that I felt this way about, but I do love Tucker, though God knows why. You heard he's left town?"

She was resigned to the fact that they would never be together. After she had thrown him out of her grandfather's suite of rooms, she had known that he would pack his bags and run from his feelings. It was what he always did, and this time she didn't expect him to return.

"Yes. I know."

"The doctor is coming back to work on Monday, and Lucas and I, we'll be returning to Tombstone. It's time."

"I'm sorry, Sarah. I wish you could stay."

She nodded. "I'm sorry, too. But I can't remain here and wish that Tucker loved me enough for us to be together. I can't face this town every day with the knowledge that he didn't love me enough to stay."

Brad stuck his hands in his pockets and shrugged. "Don't give up on Tucker just yet. He still may come around."

Sarah shook her head. Why should she continue to wait with false hopes on a man who could never be committed to her and their son? "No, I've given up. We're going back to Tombstone, and I'm going to put Tucker out of my mind. I've loved him for over three years, and before that I had a crush on him. It's time to move on."

"I'm sorry, Sarah. I wish you the best of luck, and if it makes you feel any better, I think Tucker must be blind not to see what he's giving up."

"Thanks, Brad. Maybe he's not half as blind as I am for still loving the man, even after everything he's done. But for some reason, he can't say those three little words that I insist on hearing."

Eighteen

A month later, Tucker sat huddled under his slicker on a mountaintop in the Oklahoma Territory. It had been drizzling rain for the last week. He was wet and miserable, and for the last three weeks all he had done was follow this band of outlaws from one place to another with strict instructions not to interfere, but rather to keep track of their activities.

He was living his dream, and he was miserable. He missed Sarah.

There had been no time to explore new areas, meet new people or see much besides the top of this mountain. For three weeks, he had watched these men, making notes of who came and went from the outlaws' den. He hadn't expected the job to be all excitement; but this was downright dull, and he hated what he was doing.

But worst of all, the memory of Sarah's face as she had thrown him out of her grandfather's rooms had lingered in his mind like a bad dream. And the urge to reach out and touch her was so strong that even in his sleep he extended his hands, only to wake up and discover she had disappeared like a whisper in the darkness.

The nights were lonely, and the days were quiet. There was no one to talk to, no one to taunt him and keep him on his toes. He missed the camaraderie of the men who worked the county jail, the people in town who knew him. He missed his office and his family. At the moment, he would have given anything for a friendly face.

Nothing was as he had expected. How quickly he had learned that his expectations for this job were unrealistic.

This was nothing like the days of his youth when he had spent time traveling the countryside enjoying his freedom. Though those days were not so long ago, sometime between now and then he had changed. The ground was hard. He wanted a fire, but couldn't have one. He was tired and dirty, and damn, this wasn't what he had anticipated.

And if that wasn't bad enough, he missed Sarah. Yes, he was furious with her for not telling him about Lucas. A man had the right to know about his son. But he still missed her and couldn't help but wonder what she was doing. He couldn't help but picture her smile, her flashing blue eyes when she was angry, or the way they sparkled after he kissed her.

He missed being in her arms, he wanted to kiss her, he wanted to hold her, and he wanted to make love. . . .

He placed his head in his hands. What was love besides an emotion that made women cry and men act like fools? Love made grown men rush to do their wives' bidding. Love had turned his two brothers into doting husbands and fathers. Love was an overblown emotion—one that terrified him.

The thought stunned him. Was he afraid to fall in love? Why would he be fearful of a silly emotion?

Or could it be that Sarah was right, their relationship had been more than a friendship for a long time, and he had been too terrified to admit that he had fallen for her years ago?

Could he be fearful of not being smart enough or good enough for the doctor?

God, he was the biggest damn fool. Sarah had seen through him all along. Of course they were more than friends. They had been lovers. So why was he afraid of spending the rest of his life with Sarah?

Especially when Sarah made him laugh, was fun, incredibly passionate and warm. She made him feel like more of a man. So what was holding him back?

They had a son together. Yet the knowledge of that son had come between them, because Sarah hadn't told him until circumstances forced her to reveal Lucas's parentage. And did he want to be a father?

The questions whirled around and around until he felt dizzy, and he hadn't even moved from the spot. And every single one led back to one response.

Yes. He wanted to be with Sarah and Lucas. He wanted them to be a family. He wanted more children with Sarah, though he was still afraid.

He had been wrong for so long about what he thought he wanted in life. And it had taken being shown that sometimes one's dreams were not always what had been envisioned. Being a wandering man was a lonely existence.

Everything he really wanted was back in Texas. Back in Fort Worth, where a loving woman waited for him with a son he wanted to get to know. He knew absolutely nothing about raising kids, but he was willing to learn if Sarah was willing to teach him. As long as they were together, he knew they could overcome his fears and any other obstacle that stood in the way.

God, what was he doing here? He didn't want to be a wandering man; he wanted to be Sarah's man.

A bullet zinged past his head, and he jumped. Somehow the outlaws had spotted him, and he was absolutely crazy to be sitting here like a damn target on a mountain in the middle of the Oklahoma Territory. This wasn't his fight, and he didn't want to be away from Sarah and his son any longer.

He jumped up and threw his gear on the back of his horse and leaped into the saddle. To hell with this! He was going home to his woman. He was going home to Sarah. And somehow he had to convince her that he loved her. Somehow he had to show her that she was everything to him. Somehow he had to prove to her that nothing else mattered to him anymore but her love.

Tucker rode up into the yard of the big house. In the month he had been gone, spring had brought the flowers into bloom, and his mother's roses had turned the side of the house red with blossoms.

"Hey, it's Tucker," Tanner yelled, coming out of the barn at a run. "We didn't expect to see you anytime soon."

Tucker swung his leg over the saddle and dropped down to the ground. He clasped his brother's hand in one hand and his shoulder with the other in a combination handshake hug.

"How's Beth?" Tucker asked.

"She's fine. Felt the baby kick for the first time the other day and she teared up worse than a waterfall."

Travis came around the corner of the house. "Well,

look who came in. How long are you staying this time?"

Tucker waited until they had shook hands to respond. "That depends."

Both of his brothers stopped and gazed at him, perplexed.

"Is Mother home?" Tucker asked.

"No, she and the girls went into town. I'm surprised you didn't see them when you came through," Tanner replied.

"I didn't go into town."

"You didn't?" Travis asked, frowning. "Why not?"

"Can we get out of the sun and sit a spell. I'll explain everything."

Travis gave Tucker a knowing smile. "Get kind of lonely up there in those hills?"

Tucker frowned and went up the stairs to the covered porch. There he leaned against the railing, his arms crossed over his chest.

"Damn it. You know, Travis, you have this irritating habit. You've always got to be the know-it-all."

Travis smiled and shrugged. "I can't help it if I was born first. You know, the city hasn't filled your old job yet. I'm sure they would be glad to hire you back."

"You're not in some kind of trouble?" Tanner asked.

"He's in way deep, I'd say," Travis said, laughing.

Tucker sent his brother a look that he hoped singed the edges of his cowboy hat.

"Now, don't get mad at me, Tucker. You're the one who used to give me fits about Rose. I think it's only fair that I return the favor."

"Damn it, Travis. It's not funny. I don't know what to do. I'm miserable without Sarah. I haven't seen her in a month, and I can't get her out of my mind. I miss her. God, how I miss her."

Tanner started to chuckle. "But I thought you wanted to be an independent man who had no responsibilities, who traveled across the country."

"I did. But . . . it's not like I thought it would be. I'm not enjoying being away from Sarah. And worse, we didn't part on the best of terms. The last time I saw her, she threw me out of her grandfather's suite."

"Why did she get mad at you?" Travis asked.

Tucker glanced at his brother, looked away and then returned his gaze to him. "She told me we'd been more than friends for a long time, and I was just too blind to see. But she didn't tell me about Lucas."

Travis and Tanner glanced at each other and smiled. Then Travis cleared his throat in a way that let Tucker know he was trying to keep from laughing.

"I'm sorry, little brother. Really I am. We've been where you're at, and I ache for you. Do you feel like part of you is missing? Like the one person in the world who understands and accepts you is gone? Do you hurt so deeply inside that you don't know where the pain is coming from?"

Tucker gazed at Travis. "Yes. How did you know?"

"You're in love, Tucker. You love Sarah," Travis said. "Just marry the girl. You'll feel better."

Tucker laid his head back against the post that was supporting him. "I know. That's why I came home. All my life I've wanted to be different from you two, and now I find I'm just like you. I fell in love with the woman Mother picked out for me."

"No," Travis said. "Mother recognized you were in love with Sarah long before you did. You picked her out, but just didn't realize it was love you felt for Sarah."

"But I didn't want to get married."

"Why?" Tanner asked. "Why are you resisting?"

"I wanted to experience the world. I didn't want to be tied down."

"Then, why did you come home?" Tanner asked.

"Because, damn it, all I can think about is Sarah. I wasn't enjoying being away from her and, and"—he took a deep breath—"I realized I loved her."

Tanner snickered. "You've got it bad. I agree with Travis. Marry the girl."

"But marriage seems so permanent, so final. And she's already turned me down once. What if she does again?"

Travis smiled. "Marriage is final. But it isn't suffocating. My life is better with Rose in it. I'm glad I married her. As for turning you down, at the time you probably deserved it. She knew you weren't ready."

Tanner nodded. "Beth is my foundation. My rock that keeps me steady. And if you love Sarah, she'll be your guiding influence, too. Never suffocating, just always there for you."

Tucker looked up at his brothers. "God, I never thought I'd hear the two of you say things like I've heard this afternoon."

"And if you repeat any of it, we'll kick your ass," Travis teased, and then grew serious. "I would recommend that you consider your words carefully the next time you see Sarah, because I'm afraid this will be your last chance with her."

"What makes you say that?"

"Try looking at the last three years from Sarah's perspective, Tucker. You spent one night with her, and she became pregnant. She carried your son for nine months all alone, with no one to help her. She comes home, and once again, you show your lack of commitment. Tread lightly, little brother."

Tucker frowned. He hadn't really given that thought much consideration. But Sarah had been alone and pregnant. She had probably felt used and abandoned. Shame filled him. If only he had known. "So how do I convince her I love her?"

"I don't know; but you better do something, and you better do it quick or you can forget about Sarah."

"I've been the biggest damn fool in Texas. But I don't know how to be a husband, let alone a father."

Travis chuckled. "You have been pretty stubborn, so you're going to have to do some major groveling. But do you think either of us entered into this knowing what we were doing? You'll learn just like we did. One step at a time."

"I think I'll get cleaned up and then go into town to see Sarah."

Quiet descended upon the men as his brothers glanced at each other, a troubled look passing between them.

"What's wrong now?" Tucker asked.

"Sarah left town the week after you. She's gone home to Tombstone." Travis quietly informed him.

"Damn! Well, I guess I'll be making a quick trip to Tombstone," Tucker said, putting his hat back on and hurrying down the steps to his horse.

"Aren't you going to at least stay for supper?" Travis asked.

"Nope. I'm in a hurry. Wish me luck!"

Sarah had been home little more than two weeks, and already she had fallen back into the routine of working four days and spending three with her son.

Lucas had recovered completely from the kidnapping, and she was grateful he hadn't suffered any lasting effects.

Though her days had returned to a familiar pattern, she had no energy, and nothing excited her. Many days, all she wanted to do was sit quietly and cry, but she refused to give herself that luxury. She knew what the problem was, but she refused to acknowledge that Tucker had left her heartbroken once again. At least this time she would make certain it was the last time he had the opportunity to wound her soul.

She sat in her office trying to concentrate on a new medical book Dr. Wilson had given her in Fort Worth, but the words kept blurring before her eyes with a wet, dewy substance that continually leaked from the corner of her eyes.

She was not going to cry. She was not.

The bell jangled above the door, and she looked up to greet her next patient—and blinked her eyes, trying to remove the dream of Tucker in her doorway from her vision. But after she cleared her eyesight, he was still there.

Oh, my God!

She stared up into Tucker's brown eyes and swallowed. What was he doing here? He was clean-shaven, his clothes were neater than she could remember and he smelled of peppermint.

"Hello," he said, holding his hat in his hand which was visibly shaking, surprising her even more. He was never one to show nervousness outwardly.

She stood and came around her desk, her knees quaking. Something about him was not the same. His expression seemed different, tense and uncertain, as he stood there.

"Hi. I'm surprised to see you. Do you have a case

here in town?" she asked, wondering how she was going to deal with seeing him every day.

There was no one else in her office this morning, and somehow she was suddenly glad they were alone.

"No. I came to see you."

Her heart began to race, and she stared at him, flabbergasted.

"Me?" she asked. "I thought we'd said everything in Fort Worth."

"We did at the time. But when you're sitting up on a mountain all alone, a man can do a lot of thinking." He twirled his hat in his hand.

"Is that so?" she said, feeling confused. What was he doing here?

He cleared his throat nervously. "I . . . I had to come tell you, you were right about a lot of things, Sarah."

"I was?" she asked, suddenly trying to recall everything they had said to each other at that last meeting.

"Yes. We've been more than friends for many years, and I just haven't had the courage to face the truth about us."

She swallowed, suddenly feeling almost giddy. "You haven't?"

"No. I guess one of the reasons I left this town so abruptly three years ago was the fact that being with you was the most wonderful night of my life. It scared me so bad that I ran." He paused. "I'm not exactly proud of my actions, but I ran that night because I didn't know what else to do. I never even considered that we might have conceived a child that night."

"I was rather surprised myself."

"I'm sorry I wasn't here for you then."

She nodded, speechless for a moment that he was

apologizing. She hadn't expected him to say he was sorry.

"It wasn't an easy time," she offered slowly, remembering her feelings of loneliness and despair.

"I'm sure it wasn't. But I had no idea you were expecting our son. And to be honest, I don't think I was ready. But . . ." He took a deep breath. "Sitting up on that mountain I had a lot of thinking time. I'm no longer working for the government, Sarah."

She managed to hide her startled response except for the widening of her eyes.

"I was miserable in that job. Being a wandering man was a kid's dream. I'm no longer that kid." He stepped closer to her. "The reason I was unhappy was because I missed you. I know I've been a complete jerk to you since you came home to Fort Worth. Hell, since before then. I haven't been there for you in years past. I've come to realize that you make my life complete, and when you're not in it, I'm lost."

Sarah felt her heart start to melt, and the tears that had earlier been so near the surface slipped down her cheek.

He reached out and swiped a tear away. From outside the window, she heard a band playing and glanced out to see the entire town gathered, listening to the music in the early morning sun.

While the band played, Tucker bent down on one knee.

"Oh, my God," she said, laughing and crying at the same time.

"I love you with all my heart, Sarah. I promise I'll spend the rest of my days trying to make you happy if you'll do me the honor of being my wife. I promise from now on I'll be there at your side and not a wandering man, but your man."

She stared outside through the window, at the band that was playing, wanting to capture this moment in time for the rest of her life.

He had returned for her. He was asking for her hand in marriage. He had hired a band to serenade her while he asked her to marry him. But most of all, he had said he loved her.

Was this the same man she had grown up loving, yet fearing he would never settle down?

She gazed down at him, looking for outward signs of the changes that she sensed must have taken place within him.

"You know, Tucker, you're right. You have been an insensitive cad. I've loved you for years, and you thought we were only friends. How do I know you've really changed?"

Tucker looked up at her and sighed. "You don't. You're going to have to take a chance on me, Sarah. But . . ."

He paused, and she could tell he was carefully considering his words, which was a first for him.

"I've been afraid to let you close to me. I've been frightened of committing myself to you. Deep down I probably knew that I loved you, but I was so scared of those feelings. Now, I'm willing to try. I can't say I will always get it right, but for the first time in my life, I want to try to be a good husband to you."

"How do I know if you want to marry me for me or for Lucas?"

"I don't know how to be a father. Fatherhood is new to me. But I know how to love you, Sarah. I've probably loved you for years and just didn't admit it to myself."

Sarah could hardly believe what she was hearing.

The old Tucker would never have admitted he might make a mistake.

"I should really give you a hard time. I should make you wait, like I've waited for so long. I should give you hell. But I can't. I love you, Tucker Burnett, and it's taken you way too long to say those words to me. Yes, I'll marry you."

Tucker jumped up from the floor, and Sarah stepped into his arms, her lips caressing his in a kiss that was hungry and promised so much more. She leaned back, breaking their kiss.

"You're a damn fool, Tucker Burnett, but I love you with all my heart."

"Oh, Sarah, I was so afraid you'd given up on me. It took me a while to figure out what was really important."

"I'd say. But now that you have, I don't want to wait a moment longer. Did you happen to bring the preacher with that band you hired?"

Tucker laughed. "No, but I think I did manage to find the justice of the peace, and he's outside waiting. If you happened to say yes, I didn't want to wait a moment longer."

"Grab him," she said. "Before you change your mind."

"I won't change my mind, Sarah. My life is incomplete without you in it. And this time, I want to be there when our children are born."

"And you will be," she said with a sigh as she leaned into his kiss.

Outside the band played on. . . .

Nineteen

Tucker glanced around the room at his siblings and their spouses. Baby Desiree was crawling on the floor, and the newest member of the family, baby Carter, lay sleeping in his mother's arms.

"So when are the two of you moving back to Fort Worth?" Travis asked.

Tucker glanced at his wife, and she smiled. Just the fact that he had looked in her direction, before he spoke, had her grinning at him. They were a team and consulted each other through private signals, reading each other's thoughts from across the room. It was odd, but since they had married, they had this silent communication. With just a look, he knew what Sarah was thinking.

"I've accepted the job as marshal of Fort Worth again, and we're back for good. Sarah is going to take over Doc Wilson's practice now that he's retiring, so we'll be moving into town just as soon as we find a house in a respectable area of town."

"How exciting!" Beth exclaimed, rocking the baby gently as little Carter stirred in her arms from the unexpected noise.

Travis glanced out the window. "Have you told Mother yet?"

"No, we were going to wait and tell her and Mr. Kincaid tonight at dinner."

"Where are those two?" Sarah asked. "They took off with Lucas, and I haven't seen them in a while."

Travis pointed outside. "They're outside watching Lucas play with his new ball."

Beth started to giggle.

"What's so funny?" Tanner asked.

"I suddenly remembered when we were all sitting around together trying to find someone to match Eugenia with." She laughed and pointed out the window. "The perfect person for Eugenia has been right before us all the time."

Everyone glanced out the window at the couple, who were busy playing ball with Lucas.

"Of course. My grandfather! We could fix Eugenia up with Grandfather," Sarah said, and then laughed.

Travis smiled and shook his head. "Oh, no, here we go again."

"So how do we get these two together?" Tanner asked.

"The same way she helped us find wives," Tucker replied. "Whatever it takes."

The women glanced at each other and giggled.

"Ah, sweet revenge," Tanner said.

"God help us," Travis replied.

ABOUT THE AUTHOR

SYLVIA MCDANIEL and her very supportive husband, Don live in Texas with their teenage son, Shane; Fats, the rotten dachshund; Putz, a miniature dachshund; Sam the touch-me-not cat; and four of the hungriest fish to come from the pet store. During the day Sylvia works for a major telecommunications company in the Dallas-Ft. Worth area.

Hooked on romances at a very young age, she is now hopelessly addicted to writing and gets up at 4:30 A.M. four mornings a week to write for two hours before going to her day job. Plus she spends at least three evenings a week in front of the computer working on her dream of publishing a best-selling romance.

Currently, she's written six novels, is working on her seventh, and is in the process of planning her eighth book. A 1996 Romance Writers of America Golden Heart finalist and the 1995 President of North Texas Romance Writers of America, Sylvia is very involved with the North Texas RWA and a member of Dallas Area Romance Authors. You can write to Sylvia at P.O. Box 2542, Coppell, TX 75019 or visit her Web site: http://www.SylviaMcDaniel.com

COMING IN AUGUST 2001 FROM
ZEBRA BALLAD ROMANCES

__WOLF AT THE DOOR: *Dublin Dreams*
by Cindy Harris   0-8217-6913-8 $5.99US/$7.99CAN
Millicent is determined to become a "modern" woman—and her spirit intrigues Captain Alec Wolferton—a reputed scoundrel! Thrilled by her own passionate attraction to this blackguard, Millicent suddenly finds herself swept up in a romantic adventure.

__STRANGER'S KISS: *Midnight Mask*
by Maria Greene   0-8217-7103-5 $5.99US/$7.99CAN
Rafe Howard returned to England after the war, but a head injury had erased any recollection of his previous life. Finding his estranged wife is the first step in reclaiming an identity he cannot remember. Does beautiful Andria Saxon hold the key to Rafe's past?

__GRAND DESIGN: *Hope Chest*
by Karen Fox   0-8217-6903-0 $5.99US/$7.99CAN
Artist Cynda Madison wants more from life than restoring old paintings for the historical society. Then she begins working on the damaged portrait of the handsome Prince Dimitri; she is transported back in time to 1887 and meets the prince himself. Now Cynda must prevent the prince's death in order to return to her own life . . . but can she prevent herself from falling in love?

__LOTTIE AND THE RUSTLER: *Bogus Brides*
by Linda Lea Castle   0-8217-6831-X $5.99US/$7.99CAN
Lottie is quite satisfied to live without a man. Taking the name Shayne Rosswarne from a wanted poster, she's invented a long-lost—and conveniently absent—husband. She is running her successful dress shop in peace, until the real Shayne Rosswarne shows up—and wants some answers. . . .

Call toll free **1-888-345-BOOK** to order by phone or use this coupon to order by mail. *ALL BOOKS AVAILABLE AUGUST 01, 2001.*

Name _____

Address _____

City _____ State _____ Zip _____

Please send me the books that I have checked above.

I am enclosing	$_____
Plus postage and handling*	$_____
Sales tax (in NY and TN)	$_____
Total amount enclosed	$_____

*Add $2.50 for the first book and $.50 for each additional book. Send check or money order (no cash or CODs) to: **Kensington Publishing Corp., Dept. C.O., 850 Third Avenue, New York, NY 10022**

Prices and numbers subject to change without notice. Valid only in the U.S. All orders subject to availability. **NO ADVANCE ORDERS.**

Visit our website at www.kensingtonbooks.com.

Enjoy *Savage Destiny*
A Romantic Series from
Rosanne Bittner